WILL'S
CORVETTE

WILL'S CORVETTE

A NOVEL

William j Barry

Deeds Publishing | Athens

Published by Deeds Publishing in Athens, GA
www.deedspublishing.com

Printed in The United States of America

Cover design by Mark Babcock.

ISBN 978-1-950794-76-8

Books are available in quantity for promotional or premium use. For information, email info@deedspublishing.com.

First Edition, 2021

10 9 8 7 6 5 4 3 2 1

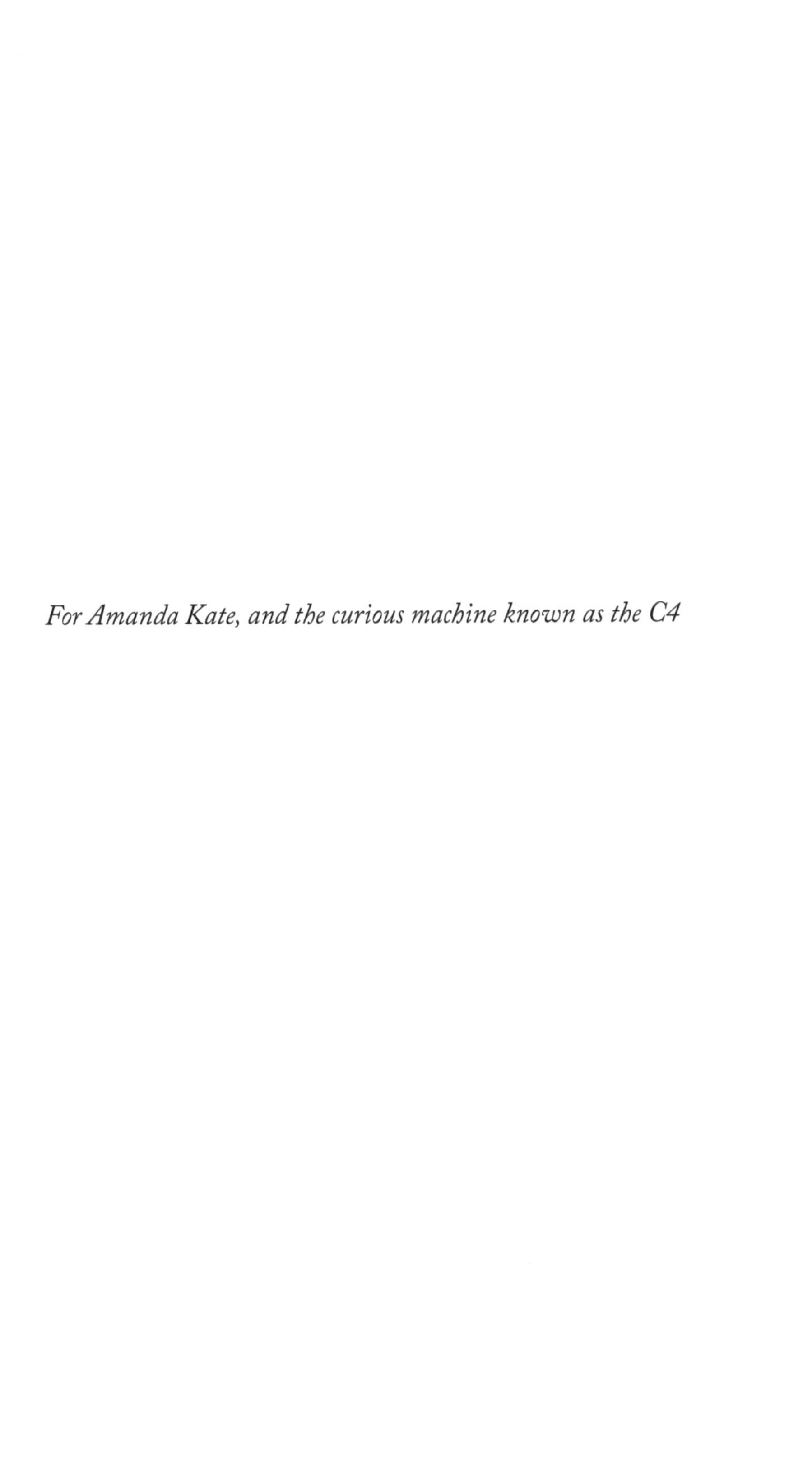

For Amanda Kate, and the curious machine known as the C4

ONE

If life was a car, and the choices we made were the roads that we took, who would be our passengers? And how long would they stay? While some drivers play life safe, others are reckless; and while some are courteous, others think they own the road.

But in the end, what really matters, is how you got from point A to point B.

Will's heavy eyelids weighed two tons. The sunlight was exceptionally bright today as it shone through the gaps of the window blinds. A slight universe of dust particles swirling in tranquil chaos through the sunbeams, began to come into focus as he wiped the sleep from his eyes.

He caught a glimpse of his high school biology textbook, still opened, resting on the edge of his bed. Last night was a late night of studying for first period's exam.

What time was it? It was still early, but the moment held an ominous feeling of lateness.

His authentic 1980s flip-clock read 1:20 am, it must have completed its last flip in the middle of the night.

A pinch of panic coursed through his veins as Will grabbed his cell phone from the night table by his bed. The time was, in fact, 8:25 am.

"You vintage piece of junk!"

The broken flip-clock was unphased by his insult.

"I'm late for school!"

Will grabbed his textbook off the bed as he jumped to his feet, and ran into the hallway.

Nala, their short-haired, red, miniature dachshund, came bounding down a dog ramp at the end of his bed where she'd been sleeping. Chasing him downstairs, she let out a couple of excited barks at his haste.

After kicking a grease-smeared ratchet away from the tire, Will threw his bookbag into the passenger seat of his 1976 Chevy Camaro project car that sat in the garage. It was a two-car garage he shared with his mother, Beth. But she, and her Honda Civic, were already long gone for the day.

As he plopped down into the sketchy embrace of the driver's seat, he fumbled the car keys out of his pocket and put them into the ignition.

The engine turned over with hesitation, and was too weak to fire up. He turned the key again, but the Camaro just hacked on and on, like an old man that had just finished a carton of cigarettes, and was trying to bum some money for more.

"Come on," he coaxed the car to no avail.

He had put so much blood, sweat, and time into getting the vehicle running, but the ungrateful car seemed to turn a blind-eye to his efforts. On a good day, the car would start right up without a second thought, which never, it seemed, were on days he actually needed it.

As he popped open the hood, his eyes poured over the grimy, oil-stained engine bay. A choice presented itself: troubleshoot the Camaro's engine, and possibly get it started, but equally possibly not; or…his eyes traveled to the moped sitting in the back of the garage; take a slow, but sure thing, that he knew was running.

The 50cc engine roared beneath him as he started up the moped. This bad-boy could do all of 30 miles an hour when wide open, provided you weren't going uphill. Taking the shortest and fastest route to school would mean risking life and limb on some five-lane roads, but it was the best compromise he could come up with.

As a senior, it was embarrassing to show up at high school on a moped. It seemed everyone had cars, or rode with someone who did. Oh, except for Arthur Tilson, and even he had a more powerful scooter, verses a moped. But you didn't want to be associated with Arthur on any level anyway.

Arthur was so unpopular; his name even sparked its own colloquial. If a house party got *Tilsoned*, too many dorks had shown up, and the gathering had become lame. You never wanted your party to get Tilsoned.

Will knew there wasn't anything inherently wrong with mopeds, per se, they performed the job they were meant to do. But the sociopolitical structure of high school was a tricky place, and though it was trivial, it was best not to draw the wrong kind of attention. At least most everyone was already in class, so they wouldn't witness his grand entrance. The same might not be able to be said for his exit, but he would worry about that later. As if he needed something else to raise his anxiety. He was so late.

A few small paint chips flaked off of the large wooden double-doors of the school as Will burst into the hall.

As his feet trotted down the old hardwood hallway bordered with grey lockers on each side, the bell sounded overhead. It was the end of first period, he had missed the biology test in its entirety.

Will's trot slumped into a defeated walk as students began to pile into the hallway from the surrounding rooms.

"I saw you brought the hog today," Arthur's nasally voice rang out as he walked up beside Will.

Will looked at him. "What do you want, Arthur?"

"I could see you, out the window of my classroom, as you pulled up on your moped." Arthur smiled. "Your bike's nice. Let me know if you want to race sometime."

"No, I don't want to race you. I don't want to have this conversation either."

Arthur swelled up with pride. "Smart man, smart man."

Will's eyes couldn't roll any harder as Arthur wandered off into the crowd of students in the hallway.

If Arthur had seen him from a classroom window, he was sure some other students did too. But he didn't have the emotional energy left to be concerned with his pride.

It was then that he happened to glance over and see her, the new girl, opening her locker. Whenever he caught a glimpse of her, it was like seeing the triumphant ending of every romantic John Hughes movie he'd ever seen, all rolled into one. It was an epic affair, even if it resided only in his own heart and mind. From the information he'd gathered from friends and acquaintances on the down-low, she was a junior named Katie.

He wasn't expecting her to notice him, but she looked up, and her eyes caught his. The edge of her lips curled up, and offered him a soft smile.

As her eyes returned to the contents of her locker, Will was jarred from his momentary daydream bliss by a painful elbow jab that threw him back, and slammed him against a set of nearby lockers. The bookbag fell from his hand.

"Oh, sorry Butt-Face, I didn't see you there," Doug said in his familiar sarcastic tone.

The pain shot through Will's arm. "Come on, Doug, not today."

It was the perfect way to continue a perfectly terrible morning. It was Doug Hanger, the self-proclaimed 'King of High School'. In truth, he wasn't popular at all, most everyone avoided him like a plague, he was more like the biggest creep in high school. Smoking, drinking, and starting fights kept him on the edge of getting expelled on a weekly basis, but somehow, he was still here. One deadbeat, abusive, alcoholic, illiterate, road-raging adult in the making. Oh, and he had a special fondness for hassling Will in particular.

"Oh yeah today," Doug replied. "Today and every day, Will. You're bad fruit from a bad tree, you're just like your dad, you only think about yourself." Doug gazed off into the air as if his words had some greater philosophical meaning. "And I'm here to remind you, every day, that the world doesn't revolve around you."

Picking up his bag from the floor, Will stood up straight, and tried to continue down the hall, away from the bully.

Putting his scarred, dirty arm around Will's neck, Doug pulled him close. "I couldn't help but notice that you were admiring the scenery."

"What are you talking about, Doug?"

"The new girl, she's going to be mine." Doug eased closer to Will's ear. "She just doesn't know it yet."

"I hope she likes disappointments."

"Ha-ha-ha," Doug fake laughed as he sucker-punched Will in the gut. "So, I don't need you getting any crazy ideas."

The pain shot through his mid-section, and Will bucked over from the punch to his stomach.

"You know, like talking to her." Doug pulled Will back up to stand straight. "Understand?"

"I don't know, Doug, you might need to explain it to me some more."

"You're such a wise-guy, Will."

Will couldn't help but wince as Doug reached his arm back preparing to slug him in the gut again.

"Hey, Honky-Kong, take that junk down the hall," Kahlil said.

Doug pulled his arm back in, and played it off as if he were an old friend dusting off Will's shirt. "Looks like your big, black, football buddy is here to save you again," Doug said.

"About to big-black your eye, psycho," Kahlil replied.

"But he ain't always gonna be around," Doug whispered to Will. He then looked at Kahlil and raised his eyebrows. "Hope you don't get injured on the field this season. That would be a shame." His voice oozed of sarcasm.

"Why don't you head on home," Kahlil replied. "I think your dad has another cigarette he wants to put out on you."

The bully released Will from his tight grip, turned, and began to strut down the hallway. "Who's the king, baby?" He yelled through his hands, cupped like a megaphone.

"Today sucks." Will mumbled, shaking his head.

Doug called out to his Latino buddy that happened to be passing by, "Hey Juan, look who it is." He pointed back at Will.

A large smirk grew on Juan's face as he called out, "Hey Puta!" in Will's direction, then went about his way.

Will rubbed the area of his neck where Doug had wrenched it with his arm, then turned to Kahlil. "You know I can take care of myself."

"Yeah, but isn't it kind-of hard to do CPR on yourself?" Kahlil kidded.

Will gave him a look.

"Yeah, yeah, of course." Kahlil nodded. "I just happened to be passing by."

"It's cool, I appreciate it. I just wish you happened to be passing by a minute earlier, before I got that sucker punch to the gut." Will lightly tapped the stopwatch that Kahlil wore around his neck. "I figured with your stopwatch you'd be on time."

"First, you don't want my help? Then I can't get here quick enough?" Kahlil chuckled. "You want me to go tackle the guy? I'll start the stopwatch and drop him right here in the hallway, I like timing my drills."

Will smiled through his easing stomach pain. "It's all good. But I may need your help sometime in the future if his goons are with him."

"You know I've got your back."

Will knew Kahlil always had his back; he'd had it for years. He'd been wearing that stopwatch for years as well. Kahlil played off the accessory as being useful to time his workouts and football drills. But the frequency that Kahlil glanced at it, seemed a little obsessive. He supposed there were worse things to be obsessed with than the time, so he never gave him too much grief about it. Just playful jabs here and there.

Kahlil kept pace with Will as he made his way down the hall.

"How are things going with the new girl?" Kahlil asked. "Talked to her yet?"

"No," There was some disappointment in Will's tone. "But we had a real breakthrough today, she smiled at me."

Kahlil laughed. "That's a good sign, man. I mean, if she smiles at you, knowing how much you look at her in the halls, and she's not creeped out. Wait, it wasn't a nervous smile, was it?"

"No, and I don't stare at her *that* much, do I?"

"I've even noticed your ex noticing how much you stare at the new girl," Kahlil replied.

A defeated huff escaped Will's lips. "Uh, her."

"Well, you're going to have to step up your game quick if you plan to ask her to the dance," Kahlil went on. "It's coming up soon. And don't think it would be cool if you came stag, because it's not."

"I'm going to ask her, I promise," Will replied. "I'm completely confident. I've already rented my tux for the dance."

"Bold move, I can admire that," Kahlil said. "But maybe start out with small talk, like, 'hello'."

"I will, this week," Will assured him.

"So, how'd the bio test go?"

"I wouldn't know," Will replied. "I overslept, and I couldn't get the old Camaro started."

"Sorry. The good news is you'd have more chance to talk to the new girl if you have to repeat your senior year."

"Thanks." Will didn't appreciate his joke. "Yeah, I was on my way to talk to Denzie, to see if I could make it up."

"Oh man, good luck, Denzie is a curmudgeon, for real."

"I know." Will shook his head in frustration. "And

sometimes I feel like he's extra tough on me in particular. I don't know why he has it out for me."

"Just lucky, I guess."

"But I think I'm finally going to get rid of the Camaro. I just can't get it running well enough to depend on it at all."

Kahlil smiled. "That's great, then you could get a car made this century, and it might actually work."

"I'm not saying all that," Will said. "I just need something I can get to be more reliable."

"Old muscle cars." Kahlil grinned. "You and your outdated antiques."

"Vintage antiques," Will corrected him. "What I really need is a weekend job, so I could buy more car parts."

"Or a new car." Kahlil shook his head. "So, you're not going to get a new car with a weekend job, but just buy parts to fix a broken old one?"

Will smiled. "Pretty much."

"Remember, you're trying to ask a girl out. Girls like modern conveniences like, air conditioning, and a door that doesn't fall off." Kahlil patted him on the shoulder.

"The door just fell off that once, and you're still bringing it up?"

"Just once?" Kahlil laughed. "Doors don't just fall off normally. And yes, I still bring it up cause I'm still a little traumatized. I was the passenger and it was the passenger side door."

"You had a seatbelt on."

"Man, the door fell off." Kahlil threw up his hands. "The seat belt was probably falling off next."

Will nodded in agreement. "Yeah, maybe."

"Oh, wait, did you end up bringing your moped here?"

Will let out a sigh. "Yeah, my favorite way to risk my life."

Kahlil playfully nudged him with his elbow. "Yeah, but the girls dig a moped-man."

"They do?"

"No," Kahlil replied with a laugh. "You see Arthur drowning in the females wearing that dorky helmet? It's definitely not that first impression you want to make on the new girl you've been eyeing."

"You've got a point, but I was desperate."

"And you missed the test anyway." Kahlil glanced down at his stopwatch. "I think I have enough time," he mumbled to himself as he began veering off toward the bathroom. "Here's my stop," Kahlil said. "Good luck with Denzie."

"Thanks," Will replied. "And thanks for your help with Doug."

"Anytime." Kahlil smiled as he turned and walked through the bathroom door.

Mr. Denzie gave a quick glance up from the summit of his small mountain of paperwork, then returned his gaze back down as Will entered the room.

"William, good news," the teacher said with a monotone annoyance. "I already have your test graded."

"Mr. Denzie, I can explain, see I–"

"In the real world there are seldom 'explanations'," the teacher interrupted him. "You either succeed at something, or fail at it, or wing it, but in that case, you still sometimes succeed at it. The latter is what you've been doing so far in this class. But today you failed."

"I know."

The teacher looked up at him with a most disappointed gaze. "You're better than this. You're smart, and you have a good head on your shoulders. I expect better from you."

"I understand."

"So, you'll also understand why you won't get a makeup test?"

"Mr. Denzie, come on," Will begged. "I studied till late last night, and my alarm didn't go off, and then my car wouldn't start. It was one thing after another."

"In general, when you start stacking excuses, it seems less and less believable."

"It's the truth. I know the material; ask me anything."

"Why are you trying to fail my class?"

Will held his palms open. "Biology questions; you know what I mean."

"I believe your excuses," there was a hint of sincerity in Mr Denzie's voice. "But just like in life, do-overs are seldom."

Will's stomach hit a cold iceberg, and began to sink. He knew his current average in the class couldn't withstand a zero on the test.

"Test scores aren't dropped in the real world either," Denzie continued. "But that's what I'm doing."

"What?" Will was confused, that wasn't very Denzie-like.

"Yes," the teacher went on, taking his reading glasses off

and laying them down on the desk. "I haven't told the rest of the class yet, but I'll be dropping the lowest test score this semester."

The relief began to set in. "That's great news, Mr. Denzie, thank you!"

"Be better, Will. It's time to start living up to the potential I see in you."

"I will."

"I hope so," the teacher replied. "Now get out of here before you fail someone else's class."

At least the morning hadn't set the tone for the entire day. It had started out rough, but somewhere along the way, it got better.

Later in the afternoon, Will had a few of his books beneath his arm as he was walking into his free period.

"Hey Will," a voice from behind called out.

Will turned around to see his friend, Pedro, with a pair of drumsticks in his hands, as usual. Pedro always had a pair of drumsticks with him whenever possible. It was as if they were his security blanket, something that could give rhythm and structure to a free-time, anti-meter world.

"What's up Pedro?" Will asked.

"Where's your guitar?"

"I don't have it," Will answered. "My car didn't start this morning, and I had to take my moped."

"Man, you should've strapped the guitar to your back," Pedro replied. "Did you forget today?"

"Oh, no." In all of the tumult of the morning, it'd

slipped Will's mind, but now he remembered: Today was the day his band was trying out in front of the school's principal. It was for the opportunity to play one song live at the upcoming dance. All the set-up and take-down of musical equipment just to perform one song seemed like a lot of work. But for a fledgling high school band, just trying to make a name for themselves, the exposure would be an amazing opportunity. And in the eyes of the band, it was more than worth it.

"Principal Finner is coming to the band room in, like, 15 minutes to hear us play," Pedro said. "And if we're not ready, he's just going to pick one of the other bands fighting to get this opportunity. Only one band gets to do it, and this is our only shot."

"I'm such an idiot, I don't know where my head's been at lately," Will said.

"Well, you better find it. Lucy is going to be so disappointed if we mess this up, she's already in the music room with her bass."

"I wonder if Principal Finner's mom ever said 'Don't be late for dinner, Finner,'"

Pedro shook his head, disappointed by Will's joke. "Or he'll get thinner? Focus, Will."

"Okay." Will thought for a moment. "Isn't there an old guitar in the cabinet of the music room?"

"Yeah, I think so," Pedro replied. "It's kind-of junky, and I don't know if it has all its strings, but maybe."

"I'll use whatever strings it has," Will said. "We need this gig."

Their friend, Lucy, a petite girl of Asian descent, was tuning her bass in the music room as Will and Pedro entered the room. Compared to her small stature, the instrument was almost comically large, but somehow, she wielded it well.

"If it isn't my Wee William," Lucy said, in a poorly executed Scottish accent, seeming relieved when they walked into the room.

"Hey Lucy," Will replied. "I'm still not Scottish, and your Scottish accent is still terrible."

"Will forgot his guitar," Pedro said.

"Will, you idiot!" Her clenched lips made no effort to hide her frustration.

"It's okay," Will tried to calm her. "There's a guitar in the cabinet here ... I think."

"That piece of junk? Yeah, it should be in there." Lucy said. "You're going to have to play your butt off to make that thing sound good."

"That's the plan." Will replied.

There were scratches and dings on the old wooden cabinet that were older than Will. The piece of furniture looked as if it had somehow found its way to this music room in an attempt to seek asylum from the gritty, wood-paneled 1970s. And if it had, who could blame it?

Will opened the cabinet doors to reveal a dusty black guitar case.

Lucy rolled her eyes. "Will, you're a mess."

"But you're our mess," Pedro said.

"I know, I know," Will replied.

Will gazed down into the case he had opened. It was

clear the cheap guitar hadn't been played in a long time. His eyes glanced over the instrument further as he picked it up. "Looks like it's got all of it strings, that's a plus. And the neck isn't too warped."

"You're too warped," Lucy mumbled.

"Excellent," Pedro said, as he took a seat behind his drum set.

Maybe the guitar had all of its strings, but they looked old and brittle. It would be a miracle if they made it through a whole song without breaking. Heck, it'd be great if Will made it through the song without breaking as well, considering the day he was having.

Will strummed a C cord. It sounded atrocious; the guitar was drastically out of tune. Pressing down the thick strings felt like holding down chunky little powerlines.

"Yikes," Lucy said.

"Yeah, that's pretty bad," Will replied. "Hey Lucy, give me a low E."

She played the fattest string on her bass, and Will began to tune the guitar to her instrument as carefully as possible, so as not to snap any of the strings. He knew her bass was in perfect tune; she was very meticulous about that.

The band had a good chemistry together, and they tried to meet once a week to practice. They had a number of potential songs in the repertoire that they could perform for the dance.

"Did we decide what song we're playing?" Will asked.

"We only get to play one song, so I think it should be an original," Pedro said.

"I agree," Lucy said. "Maybe we could play a cover song

if we end up performing more than one song, but with just one, we need to showcase the band's material."

"That's a good idea." Will continued to tune.

Pedro turned to Will. "What about that new song you just wrote? I like that one a lot, and your voice sounds good singing it."

"Yeah, the one Will said he came up with 'out of the blue'," Lucy said. "But it's clearly written about that new girl in school."

"Do I sense a note of jealousy?" Will kidded her.

"Not at all." Lucy chuckled. "But if I was into dudes, you'd be at the top of my list, Will."

"Thanks for throwing a line to my fragile ego," Will replied.

"…Of guys to dump," Lucy mumbled.

"I heard that," Will replied.

"I didn't say anything, I'm here for your fragile ego." Lucy offered a big cheesy smile. "That and the sarcasm you don't always pick up on."

"I agree with you guys," Will said, refocusing the conversation. "That song is pretty tame and Principal Finner is a…"

"Is a what?" Principal Finner, who had just walked in behind Will, asked in his trademarked disapproving tone.

"Principal Finner is a…connoisscur of good music, a man of distinguished taste," Will said with a smirk and slight exaggeration. "So only our finest material will do."

"I'm sure." The principal's eyebrows flattened.

Will glanced at Pedro and Lucy, who were barely able to contain their laughter.

The principal found a chair across from them and sat down. "I'm pretty busy, so you can start whenever you're ready. And by that, I mean now."

Will had just finished tuning the guitar, and prayed it would stay in tune for an entire song. Getting out his wallet, he procured a guitar pick; he always kept one in there. What self-respecting guitar player didn't always have one on his personage?

Will turned to face Principal Finner. "We are Oblivion Cubed…you know, cause there's three of us…and we'd rather be sleeping."

"I got it," Principal Finner replied in a tired voice.

"I think you'll think this song is a winner, Principal Finner," Will said.

The principal glared at him. Perhaps it wasn't the best time for a rhyme.

Will turned to Pedro and Lucy and gave them a confident smile.

A tapping of Pedro's drumsticks counted the song in. Will brought the pick down on the old strings of the guitar, which, surprisingly didn't snap, at least at first. Oblivion Cubed began their song.

TWO

Though the day had gotten significantly better than its start, Will just wanted to put it all behind him as the final bell rang. He feet trudged to his trusty moped in the school parking lot.

He hoped not to be noticed by anyone as he mounted his 50cc hog, and put on his helmet. Now that time wasn't a factor, perhaps he could take the safer backroads to get home. It would take a good ten minutes longer, but at least it was more scenic.

Then Will caught a glimpse of her, as he began to roll through the parking lot. She was approaching what he could only assume was her car. It was a blue, fifth-gen Camaro SS, maybe later in the series, like a 2014 or 2015 model. He was impressed, not that Camaros were rare by any means, because they weren't. They were everywhere if one bothered to look. But he was impressed that she had an enthusiast's car at all.

To Will, sure, most cars had good aspects to them,

but muscle and sports cars had a strength and a soul not found in most other cars that were simply meant to get you around. He liked cars with a little more character, and he'd met girls that had reached this bodhi, but it was less common in his experience.

His feelings of approval and admiration quickly turned to ones of apprehension and fear as he remembered his current state. He glanced down to see his fingers wrapped around the throttle. She was about to see him mopedding along, in all his goofy-helmet glory. It's just that the moped wasn't representative of who he was, vehicularly speaking. And in most cases, a young man in high school trying to make a good impression, is, if nothing else, insecure.

Maybe she wouldn't notice him if he kept rolling slow and quiet, don't gas the *beast* of an engine. *Don't look, don't look, don't look*, the mantra Will repeated to himself as he tried to keep the bike's engine noise to a minimum.

He watched her throw her bookbag into the backseat, and close the door. As she was about to get in, she turned her head and noticed him.

No, he thought. She had caught him there, lurking by on his twelve-inch tires.

She smiled, but it wasn't a cruel smile as he assumed it would be. It was a sweet one. It was followed by a casual wave.

Something about the look on her face dispelled his embarrassment, and he began to feel silly for being ashamed of his ride. He smiled and returned a wave.

By this time, his eyes had been off the road for a good 5 to 10 seconds. And as he was beginning to feel his confidence return, the moped tire caught a curb. The harsh impact launched him into the air, landing him into the open arms of some nearby bushes, which did the bare minimum to lessen his hard fall to the ground.

Will opened his eyes as he lay there on the ground, mortified. There was now a new, more legitimate reason to be embarrassed. Maybe he'd just stay here. Live out the rest of his days in these bushes, so that he'd never have to leave and see anyone's face again. Years from now, the legend will be told about the Bush-Man, that lives in these bushes, and is never seen.

Gazing at the sky, he tried to gather himself, his pride hurt more than any physical pain he was feeling. If not yet, there were no doubts he'd made an impression on her. And not a good one. If he were not to become the Bush-Man, perhaps he could just write his own obituary, the title of which: 'Well-Meaning Boy, Trampled to Death by Monday.'

"Are you okay?" A girl's voice asked as he laid motionless in the middle of the bushes.

Her face entered frame. With the clouds above her in the sky, setting the background, the view made her appear an angel looking down.

"You look like an angel." *What did I just say?* Will immediately wished he could reach out and grab his embarrassing words back.

She giggled. "I think you may have hit your head."

Will smiled, raised his arm, and gave her a thumbs up. "My head is fine, thank you. Well, no worse than it was before I crashed."

"Thank God for that cool helmet." It was obvious she was poking fun at him.

"Right?" He tried to pull himself up.

"Here, let me help you." She reached down to take his hand. "I didn't know anyone at this school was into extreme moped-sports."

"There's such a thing?"

She motioned toward him. "Evidently."

Escaping the clutches of the branchy bushes, Will bounced back to his feet, acting as if he was fine, but he knew that he'd be sore the next morning.

"I'm Katie."

"I'm Will, it's nice to finally meet you."

"Yeah," she replied, with a beautiful smile growing on her face.

Reaching down, she picked up his book bag and handed it to him.

The moped laid on the pavement. It had sustained some scrapes and other damage. The front wheel that had struck the curb was blown out as well.

"Your moped looks pretty torn up."

"That's the price of extreme moped-sports," he kidded.

"Do you need a ride?" She asked.

"Oh, I couldn't ask you to –"

"You didn't ask," she interrupted. "I offered."

"Yeah, sure, thanks."

Will walked his moped back to a nearby spot at the edge of the school parking lot. It would have to sit there until he returned later.

"Do you want to try to fit your moped in the trunk of

my car?" Katie tilted her head as she looked between the bike and the trunk of her car, trying to gauge the plausibility of her offer. "If it'll even fit."

He smiled. "I'm flattered that you think I'm strong enough to lift it in there. Nah, my friend Kahlil has a pickup truck. He's at football practice now, I'll have him help me get it home later."

"Always nice to have a friend with a truck."

"It's nice not to be the friend with the truck," he kidded.

Easing back into the front passenger seat of Katie's Camaro, Will laid his bookbag on the floor at his feet. The interior of the car was immaculate, and spoke to the care in which it was maintained. The vehicle was a number of years old, but had a shine almost as if it was new. Either she had just gotten this car, or assiduously took care of it.

He'd always admired the aggressive exterior retro-future looks of the fifth-gen Camaros, but had yet to be inside of one. The interior wasn't bad either, providing you weren't trying to ride in the back seat, or see anything out the back window.

The car offered a pleasant growl as it started.

"So, where are we headed?" She asked.

He gave her his address, and after she entered it into her navigation, they were off.

As Will's new taxi neared where the school parking lot met the main road, he happened to glance over and notice Doug, sitting in his Mustang, staring at him sitting in Katie's passenger seat.

Ah great! Will thought to himself. Doug was going to have something to say about this the next time they bumped into each other. The bully's stare was mental, seeming dead behind the eyes, all except for a festering anger. Geez, he had such angry eyebrows. But Will didn't want to think about the consequences as he and Katie merged onto the main road, he was just excited to have a chance to talk to her.

His eyes poured over the dashboard of the car as she drove, Will's gaze then wandered up to her. He couldn't help but be taken aback by her brown eyes, long brown hair, the soft lines of her face, and her full red lips. At the start of the day there's no way that he could have anticipated that he'd be here with her.

Wait. The thought flashed across his mind. He shouldn't stare. Kahlil had already called him out for staring too much in the hallways at school. And the last thing he wanted to do was weird her out.

She glanced at him and gave him a timid smile, seeming a little embarrassed by his gaze.

She noticed me staring! Will was frustrated with himself for the rookie mistake. Getting to know a girl you're interested in is like walking a tightrope, any off-balance step could send you plummeting down to a harsh landing in the friend-zone, or worse, the creep-zone. He scrambled to come up with an excuse to ease the awkwardness of the moment. "Oh, I was just noticing the stitching on the headrest behind your head." *Ah, that excuse should do it.*

She laughed. "Sure, you were."

Will couldn't help but cringe a little as he turned his gaze back straight.

Katie shifted the Camaro into the next gear, reached over, and gave his leg a playful push.

Looking over at her, he noticed the grin growing on her face. In that moment, he got a reassuring feel about her personality, he knew he could let his guard down, just an ounce, and push away his nervous paranoias, within reason.

"So, you like the car?" She had an amused tone. "Or just the headrests?"

"Both," he replied. "What year is it?"

"It's a 2014 SS model; it's my baby."

He couldn't believe it. How perfect could she seem? She was beautiful, kind, and had a love for cars?

"Do you work on it yourself?" He asked.

She chuckled. "No, but I make sure it's well serviced, and I wash and wax it often. My father always taught me the importance of taking good care of your vehicle."

"I have, like, the great-grandfather of this car, a 1976 Camaro project car that I've been working on. I haven't quite gotten it to the stage of 'reliable transportation' yet, hence the moped."

"My dad could probably help you with that," she said.

"I appreciate it, but I've been thinking about getting something else anyway." Will gazed out at the traffic outside of his window. "There's a guy that's been wanting to buy it from me for a while now, and after today, I think I might just let him."

Will was amused, and smiled to himself at the thought of working on a car with her father, and how awkward that might be.

"That's cool that you work on cars." Her admiration seemed genuine. "Are you into the car modding scene?"

"I've seen some modifying that actually looks and performs great; really clean builds," he said. "But I've seen a lot more that are just terrible, and some just hilarious."

She chuckled. "Yeah, I've seen and heard it go pretty bad sometimes."

"Everyone is different, and I can respect that, it's an expression of yourself. Making the car *yours*," he said. "As for me, I think some tasteful exterior mods could be cool, nothing too gaudy though. A few goodies under the hood to increase power certainly aren't bad."

"LS-swap everything." She smirked.

Will laughed. "Yeah." He was impressed, she definitely knew something about cars. "Maybe an upgraded stereo is fine too. I don't have any 8-track tapes."

She looked confused. "Any what?"

"Never mind." Will smirked. "My project car is pretty old."

"I think I'm on the same page with you about the mods, I appreciate subtlety, at least for the exterior," she said.

"I wouldn't mind getting a C4 Corvette," Will said. "They've gotten less expensive the past few years, and I've always wanted one."

"What years is that gen?"

"They sold them from 1984 to 1996," he explained. "They had a number of different engines in them. I like the digital dash of the earlier models, but I'd like to get one 1992 or newer. Those base models had the LT1 V8 engine, unless you got the ZR-1 version, which I can't afford. But the base model is still really great."

She thought about it for a moment, recalling Corvettes

from that time period. "That's cool, I like those. They're pretty retro, but I mean that in a good way."

"I guess for me, my dad and I used to help my uncle Zac work on his 1992 Corvette, and that's how I first got into cars. Those are some of my favorite times with my dad and uncle."

She smiled at him. "Sounds like you'll already know how to fix it if you get one."

"Yeah, that's a bonus, I guess," Will said.

"Do you consider a Corvette a muscle car?"

Will pursed his lips. "Nah, it's a sportscar. It has a lot of similar aspects, though. It's even shared engines with Camaros before. I feel like it's close enough to scratch the itch if you're a muscle car person. New Mustangs and Camaros are more like sports cars these days anyway."

"I can see that." Katie nodded in agreement. "Gone are the days of the misnomer that they can't go around curves."

"That's true."

"Does your dad ever help you with your old Camaro?" She asked.

"No, my dad passed away a while back." He thought for a moment. "I guess it's been five years now. And that's long before I got the car."

"Oh, I'm sorry." It was obvious Katie felt embarrassed. "I didn't know."

"It's okay, how could you know? It's been a while anyway."

Her tone somewhat softened. "What was his name?"

"My dad's name was Steven."

"I couldn't imagine how rough that must have been, being so young when it happened."

"It was, but like I said, it's been a while," Will said, detouring away from the topic. "My uncle still has that 1992 Corvette though. But I don't get to see him much these days."

"That's a shame."

"Yeah, but he's been really busy," Will said. "And so have I." He pivoted to another subject. "So how do you like it here so far?"

"I'm still getting used to it, but I like it so far," she said. "I miss some of my old friends, but I've made a couple new ones since I've been in school."

"Yeah, they're some cool people at our school; some idiots, but I have some good friends too."

Her lips betrayed a mischievous smile. "I just hope your girlfriend isn't jealous that I gave you a ride home."

He chuckled, picking up on her fishing for his dating status. "I'm not seeing anyone at the moment, so you're good. There's always that one psycho ex though, but I think that goes for everyone."

"Yeah, isn't there always at least one?"

The ride continued with a pleasant flow of surface chitchat, that was, even at times, humorous. Their conversation glided with ease; he didn't know if he'd ever felt this relaxed talking with someone that he had just met. Especially someone that he had a crush on. It was as if perhaps their souls knew each other from another lifetime, and were just catching up after a short absence away from each other.

She turned onto the street where he lived, and stopped at the curb in front of his house when they arrived.

Will was disappointed the ride was over so soon. "Thanks for the lift," he said. "I owe you one, let me know if you ever need anything."

Her glistening eyes hinted her intent. "Maybe you could show me around some of the cool places in town sometime?"

"Yeah." Her eyes and words caught him off guard. *She wanted to spend more time with him?* "I'd be happy to," he said, playing it as cool as possible.

"Maybe like a good restaurant or something?" She asked. "Maybe on a Friday night?"

His brain had turbo-lag, but it finally registered that she was asking him out. "Oh, yeah, how about 7:30 PM this Friday?"

"Sounds good to me." She had a contagious excitement in her smile. "And I can pick you up. I don't want you to stress about getting your car or moped running by then."

"That'd be perfect." He grabbed his bag and got out of the car. As he was about to close the car door behind him, he turned back to her. "By any chance do you think you'd like to see the old Camaro?"

"Sure." She got out of her car, closed the door behind herself, and began to follow him up the driveway.

Will felt around in his bookbag until he found the garage opener, and pressed the button. The door rose slowly; a dramatic stage curtain revealing the anticipated show.

His old project car sat there, staring back at them.

"She's old and dusty, and slightly rusty, but I thought she had potential," he said.

"Ah, you're a poet too."

"You should hear me rhyme stuff with Principal Finner's name."

She smiled, then began looking over the car, running her index finger along the edge of the hood. "I can definitely see the potential."

"Some people hate on this gen Camaro, and a lot of the muscle cars from the 1970s through the 1990s, and I get it, especially in the late 1970s, early 80s, a lot of them were severely underpowered. But there were a number of really good cars in that timespan too."

"Ah, forget the haters," she replied as she looked into the driver's side window at the interior. "Plenty of those cars are classics in their own right. If you're just loving a car because of the specs you read in a magazine somewhere, you're probably the wrong kind of car-guy. How does the car make you feel?"

"It makes me feel great." Will smiled. "When it's not making me feel frustrated."

She chuckled. "There are a lot of reasons to love a car. Cars are deemed *classics* simply by people holding them in that regard. So, to me, this is a classic, because that's what I see and feel when I look at it."

It was nice, so many people didn't get it, but somehow, she did, and her astute outlook made Will feel better.

"I should get going." She glanced back at her car, then back at him. "Let me give you my number."

He put her number in his phone, and sent her a text so she'd have his.

Will watched her drive off in her Camaro, he was still

in a bit of daze. So much could happen in the span of one car ride. It seemed all the time he was noticing her, she, in turn, was noticing him. For a school day that had started out so bad, it was ending the opposite.

As he entered the house, he could hear his mother speaking on the phone. It was odd that she was home this early from work.

Their pup, Nala, came running up to him. He bent over and gave her a little pat, then continued toward his mother's voice.

As he neared the living room, he began to make out the words she was saying. Her tone was distraught, on the verge of tears. "He doesn't have any good male role models left in his life, he already lost his father, and now–" She stopped midsentence as she saw Will enter the doorway. "I've got to go, he's home."

A terrible sense of dread began to well up within him. "Mom, what happened?"

She laid down the phone, and turned to him with tears in her eyes. "It's your Uncle Zac. I'm so sorry…he's been killed."

Her words had claws that tore the insides from his chest, and left an empty gaping hole for a cold wind to blow through.

His fingers loosened and his bookbag dropped to the floor. Time and reality were numb as he stood in shock, with no words. Beth went to him, and wrapped her arms around him tight.

He could feel her tears running down onto his shoulder as he stood there in an anesthetized stupor.

A familiar echo from his life rang back to him: no matter how good it may be, in time, every story had a sad ending.

THREE

The sights and sounds of the following few days were a blur. Will was on autopilot, going through surreal motions and reactions with Uncle Zac's funeral, and the wave of sympathy wishers that it brought.

The mystery and suspicious events around Uncle Zac's death did not stop with his untimely demise. There had also been a glitch in the computer scheduling system at the funeral home, and the body was prematurely cremated, well ahead of schedule. It's not as if they were planning on doing an autopsy on him, the bullet wounds were a pretty cut and dry cause of death, but the glitch was an odd occurrence that sat strangely with Will.

Will hadn't been to many funerals, just his father's and one grandparent, but his Uncle Zac's funeral seemed like quite a big affair.

It was known the turnout would be far too high for the funeral home to handle at their facility, so it was held at a larger community center. The event was catered, and had a

DJ that played introspective music between the individuals speaking about Zac's achievements, and their personal experiences with him. On paper, the extravagance of the event might have seemed in poor taste, but it somehow wasn't, due to its tasteful execution.

The event itself furthered the surrealism of his uncle's death. *Where do you even find a funeral DJ?*

The sight of family and friends he hadn't seen in a long time brought some comfort to Will, but he had never seen the majority of the people there. Will heard the attendees were an ensemble of the who's-who in technology of the region. His uncle Zac had worked with a number of ground-breaking computer and software companies on many projects, bolstering his exemplary reputation all along the way.

If the parking lot was any indicator, there were plenty of affluent individuals in attendance. Will couldn't help but notice, beyond the overly abundant Mercedes and BMWs, there were several Porsches, including a GT4. There was also a BMW i8, a Mercedes AMG GT Roadster, an Aston Martin, and a Bentley. One vehicle that caught Will's eye in particular, was an early 1990s Ferrari Testarossa. The car was so wide and so low, it was hard not to notice. Unless, of course, it was behind your monstrous SUV in traffic. It was quite a selection; the parking lot was a low-key car show. But Will was in no mood to enjoy all the sights on four wheels.

While many people found it cathartic to hear the speakers rehash their nostalgic tales about Uncle Zac, it was difficult for Will. Every story just reminded him of

Zac's great sense of humor, and general goodness as a human being. It made him think about how he could never be replaced, and how big of a hole his departure had left in the world, and his heart. All he could do was look up at the large framed picture of Zac that sat next to the urn that held his ashes on the table.

As Will sat there, fixated on his uncle's picture, he noticed a slender woman in a black dress approach the urn and lay red roses next to it. If he had to guess he'd say that she was in her mid-thirties, but he was bad at guessing ages. Maybe it was her looks, the style of her clothes, long blonde hair, or the way she carried herself, but Will thought perhaps she was a model or an actress. She was beautiful. He didn't recognize her though.

The woman seemed overcome by her emotions. Putting a hand to her face, she wiped a tear away, then stole off into the crowd, disappearing into the myriad of mingling mourners.

When Will thought that it had become too much for him to bear, people stopped approaching the microphone, and the music began once again. Most of the family were stationary near the front of the venue for a while, but it wasn't long before even they began to disperse among the crowd.

"Hey, my name is John," a man introduced himself to Will and his mother.

"Hi, I'm Beth," Will's mother replied. "I'm Zac's sister, and this is my son, Will."

Will nodded a cordial acknowledgment to the man.

"Thanks for coming," she said.

"Of course," John said. "My sincerest condolences."

Beth gave him a nod. "Thank you."

"Zac, what a guy, what a guy," John went on. "I can't believe he's gone." There was an odd awkwardness to the man's mannerisms, and while his intentions may have been well-meaning, it made the conversation uncomfortable.

"He was great," Beth said, trying to ease the awkwardness.

"He was brilliant, thought circles around his peers," John said.

"Yeah," Beth replied. "Even as a kid he was smart."

John put his thumbs in his front pockets, and patted the outside of his pockets with his exposed fingers, as he rocked back and forth on his heels. "He was so innovative with some of the stuff he came up with, I wonder where his notebooks are." John chuckled.

Beth looked at him and shrugged. Will could read her expression: at that moment she wished to be anywhere else in the room, perhaps even in the urn, rather than the conversation she was in with this guy.

"Well, I just wanted to offer my condolences," John said. "What a guy, what a guy." He shook his head in disbelief as he wandered off.

Will looked at his mother. "What a guy." He rolled his eyes.

"Oh, that guy?" She asked. "I know, right?"

"Maybe we can find Uncle Zac's notebook for him," Will kidded.

"Yeah, and stick it right up his –" She stopped her sentence before it got graphic, pursed her lips and gave a fake smile. "I'll get right on that."

The whole scene was all-too-familiar for Will. It wasn't too long ago that he had gone through all of this with his father. Though that funeral was far less extravagant.

All of the people offering condolences, and the ones seeming to give more condolences for Zac's lost future achievements, wearied Will. All he wanted to do at the moment was go outside to get some air.

"Hey Will, this is Dylan," his mother said, introducing him to yet another person he had no desire in meeting at the moment.

Will didn't quite snap out of the haze he was in. "Nice to meet you," he said politely, barely glancing at the man. "Hey mom, I might go outside and get some air."

"That's fine," she replied.

As Will sat down on the edge of the outside steps that led to the parking lot. He took a deep breath as he ran his finger over the rough edge of one of the brick steps nearby. Was having a heart as jagged and cold as these bricks the only way to survive in this life? This was all so ridiculous.

Something in the lot caught his eye. It was someone opening the driver's-side butterfly door on the BMW i8 that he had seen earlier.

John, the guy who had made super-awkward conversation with him and his mother was getting in the car.

He was the one with the i8? That's a shame, Will thought.

It was a cool car, but even it couldn't compensate for that guy's personality.

As Will watched the i8 leave the parking lot for the main road, he noticed the police officer directing traffic in and out of the venue.

He hadn't looked at the man closely when they arrived, but now, Will recognize him as Joe, a cop that had stopped to help him once when his Camaro project car had left him stranded on the side of the road. Joe actually knew a thing or two about cars, and helped Will get the car going so he could get it back home.

Will had stopped a time or two after that, to talk to Joe when he saw his patrol car sitting at the side of the road.

After Joe had let the i8 out onto the road, he happened to glance over and notice Will sitting there.

Will raised his arm and gave him a wave.

Joe returned a friendly nod back.

When there was a lull in the funeral guest traffic, Joe walked over to where Will was sitting.

"Hey Joe," Will greeted the officer as he approached.

"Hey Will," Joe replied. "I was sorry to hear about your uncle."

"Thanks." Will glance down toward the ground, then back up at him. "Crazy that you're directing traffic for this thing. I mean, it's nice to see a friendly face." Will tilted his head. "Wait, how did you know he was my uncle?"

"You mentioned him once when we were talking, and I already knew who he was. He was pretty well-known, locally at least. I remembered again when I heard the news. I figured I'd volunteer, it's the least I could do."

"I appreciate it," Will said with a sincerity he had reserved for only a few at the memorial.

Joe's eyebrows straightened. "I just wish we could catch the monster that was behind this."

"The investigator said they thought it was random, and sounded doubtful about catching them," Will said.

"Yeah, well, that's not going to stop me from looking into it, and keeping my ear to the street."

Will nodded his head, the officer's kindness and support was more than he expected.

"If you ever need someone to talk to, you know where to find me."

Will gave an amused smirk. "Yeah, I know where you stake out waiting for speeders. Thanks. I'll come find you if I do. Or just drive by really fast."

"Alright." Joe smiled. "Oh, is Cade still giving you grief?"

Will sighed. "Only when he sees me."

"I've been meaning to say something to that kid. Maybe he means well, but that ego of his isn't doing great things for the department's reputation. He's new, some of us veterans will have to sit him down and give him a talking to."

Will nodded in agreement. "That would be helpful."

"How's the Camaro?"

"Still hit or miss…mostly miss," Will replied. "I may get rid of it; take on a new project."

"I understand," Joe said.

The blonde woman in the black dress that had left the roses by the urn hurried by, passing Will and Joe. She kept her brisk pace into the parking lot.

Will watched her as she made her way to a little red Porsche Boxster S that already had its top down. Reaching into the glove box, she retrieved a pair of designer sunglasses and put them on.

The woman started up the Porsche, zipped through the parking lot, and merged onto the street.

Joe turned his head, joining Will watching her drive off.

The woman laid a lead foot on the pedal, and her tires gave a slight squeal as she raced off around the corner out of sight.

Joe glanced back at Will, smiled, and shrugged his shoulders at the woman's reckless driving. "Well, it looks like I should get back to my post."

"Thanks for coming over," Will said. "And for volunteering."

"Yeah," Joe said. "I'm serious, if you need me, come and find me in my stakeout spot, or call the station."

"Thanks Joe."

The officer returned to take his spot where the parking lot met the road.

Will found some solace there, sitting at the edge of the steps. It helped that a wave of people weren't offering condolences to him there. It helped that he didn't have to be forced into awkward conversations with people he didn't or barely knew.

Life wasn't fair, his uncle Zac didn't deserve this. Will's mind kept churning, replaying a supercut of his favorite moments spent with his uncle.

Little by little, people began to trickle by, walking to their cars after paying respects inside. Will was ready for this all to be over with, but judging by the number of vehicles remaining in the lot, there were plenty of people still lingering.

The nearby door swung open again, and an older gentleman stepped out of the doors, in what was, no doubt, a very expensive suit.

"Well Zac," the man said out loud to himself. "You would've been impressed with the turn out, and all the nice things people had to say."

As the man began to descend the stairs, he noticed Will sitting there. As he took another step, he did a double-take as Will glanced up.

"Hey, are you Will?" There was a distinction in his voice, that rang of refinement and privilege.

"Yes sir," Will replied.

"I thought that was you." The man stopped at the bottom of the stairs and turned to Will. "Your uncle Zac showed me pictures of you guys working on his car."

"Oh, yeah?" Will replied. "My dad and I used to help him do a lot of the work on his Corvette. That's pretty much what got me into cars."

"Well, he certainly thought highly of you," the man said. "He spoke of you often, even though, as I understand it, he didn't get to see you much as of late. He would tell me about a Camaro or something you were fixing."

The knowledge that his uncle was proud of him warmed Will's otherwise frozen spirit for a moment. His uncle had even thought highly enough of him to mention him to his colleagues.

"Where are my manners? My name is Alexander Lewis," the man said. "You can call me Alex."

"It's nice to meet you, Alex," Will said, truthfully happy to make his acquaintance, unlike most of the people he had met inside that day.

"Your uncle did some great work for my company," Alex said. "In turn, I let him use some of our resources for his private projects. He seemed to appreciate that arrangement. I'll tell you one thing," Alex went on. "I would've traded ten of my best techs for him."

Will chuckled. "That good?"

"I'm not just saying that." Alex's face offered a warm smile. "We also shared a love for vintage 1980s and 1990s cars."

"I think he passed that along to me." Will glanced at the ground.

"He used to tell me that you gave him hope for the future, a kid that still got a thrill out of shifting his own transmission."

Will chuckled. "That's me."

"Yeah, the smooth ride of a modern car is nice," Alex went on. "Especially on long trips. But a lot of those older cars really connect you to the road, and give you a much more visceral driving experience. It's easy to get passionate about driving them."

"So many people don't understand that," Will said.

"I certainly do." The man thought for a second. "I know today is a terrible day, but I have an idea of something that might help get your mind off of things."

"What's that?"

"Come with me," Alex said.

Will was cautious as he followed the older man across the parking lot. The man didn't seem like an abductor, but one could never be sure these days. Will didn't see a white conversion van in the parking lot. Abductors could have any car, but classic abductors tended to gravitate to white conversion vans. Nobody knew why; perhaps abductor status quo. He glanced over at Joe. He could always yell to the officer if things started to get weird. But Will didn't get that vibe from the man.

His face lit up when Alex approached the Ferrari Testarossa.

"I'm into redheads," Alex said.

"What?"

"Testarossa or testa rossa translates as redhead," Alex explained.

"You've got to be kidding, is this yours?" Will was elated.

"I told you, I had an affinity for 1990s cars. This is actually a 1991 Testarossa."

"You did."

The deep side-scrape design was amazing, even more majestic up close.

Alex held out keys to him. "Do you think you're up for taking it around the block?"

"Really?" Will couldn't believe his ears. "You trust me?"

"You come highly recommended, by your uncle, plus I'll be with you."

"Wow." Will thought it over. If he was going to get abducted, he was going to get abducted in style.

Alex smiled. "If you're not living on the edge, are you even really living? There's a little thing called insurance too."

Will held his nerves about crashing the car at bay, there was no way he wasn't going to take Alex up on the offer. It was perhaps a once in a lifetime opportunity.

As they pulled out of the parking lot onto the main road, Joe noticed him behind the wheel of the supercar as he held back traffic for a moment. The officer's look of surprise was followed with a smile of support and approval at his opportunity.

That afternoon, Will redefined the art of *driving like a grandma* as he eased out of the parking lot, and onto the road. He took it all in: the steering, the pedals, how it sat so low to the ground it almost felt he was inches away from sitting on the road itself. Driving a car manufactured with a gated shifter was on Will's bucket list, and this car had one. The car screamed 1990 supercar, both the polished and unpolished aspects. It was everything that he imagined it would be and more.

"You know, your uncle could've had a Ferrari," Alex said. "But he always wanted that Corvette for some reason, and the base one at that." He shook his head, still baffled.

"That was his dream car," Will replied. "Always was; he said he wanted it since he was a kid."

"He always loved the fact that he could work on it himself," Alex said. "He always had that blue-collar streak hidden deep down inside, no matter how successful he was."

"He found value in it," Will said.

"Indeed, maybe there is value in it."

Will smiled as he continued to drive along below the speed limit.

"The Testarossa is an amazing car," Alex explained, "but its actual specs might seem more like luxury specs than performance-oriented specs when it comes to Ferrari numbers. But don't tell that to anyone who saw Miami Vice as a kid. Still, it's fast, and amazing to drive."

"I've never driven anything like it," Will said. "I mean, obviously, but yeah, it's really amazing."

It wasn't long before Will had rounded the block, his joyride was coming to an end. He pulled the Ferrari into the parking lot, but didn't return it to a space. He decided to turn the reins back over to Alex before he put a scratch on it.

"Thank you, Mr. Lewis, that was brilliant experience, you don't know how much that opportunity meant to a car guy." Will stepped out of the car.

"Oh, I think I can imagine; and you're welcome." Alex got out of the passenger side of the vehicle and took his place behind the wheel of the car. His eyes seemed full of understanding as he looked up at Will. "Keep your chin up, kid. You're one of the promising youths; one of the good ones. Things will begin to look up soon."

"I will, sir," Will said.

Alex smiled at him as he drove off in the redhead.

Will didn't return to school for the rest of the week, or even bother to answer calls or texts from his friends. He might have answered a text or call from Katie, but she hadn't called.

Despite not seeing Uncle Zac much in the time leading up to his death, Will never doubted their closeness. They were not only family by blood, but kindred spirits when it came for their love of automobiles, and that was another type of family on its own. Will just needed some time.

By Friday morning, Will had almost begun to lose track of what day it was. But of particular significance this morning, was what he found when he looked out of a downstairs window that faced his driveway.

Will rushed out of the front door to find his moped in the driveway. All of the scratches and dings that were inflicted on it from the crash earlier in the week had been touched up, and the blown-out wheel had been fixed. His mother denied having anything to do with it, and seemed as surprised as he was. He wasn't sure who else would have been responsible, but he had a suspicion.

On Friday, Will decided to call the individual interested in purchasing his old Camaro, and sell it to him. The man wasted no time in coming over, perhaps afraid Will would change his mind. Will's old project car was towed away by lunchtime.

Will was sitting on the edge of his bed, later Friday afternoon. He gazed at the fingers of his left hand holding the shape of a chord as he strummed his red guitar. He let the cord reverberate through the emptiness in his hollow soul.

The incoming-text tone chimed on his phone. He

put the guitar back on its stand and reached over for his phone.

The text was from Katie: *Hey, haven't seen you at school all week, are you okay? Are we still on for tonight?*

His silence to her wasn't intentional, he had intended to text at some point. He'd been putting it off. Perhaps his subconscious was waiting to see if he'd be up to going on the date when the time arrived.

His reply to her was honest: *We lost my uncle Zac this week, it's been rough.*

I'm so sorry, that's horrible! She replied. *That's the uncle with the car you were telling me about, right?*

Yes, he texted. *I'd like to see you tonight, but I don't want to bring you down.*

If you want some company, I can come over and just sit with you, she said. *You won't bring me down, I promise.*

He still had some apprehension about seeing her, mostly concerned that his state of mind would be off-putting. But seeing her was the only thing he knew would distract him from his grief.

I'd like that. He replied.

Okay, see you soon.

As Will was about to put his phone down, he noticed he had a voicemail. It was from his bandmate, Pedro.

Will pressed play and held the phone to his ear.

Hey Will, haven't seen you around school this week, hope you're doing okay. I hope you're not sick. The cafeteria lunch on Monday was nasty, maybe that did you in. Anyway, I just thought I'd pass along the good news: Finner picked us to perform a song at the dance. I can't believe it, even with that junk guitar. You still pulled it off… we pulled it off. Lucy is super excited too. This is so great. Well, give me a call, man. Later … The message ended.

It was good news, no doubt, not enough to raise his spirits at the moment, but he was glad they got the spot performing at the dance. The dance was still weeks away, and he was pretty sure he'd be up to performing by then.

One foot stretched out through the open window of his room and found its footing on the roof. Will climbed out of his second-story bedroom window, and after taking a few steps across the roof, laid back, out across the shingles.

This side of the house faced their well-kept backyard, which would have been a nice enough view, but his eyes always travelled upward toward the skies. The stars began to come into view as twilight faded into night. As Will began to get lost in the heavens, he once again succumbed to memories of times he'd spent with his uncle, re-mastered for nostalgic grieving. As he laid there, he lost track of the time that flew by.

"Hey," Katie greeted him, sticking her head out of his bedroom window.

Startled, he snapped out of his twilight daydream. "I'm sorry, I didn't realize the time."

"No worries, your mom said you were up in your room." She glanced around at the view. "I guess she was close. Anyway, I'm sorry to intrude, your door was open."

"It's fine." His tone was nonchalant, but his mind raced

to remember if he had left anything embarrassing lying about. Nothing crossed his mind. Wait; did he pick up that pair of underwear he threw at the clothes hamper this morning that had missed and fallen on the floor? *Oh, yeah.* Relief settled back in as he recalled that he had put them in the hamper.

"This was on your shelf." Katie held out a Rubik's Cube in one of her hands. "Are you good at this?"

He shook his head *no*. "Not great, it takes me awhile. That was my dad's old Rubik's Cube."

"I tried to solve one once when I was younger," she said.

"I know it seems simple, but there's something about old games and toys that's kind of interesting to me," he said. "I don't know, maybe it's some kind of phantom nostalgia."

"Maybe you have an old soul."

Will shrugged. "Maybe."

"Oh, but *seems simple*?" She raised her eyebrows. "I just remember getting frustrated with it and wanting to peel the stickers off and re-affix them to look like I solved it, but I couldn't bring myself to cheat." She ducked her head back into the window to put the cube back.

"I like your red guitar too," Katie said from inside his room.

"Thanks, it's a Gibson EC-10," Will said. "I'm actually in a band."

"Really?" Katie stuck her head back out of the window. "That's cool. Unless you're making out with all the groupies."

Will smiled and rolled his eyes. "Even if we had groupies, I wouldn't be making out with them."

Katie cocked her head and gave him a silly look. "You say that now, but…"

"If you're done going through all my stuff, why don't you come out?" Will asked.

From the window, she glanced over the edge of the roof and noticed how far above the ground they were.

Will could see the nervousness on her face. "It's not steep, just be careful."

"Okay." She took a deep breath, exhaled, and overcame the apprehension she was experiencing, and began to crawl out of his window onto the roof.

She scooted across the shingles, trying not to scuff up her jeans too much, until she reached a spot near him and settled in.

As she laid back onto the roof and looked up at the sky, she smiled. "This is nice," she said in a soft tone.

"I come out here to think, and sometimes to *not think*," he replied.

"This is a great place for that."

He smiled at her. "Did you enjoy casing my room?"

She chuckled. "It's nice to know what I'm dealing with. You could have been a psychopath."

"Unfortunately, I'm as normal as they come."

"I'm good with normal. I did see a small knife on your shelf, though," she kidded.

"What?" Will thought for a moment. "Oh, my old pocket knife. That was handed down to me. It's been in the family forever."

"Interesting thing to hand down."

"Yeah, the story is that my great, great, great grandfather…"

A puzzled look grew on her face as she did the math in her head. "About when would that be?"

"In the mid to late 1800s."

"Wow, that's old; the cowboy days."

"Yeah," Will replied. "So, he was walking near the woods with his girlfriend at the time, and found that knife on the ground. He took it over to a nearby tree and carved their initials. And that woman ended up being my great, great, great grandmother."

"I think that's the sweetest story I've ever hear about a knife."

"Me too," Will said. "Then he stabbed someone."

"What?"

Will chucked. "I'm just kidding about the stabbing part."

"That's good." There was some relief in her tone. "I noticed your name was carved into the handle. Did you do that?"

"No, that's the crazy thing. It was found like that back in the day."

"Were you named after a knife?" She kidded him.

He chuckled. "No."

She smiled. "Then it was like it was meant to be yours."

"I guess," Will replied. "Oh, speaking of 'finding things like that', did you fix my moped and leave it in my driveway?"

"Me? No. My dad, yes." She cleared her throat. "I hope that's okay."

"What? Of course, I really appreciate it."

"That's good to hear," she replied. "My dad doesn't work on mopeds a lot, but he made an exception in this case."

"The work looks excellent, I really banged it up on Monday, now you wouldn't even know it'd been in a wreck," Will said. "But you didn't have to do that for me."

"Some of the teachers were looking at it there on Thursday afternoon," Katie replied. "I think they were talking about having it removed, so I had to beat them to it."

"Wow, well, thank you; and please thank your father for me."

"I will."

"How much do I owe you?"

Katie smiled. "Nothing, you big goof."

Will smiled back at her, not completely comfortable with not compensating her for the repairs, but he'd figure out something nice to do for her.

"Speaking of having something removed," Will said. "I ended up selling the Camaro."

She nodded as if she wasn't surprised. "It was a cool car, but it wasn't *your* car. It didn't define you well enough, if that makes sense. Even I could see that."

He hadn't thought about it like that, but she was right. Will turned his eyes back upward toward the stars.

Close to ten minutes passed without a word spoken as they gazed up at the sky.

Will broke the silence. "He was killed, they think it might have been a gang or something."

"Oh, Will." Her face conveyed the disbelief and horror she found in his words.

"The police don't have any leads, and it seems doubtful they'll dig up any…their own words."

"That's what they said?"

"Yeah," Will replied. "They think it was random."

"Random?"

"Random, as in, he wasn't targeted in particular. They think it may have been one of those things: a person in the wrong place at the wrong time when a gang felt like…"

"That's terrible."

"Yeah. I don't know how this could happen to Uncle Zac; he was just the coolest guy." Will took a deep breath. "He was, like, this super-smart software developer, but he also worked on his car, played guitar, and was in a rock band that played shows on the weekends."

"He sounds amazing."

Will nodded. "He was."

They sat in silence for another moment.

"It's just, there's a point when you realize that maybe dreams don't come true," Will said as he continued to gaze into the sky. "And you find yourself in a long, dark tunnel. But there's no light at the end of the tunnel, there's just more darkness."

Will felt the gentle touch of Katie's hand, and as he opened his hand, their hands fit together perfectly, a jigsaw puzzle that had been waiting to be put together.

"There's a light at the end of the tunnel, I promise you," Katie's soft voice reassured him. "Sometimes you just have to keep going to get far enough to see it."

A sigh escaped Will's lips. Maybe in time he'd agree with her, but he was skeptical in the moment.

There were no intuitive words or finely crafted expressions of sentiment that could be said to make things better, and she seemed to understand that. He just needed her to be present; and she was present, both physically and emotionally. His appreciation for her in that moment was beyond words.

As more time breezed by in the quiet, she gradually eased closer and laid her head on his chest, he put his arm around her and held her there beneath the stars.

FOUR

Texting back and forth with Katie began to make life feel normal again, at least somewhat. Will was excited to see her again in the hallway at school between a couple of his classes on Monday.

She glanced up from some books that she was loading into her locker and smiled as he approached.

As she closed her locker, she turned to him. "Hey, so how are you doing?"

"I'm okay," he replied, and for the first time since his uncle had died, it was the truth. "I was wondering if you might want to get some pizza after school...Mario's is, like, two miles from here, and sells excellent pizza by the slice. I figured it would make up for Friday night."

She smiled. "You don't have to make up for Friday night. It was nice hanging out with you, despite the circumstances. But ycah, I'd love to get a slice."

"Great," he replied. "I can meet you there."

"You still on the moped?"

"Yeah." He flashed an embarrassed smile. "I'd offer to drive you, but it'd probably drop the moped top speed to 20 miles per hour. And out on the main road …" Will cringed.

"Are you calling me fat?" Katie asked.

Will's eyes widened. "No, no! I'm calling the moped weak."

"Relax." Katie smiled. "I'm just messing with you. And I can drive us."

Will breathed a sigh of relief that she wasn't offended. "Okay, you drive and I'll buy."

"Fair enough." She grinned.

"I've got to get to my next class," he said. "I'll see you after school."

"Sounds good."

The adrenaline rushed through his body as he walked away from her, he was more wide-eyed than any energy drink had ever made him.

He had almost arrived at his next class when he heard a voice that snapped him out of his reverie.

"Hey, Will!"

He looked over to see a girl named Mandy, leaning against some nearby lockers. These days when he saw her, his mind couldn't help but drop a record needle on an old song he knew named "Wicked Game" by Chris Isaak. It was a song he'd played on repeat awhile back, but that didn't really matter anymore. All that was left was the empty association of her and the song.

But not even Mandy could spoil his momentary bliss. Will gave his head a nod, barely acknowledging her as he passed her by. The signs she was giving off indicated she wanted him to stop and talk, but he pretended not to notice her intention.

Will couldn't pay attention in the rest of his day's classes if he tried. It was all he could do to subdue the excitement he had; he was going to get to spend some real time with Katie on an actual date.

After being consumed by daydreams about her for the entirety of the school day, the final bell rang. He walked out the front paint-chipped double-doors of the school on top of the world. Down the front steps he bounded, making his way toward the parking lot.

Will took a step off of the curb and began to cross the parking lot, when he heard an all too familiar voice call out from behind him.

"Hey Puta," Doug's cohort, Juan, called out in his slightly high-pitched voice.

This is the worst timing! Will thought.

Will turned around to see Doug, Juan, and Crazy Shane. Crazy Shane was perhaps the least mentally stable of the group, and considering the company, that was saying something.

Once, after school, Shane got a traffic ticket for failing to stop at a stop sign. It was at the edge of one of the parking lots that let out from school campus on to the main road. No joke, after the cop left, Shane got out of his car and beat up the stop sign. Onlookers could hear the continuous clangs as he kept punching until the sign was bent over, and his knuckles were covered in blood. In retrospect, the story was amusing, but it was disturbing to witness it at the time.

The whole gang of rejects were together today, and looked like they wanted to do more than talk.

Doug walked down into the parking lot and began to approach.

"Looks like your bodyguard is at football practice," Doug said. "That's too bad."

"I know, right?" Will replied.

"I thought I distinctly told you that I had an interest in that new girl," Doug said. "But then, last Monday, I see you riding in her car, with a big stupid grin on your face."

"I guess you'd know," Will said.

"Know what?"

"About stupid expressions."

Doug's face got even redder than its normal shade. "Oh, you've got a lot of nerve talking back," Doug continued, his aggressive tone rising as he continued to approach. "Then I noticed you skip school the rest of last week, like a coward, because you were scared, 'cause you know that I saw you."

Will knew that it wasn't worth correcting Doug about why he was absent last week.

Doug folded his arms. "Well, I was telling the boys about it, and they don't much like what you did either. And school may be over, but we all thought you could stand to learn another lesson."

Crazy Shane reached behind his back, and procured a knife and a big toothy grin on his face.

"So, you guys are going to teach me a lesson?" Will asked, as he dropped his bag on the pavement. "How is that fair? Three on one, and one of your guys has a knife?"

"Life isn't fair, snowflake," Doug said to him. "So why should a lesson about life be fair?"

"You're a real philosopher, Doug, right up there with Spinoza and Nietzsche," Will quipped.

"Who?" Doug asked with a confused look, then shook his head from too much thinking. "Shut up!"

The three goons began to spread out and ease closer to him.

"Time for the lesson." Doug rubbed his hands together, preparing them to inflict some damage.

As Will was emotionally preparing to get beat down, and possibly stabbed, the entire situation was interrupted by the sound of tires screeching to a halt.

Katie had skidded to a stop, twenty feet from Doug and his posse, the aggressive front end of her car staring them down. The engine of her Camaro began to roar, and smoke began to pour out from her back tires, as she began to do a burnout. All it would take would be releasing the brake pedal to potentially add three new speed bumps to the school parking lot. Speed bumps that plenty of people would be happy to drive over.

The three hooligans stopped in their tracks, and looked at the driver. All she offered was a determined look in her eyes, and a right hand giving them the middle finger.

"Wait." Doug held out his hand to stop the gang's march forward. "That girl's a psycho, you can have her!" He then turned to his cronies. "Let's get out of here."

Doug looked over his shoulder at Will as the three walked away. "This isn't over."

As the three miscreants left the parking lot, Will

looked at Katie. She stopped burning rubber, her demeanor brightened, like the sun peeking out from grey clouds, and she smiled at him. He waved back, and released the breath he'd held for a couple of minutes; minutes that had felt like a couple of hours.

Shane drove a Mitsubishi Eclipse, and Juan had a white F-150 pick-up truck, but when the gang was all together, they always rode in Doug's car. Doug peeled out in his lime-green Mustang, riding off with his two cohorts.

Will got into Katie's Camaro, and she pulled away, headed for Mario's pizza.

"Well, these *were* new tires," Katie kidded.

"You know I can fight my own fights?" Will asked.

"Yeah, of course. I know you can fight them; I just don't know if you can win them." A smirk grew on her face.

He shook his head in agreement. "Thanks for helping me out."

"That's better…you're welcome. I know you'd do the same for me."

"In a heartbeat."

"That guy is seriously the worst," she continued. "It's just a minor inconvenience to be a decent human being. I don't know why people don't get that."

"He certainly doesn't," Will said.

"Why does he seem to really have it out for you?" she asked. "You don't seem like the type of person that a bully targets in particular."

"Well, with Doug, there's a history," Will explained. "Back in the day, his father, who has never seemed to be able to hold down any job for more than six months, worked for my father briefly. My father really tried to help him. Within a month, Doug's father started missing work, which was bad enough, but then my father had to fire him not long after, when he started showing up to work drunk."

"Sounds like the apple doesn't fall too far from the tree."

"Yeah, we already have a glimpse into Doug's future," Will said. "Anyway, supposedly it was the best job that Doug's dad ever had, his best chance to do right by his family, and he still couldn't keep his act together for more than just a few months. Doug blames my dad, and subsequently me, for ruining his family's lives."

"What?" She asked. "He was showing up drunk."

"I know, it's not like his dad has been able to keep any of his other jobs before or after either, but somehow it's my family's fault that their life is in shambles."

"He just wants someone else to blame instead of his father," she said.

"Yeah, cause if he said anything to his father, he'd get a black eye," Will said. "Or worse."

"The cycle continues."

"So, anything I do that Doug has any mild grievance with, gives him cause to come after me. It didn't used to be this bad though. It's like he's getting more violent with age."

"Aging like a fine wine," Katie's sarcasm was evident.

"Yeah." Will gave a roll of his eyes. "Most recently, his annoyance has been with me talking to you."

"What?"

"Yeah, according to Doug, you're really into him…but don't know it yet." He accentuated the latter part of the sentence with air quotes.

"That is genuinely frightening," she said. "I don't want anything to do with that guy."

"Well, judging by the look on his face, and what he said, I think you may have just solved the problem with that scene back there."

"Good."

It wasn't long before the two were sitting across from each other in a booth, enjoying slices of pizza at Mario's.

The dim-lighting from the faux stained glass light fixtures over the old wooden booths gave an old-school pizza joint atmosphere. Some neon lighting accents around the place and a couple of arcade video games in the corner gave the finishing touches to a place that seemed lost in an earlier era.

"Wow, there is so much cheese on this pizza," she said, as she finished another bite of her slice. "It's so good."

"I told you this place was great."

"And I love the décor," she said as she glanced around. "See? This is why I needed you to show me around."

"I've got plenty more places to show you," he replied.

"I can't wait."

"So, you really seem to know your way around a car, where'd you learn to do burnouts like that?"

She smirked. "Burnouts aren't very hard to do, I can drift too, well, a little. You can thank my dad for my car knowledge, he's always had cars that he's worked on and raced. He always wanted to make sure I knew what I was doing, not that he encourages the crazy stuff. But he's brought me to the track and the dragstrip a couple times with my car."

"Really?"

"Yeah, he says I shouldn't drive fast, but if I ever have to, he wants me to know how to do it right."

"He sounds cool."

"He is," she replied. "I think you two would get along."

"Me too, I mean, as long as he could get over..."

"Over what? She asked.

Will didn't know what their relationship was at the moment, or where it was headed. So, he tried to keep it vague. "Over us hanging out."

"He might have to," she said with a coy smile.

After taking another sip, she put her drink down almost perfectly in the condensation circle it'd left before.

"So, what was with the whole *I can fight my own fights* before?"

"I'm sorry, it's stupid," he replied. "I feel like I get bailed out a lot whenever anything starts to get serious, usually by my friend Kahlil."

"The football player?"

"Yeah."

"Is that a bad thing?" She asked. "Sounds nice to have a friend like that." She smiled. "And a friend like me."

"I know, it is," he continued. "I just don't want to seem weak."

"You don't seem weak at all, besides maybe your ego," she kidded.

"It's weird, ever since we lost my dad, I've felt this thing, like I've got to be strong, and be the man of the house, but I don't even know what that means."

"Huh." She continued to listen with interest.

"I mean, my mom, or anyone else, they don't expect that from me. But I feel like I have to step up and fill some void. I have to be strong for her, or maybe myself, or else everything may fall apart." He let out a big sigh. "I don't know."

"You've got to know that being a man doesn't mean being some caveman brute. Just from the short time I've known you, I can tell you know that deep down."

"I do," he replied. "Things just get a little blurry sometimes."

"I can tell you the most attractive manly things about you don't include your willingness to fight," she said. "It's good that you'll fight if you have to, but that's not what girls find attractive about you."

"Girls?" He asked.

"Girl," she said it with a smile, punctuated by an innocent sip on the straw of her soda.

He smiled. "So, you're saying there's something attractive about me?"

She laughed. "I mean, I've heard there is."

Will smiled. "From a friend of a friend of a friend?"

"Actually, here's the thing about that," she whispered. "If you want to know a secret," she said, leaning in across the table toward him.

He leaned in toward her to hear the 'secret', and she laid her soft sweet lips on his.

And that moment, in a little booth, in a little pizzeria, in a little town…was the center of the universe.

As Will pulled his moped into the driveway after school on Wednesday, he realized that he had forgotten the garage door opener again. He wasn't surprised. He hadn't slept well the night before, or the week before for that matter. He'd been a little more absent minded overall since his uncle had passed.

As he entered the front door of his house, Nala, their little dachshund, came bounding out of the kitchen to greet him. He knelt down to pet her for a moment. She wagged her tail and rolled over in an attempt to get some belly rubs. Those were her favorite.

His mother heard Will come in, and greeted him from the kitchen. He went to the doorway to see her.

"How was your day?" Beth asked.

"Fine, what are you doing home so early?" He asked.

"I took off work today, there was some stuff to take care of from Uncle Zac's will."

"Oh, I didn't know," He replied. "Did he leave you anything?"

She gave a somber smile. "Yeah, some sentimental things from when we were younger. And a respectable amount of money, which I wasn't expecting, at least not that much."

"Wow, that's nice."

"Yeah, it'll help us out. Uncle Zac always looked out for us when he could. He left you a couple things too."

"Really?" Will was surprised, it was unexpected. To be honest, he tried not to expect anything from anyone.

"Go look in the living room," she said with a smile.

As he walked into the doorway of the living room, he

noticed his uncle's white Les Paul electric guitar, and Marshall amplifier.

"Oh wow," he said. "His guitar and amp."

Will rushed over and picked up the instrument. He threw the strap over his shoulder and strummed a couple of cords with the backs of his fingers.

His mother smiled at him from the doorway.

He looked up at her, a little starry-eyed. "Do you know how many shows he played with this?"

"A lot, he's had that guitar since the 1990s," his mom said. "Oh, speaking of things from the 1990s, there was one more thing he left you."

"What?"

"You obviously haven't been in the garage," she said.

"No," he replied with an air of confusion, his curiosity growing exponentially. "I forgot my garage opener again."

She reached in her pocket and procured a set of keys, then tossed them through the air to him.

He caught the keys, and examined them in the palm of his hand. His jaw dropped as he recognized them.

"No way!" His mind started racing as he scurried to the garage.

His mom smiled as he passed her by.

Opening the door to the garage, he found it there, the 1992 Black Rose Metallic Corvette that he used to work on with his father and uncle. The name of the GM paint color, 'Black Rose Metallic', could be slightly misleading to some, it was actually a unique shade of purple that had some sparkle to it. Leave it to Uncle Zac to have picked a color out of the norm.

It still had the subtle brake light and license plate louvers that he had helped put on, that made the lines of the car scream 1990s that much more.

"I can't believe it," he said, as he opened the door and sat down in the driver's seat.

Beth entered the garage and approached the side of the car. "I think your uncle knew how much this car meant to you, and he wanted it to go to someone who would love it as much as he did."

Will didn't know what to say, he was speechless as he ran his fingers over the dashboard and down to the manual six-speed stick shift. Most of the car's interior looked stock for the 1992 model year, as far as he could remember. There was the exception of a modern screen in place of where the large factory radio used to be. It was some kind of infotainment system, probably with radio/GPS/Bluetooth and the like. That's nice. He couldn't remember if the old stock radio took cassette tapes or CDs, or both, but he didn't really have either.

He noticed the Alpine subwoofer in the back, and remembered that his uncle always had an affinity for Alpine car stereos. Though they seemed like a slightly lesser-known brand in the area where they lived, he remembered his uncle recalling advertisements that he would see as a kid, showing Alpine as the stock stereo system in the Lamborghini Countach. As a child of the 1980s, if the stereo was good enough for a Lamborghini, it was good enough for Zac. It's amazing how the power of advertising reached across decades, and still had a hold on his uncle.

It seemed beyond his dreams that he would ever own

this car, it was the reason he had gotten into cars in the first place.

"I put the title on the dresser in your bedroom, we can start working on getting it put in your name this week," Beth said.

He turned to his mother. "Can I take it for a drive?"

She seemed hesitant. "I put it on our insurance already, but we still have to get it transferred over at the DMV." But she couldn't withstand the excitement in his eyes. "Okay, just be careful and try not to get pulled over. Don't stay out too long, I was hoping we could have dinner together."

"That depends."

"On what?" She asked.

"On what we're having for dinner," he kidded.

She chuckled. "I was thinking about ordering Chinese," she said. "I figured it'd been a while."

"That sounds great to me," he replied.

"Can I bring a friend?"

"Yeah, of course," she said. "Is it Kahlil? Because in that case, I might need to order a bit extra."

He laughed. "No, Katie, the girl that came over Friday…if she's free."

"Yes, of course, she seems really nice." His mom had that tone, that tone that seemed as if she was downplaying her excitement that he was bringing a girl to dinner.

"She is nice, just don't embarrass me."

"So, no naked baby pictures?" She gave him a mischievous smile.

"No." He flopped his head back, already exhausted by

her antics. "I'll let you know if she can come, and what she wants."

"That sounds good." Beth began to walk back into the house, to give him his privacy. "Oh, and Will," she said over her shoulder when she reached the doorway.

"Yeah?"

"Don't drive faster than your angels can fly," she said, then entered the house.

He smiled. "I hope they can fly fast," he said to himself.

Will dialed Katie's number, and soon she had accepted his invitation to dinner, as long as he wasn't picking her up on his moped. He then texted his mother to give her a heads-up about their guest.

Will cranked up the Corvette, and heard the familiar growl of an old friend. The car had started up with no hesitation, Uncle Zac had always kept it in as good as new condition.

After backing it into the street, Will let it idle there for a moment. He glanced down at the infotainment screen as it powered up.

Text came across the screen: *Awaiting voice command.* After flashing that message, the display reverted to a C4 Corvette logo.

"Voice command?" Will was amused. "My uncle didn't play around."

He pushed in the clutch and put the car in gear.

"It's time to roll with it," Will said with a smile.

Text appeared on the infotainment screen: "Playing 'Roll With It' by Oasis".

The song began to play, crisp and clear through the speakers.

"Oh, you thought I said ..." He was about to adjust the song, when the melody got ahold of him, and he decided to leave it on.

Will accidentally caught a little rubber as he took off. He forgot how much power the car had. Sure, it was the base model, with the LT1 engine in it, but there were several modifications done to the engine, some that he had helped install himself. These modifications made the engine much more formidable than it already was.

The car sat low to the road, and the gear changes had a real mechanical feel. It was the kind of car that would be difficult to describe how engaging the driving experience was to someone that had never experienced it.

A warmth welled up within him. It was a true connection with his uncle. And as for the car, well, it was a reunion with an old friend that always knew how to make him smile.

FIVE

He had told the infotainment system her address, and while it was strange that it didn't speak to him when he needed to make turns, it did map the way to her house on the display. He'd have to mess with it, there was probably some voice setting that was turned off.

It was a smooth shift and ride, and Will couldn't help but grin from ear to ear.

As he pulled into the neighborhood where Katie lived, he was a little taken aback by how nice the houses were.

She must come from money, he thought. While that didn't make him nervous about his relationship with her, it did make him somewhat more nervous about being accepted by her parents. His house was decent, but these homes were on another level.

As he pulled up to her house, he continued up the brick roundabout in front of her large stone-exterior home. He glanced around at the well-manicured front lawn.

Will parked and walked to the front door. Upon arriving, he took a deep breath and rang the doorbell.

After a moment, a woman answered. She looked like an older version of Katie. Of course, he knew that it must be her mother, they had the same eyes and hair. Will thought if Katie ended up aging to look like her, it wouldn't be a bad thing at all.

She reached out her hand to him. "Hello, I'm Michelle, Katie's mom. You must be Will."

"Yes, it's nice to meet you," he said as he shook her outstretched hand.

She glanced over his shoulder. "Nice Corvette, I've always liked that generation."

Is this entire family into cars? He thought. "Thanks," he replied. "I just got it."

"What year is it?" she asked.

"1992."

Michelle smiled and seemed a little wistful. "That takes me back to high school."

Katie pushed by her mom. "Stop bugging him, mom." She stepped out of the door to stand by Will.

"You're right." Michelle smiled. "He is cute." It was a clear attempt to embarrass Katie with some inside information Katie had confided in her.

"Huh?" Will looked at Katie and smiled.

"Uh!" Katie rolled her eyes at her mother and let out a sigh. "Bye mom, I'll see you later."

"Remember, it's a school night," her mom said.

"I won't be late," Katie replied.

"Yeah, and I'm really tired today," Will added, trying

to give Michelle extra assurance that it would be an early night. In truth he wasn't lying, he was tired. "It's really just dinner with my mom, and then she'll be back."

Michelle smirked. She might not have been buying his sleepiness, but she looked to appreciate his supportive attempt. "Again, it was nice meeting you, Will."

"You too," he replied. "Thanks for letting her come over for dinner."

As they walked away from her house, Katie's eyes caught sight of the Corvette.

"You got one?" Her voice echoed her excitement.

"It's not just one," he said. "It's the one. My uncle left it to me."

"Wow." She gave his arm a soft playful punch. "That's so nice, I'm really happy for you."

As they reached the car, he showed her a few things that he loved about it, like the location of the fuel door, in the center behind the window, convenient from either side. He pointed out how low the car sat, almost like an exotic car, and how close the driver's pedals were together. The pedals were so close together, he might not even be able to drive it well with boots on, not that he ever wore boots anyway. While some might complain about the close proximity of the pedals to each other, Will felt like it also made the car seem more exotic.

The pop-up headlights were another great feature. With most car pop-up lights, the headlights would just raise up and down. The C4 headlights rotated a full 180 degrees as they were raised and lowered.

Will popped the hood and showed her it's iconic clamshell design, which was easily the largest, and looked best on the C4 models in his humble opinion. He then showed how you could see how the tires were mounted beneath the hood.

She seemed interested, or she was skilled at humoring him. He was afraid that he might begin to bore her with too many details if he carried on, so he kept his tour of the car brief.

He opened the passenger door for her, and she got in. He sat down in the driver's seat and cranked the engine.

"This is really nice," she said. "And the exhaust note sounds great."

"Doesn't it? And it's got a cool voice-activated infotainment system, but it has some bugs. I'll have to mess with it."

"Nice."

"One cool thing it can do," he said. "Say the name of a song you'd like to hear."

She thought for a short moment. "You don't have anything by K.K. Slider, do you?" She asked with a grin.

"Who?"

She chuckled to herself, not answering his question, then thought for another moment.

"How about 'One of Us', by New Politics."

The song title came across the screen and then began to play.

She smiled. "I have to say, that's pretty cool."

Will smiled at her song decision. It was good. He knew that she could see through him, and it was, perhaps, an all too appropriate choice for his mental state.

After the short drive to his house, they soon found themselves around the dinner table with his mother, Beth.

There seemed to be no awkwardness between Katie and his mother. They were getting along great. Not that he expected any less, but the same could not have been said about Will's last girlfriend.

"So, Katie, what do your parents do?" Beth asked.

"Oh, my dad, Mike, owns that new car maintenance and repair shop down on Central Avenue."

"You didn't tell me that," Will chimed in. "That place is huge, and looks nice."

"You didn't ask." She chuckled. "Yeah, they do a lot of custom jobs and restoration too. They can even do mopeds, though that's not their standard fare." She raised her eyes at Will.

Beth chuckled. "Well, it makes sense why you two get along so well. Will loves to work on cars, and you're used to tolerating car guys."

"I'd say Will is far from the typical car guy I've known," she flashed him a smile. "But yeah, I'm used to the culture. I grew up around cars and I love them too."

"I think he's pretty special too." His mom offered a proud smile.

"Mom," he said with a sigh, her complements were embarrassing. "I'm okay at best."

"I think you're special too." Katie smiled and turned to Will. "Sorry to gang up on you with her." Katie turned back to his mother. "Oh, and my mom, Michelle, doesn't have an official job, she's involved with some nonprofits and charities. She definitely keeps busy."

"That's great," Beth replied. "Speaking of cars, do you like Will's new-old car?"

"I love it," she replied, which made him smile. "What do you do? If you don't mind me asking," she asked his mom.

"I'm a physical therapist at a rehabilitation center."

"I bet that's rewarding," she replied with earnest admiration.

"It is, sometimes challenging," Beth replied. "But I love the work."

The dinner continued in pleasant tone as they got to know each other. As the dinner concluded, Beth picked up some fortune cookies that were sitting together near the edge of the table.

"Oh, I almost forgot, fortune cookies." Beth handed a cookie to both him and her.

As they opened them, Will was the first to read his fortune aloud to the table.

"*Voices from your past will guide your future.*" He shrugged. "These fortunes are always so vague; you can make them mean anything."

"Mine says '*What you are looking for stands right before you,*'" Katie said as she took a couple crunches on her cookie, swallowed it, looked at Will and smiled.

"Maybe not all vague," Beth said as she looked at her fortune. "*The sun rises, and day by day, shines brighter.*" His mom chuckled. "Okay, now back to vague."

After dinner they sat in the living room, Nala hopped up on the couch, and cuddled up next to Katie. Will thought that was a good sign. Nala didn't like his ex-girlfriend,

Mandy, and she turned out bad. Perhaps the little pup was a good personality judge. Nala even tried to get some belly rubs from Katie, which were reserved for humans that had earned her upmost trust.

They enjoyed some further conversation for a short time until it was time for Will to bring Katie home. He wanted to make sure he stayed in her parents' good graces. That and he was, indeed, tired today.

As they got into the Corvette, Will turned to her. "Do you want to drive the car?"

She smiled. "Maybe another time."

Text came across the infotainment screen: "Playing 'Drive' by The Cars".

"The stereo is so buggy," Will said as the song began to play.

"It's kind of nice though," she kidded. "It seems to have good taste in music."

They set off on their way.

After riding along for a few minutes, Katie spoke up, "Your mom is great."

"She's nice. A little clingy at times," he replied.

"I think every parent of a teenager is though. It's hard for them to adjust to us needing them less and less."

Will nodded in agreement. "But I think it went pretty well tonight. I can tell when she approves of someone."

A warm smile grew on Katie's face and she reached over to hold his hand in between when he would shift the car.

The drive to her house was far too short, as was any time he got to spend with her. True, he was tired, but it was still over all too quick. And before he knew it, they were stopped in front of her house.

She seemed a little hesitant to speak. "I've been meaning to ask you, what are we?"

"Carbon lifeforms? Homo sapiens?" He kidded, knowing what she was getting at.

"You goof!" She gave his arm a playful punch. "I mean, are we exclusive?"

"I'd like that," his tone rang of sincerity.

"I'd like that too," she said. "So, tomorrow, when I tell my friend what I was doing last night, I'll have to tell her that I was out with my boyfriend."

He smiled, and nodded *yes*, playing it cool, which was no easy feat when he was jumping up and down on the inside.

She smiled the widest smile. "Good, I'm glad you're not playing me."

He laughed.

She ran her fingers through his hair. "I guess I'll see you tomorrow at school…boyfriend."

"I guess you will," he replied as he leaned in and gave her a kiss.

They continued kissing, only stopping for a moment, long enough to look into each other's eyes, then leaned back in and began to kiss again. Will was in a daze.

She stopped kissing him again, and glanced toward her house. He looked as well, and noticed her mother, Michelle, closing the shades that she'd been peeking through.

"Maybe this isn't the best place to make out," she said with a smirk.

"Especially when I'm trying to make a good impression on your parents."

"Well, I better get going," Katie said.

"Oh, you don't have to go," Will kidded.

"Playing 'D'yer Mak'er' by Led Zeppelin" flashed across the car's infotainment screen, and the song began to play in the background.

Will looked down at the stereo. "What is with this car?"

Katie laughed. "I think your car likes me too. It doesn't want me to go."

Will smiled. "Yeah, it'd seem that way."

Katie got out of the car and closed the door behind her.

She leaned down in the window to talk to him, and Will glanced away, trying his best to be a gentleman, and not glance down her shirt. He returned his eyes to the soft lines of her pretty face.

"Wait, I can walk you to the door." Will said as he got up out of the car and walked around to her.

He glanced back at the Corvette, then looked at her as they began their slow walk to her front door.

"We should do something this weekend," she said.

"Yeah, I'm game."

"Great," she said, with a contagious excitement in her eyes.

Will smiled.

Katie bumped her shoulder against his as she took another step. "You know, the world is full of people that don't understand why you take an extra glance back at your car when you walk away, but I do."

"That means a lot, I know it's not…"

"Not what?" she asked.

He thought about how to phrase what he wanted to say. "Not stereotypically the dream car of a guy my age."

"Stereotypes are something that lazy people tell themselves when they don't know what they're talking about. Sure, maybe a lot of older people drive Corvettes, but maybe it's because that's who can afford them. I've met a lot of people our age that love them too. The same could be said for Porsche 911s, and I don't consider them an older-man's car, necessarily."

"Yeah," Will agreed.

"Some people might not like the design of that era, but I think it's great. I wasn't born then, obviously, but I think the 1980's and 90's had some of the best pop culture in the last century, maybe minus the hair."

Will chuckled.

"It's fun to have a small slice of that." She smiled at him. "The more we break stereotypes, the more the world seems a better place, don't you think? Besides, it's sad to see an amazing car get dismissed by a short-sighted outlook."

"I couldn't have said it better myself," he replied.

"Sorry to get on my soapbox for a minute, I've heard plenty from different car haters over the years. Somebody always has a reason to hate someone or something. It's exhausting."

"No," Will replied. "That was great."

She began to walk away.

"Oh, there's one more thing," Will said.

"What's that?" She asked.

He didn't know why he was so nervous to ask, now it was even established that he was her boyfriend. He just had to go for it. "Do you think you'd like to go to the dance with me?"

A grin washed over her face. "I thought you'd never ask."

"Great," Will said.

"I didn't say yes," she replied. "I just didn't think you'd ever ask."

Will's jaw dropped.

Katie began to laugh. "I'm just messing with you; I would love to go with you. So … that's a *yes*."

"Excellent." Will smiled and began to walk backward toward his car. He should probably leave before he messed something up, the night was going too well.

He got back into the Corvette.

As she walked toward her front door, she glanced back at him in the car. The Corvette's right pop-up headlight rolled down and back up, independent of the left headlight, as if it were winking at her.

She smiled and turned her head in curiosity, like a puppy, at how he had done that headlight trick. She then turned and entered the front door of her home.

He had no idea how and why the right headlight had done that. Sometimes the old C4 headlights were problematic, but these hadn't given him any trouble yet. Not only was the malfunction a curious oddity in itself, but also the fact that it seemed to have perfect timing.

He shook his head and smiled. The quirky bugs in this car's system turned the car into being a pretty good wingman when he was with her.

It was so nice to kiss her again, her lips were soft and intoxicating. But it was probably for the best that she had to leave, things seemed to be moving fast between them, and he didn't want to mess up what they had. They seemed to have a really strong connection, and from what he could tell, she felt it too.

While it put Will over the moon, it also made him nervous. He just prayed he wouldn't end up getting hurt again. After all, he was really into his ex-girlfriend when they had first gotten together. But she was so different. It was obvious that Katie was kinder and had a much better heart, and better brain for that matter. And Will had never felt near the same amount of spark and connection with his ex as he did with Katie, there was no comparison. Perhaps that's what scared him the most. If the relationship went south, it could be a heartbreak that he'd never recover from.

Will pulled out of her driveway, and onto the road. He was exhausted, and felt the heaviness of his eyelids.

On the short straightaway after taking the turn out of her subdivision, Will almost nodded off, but shook himself awake. "Yikes, I've got to get home."

He was certainly going to sleep well tonight, it's a good thing it was a short drive to get to his house.

Will yawned, blinked his eyes, and then blinked again.

He found himself standing in a darkened place, gazing at the only thing visible, the Corvette. There was some mist rising from the ground in the background.

Then he saw her there, in a low cut dress. Katie gradually became visible as she approached through the mist in the darkness to the front of the car.

When she reached the hood of the car, she gently laid back on it, and eased her whole body onto the vehicle. There was a delicate grace and beauty to her movements. She leaned her head and neck over the driver's side edge of the hood, and looked at him, upside down from her perspective.

She rolled over onto her stomach and slid up onto her hands and knees on the hood, and motioned with her index finger for him to come over.

Will had always thought that pictures with pin-up girls posing with sports cars were a bit much, but in this moment, he kind-of understood. Not that it was something he'd ever hang on the wall, but he could understand that there were two things that spoke to his soul, together, in front of him. Two things that he desired most, and he could stare at them all day.

He walked forward toward her, she leaned back on her knees on the hood and wrapped her arms around him. He began to kiss her delicate lips.

He opened his eyes, and found her eyes, peering right through him.

As he continued to kiss her, he heard a voice. It sounded like his uncle. *That was odd, what was he doing here?*

Will stopped kissing Katie and eased his head back to look over her shoulder.

Standing behind the car, he saw his Uncle Zac.

"Hey Ace," his Uncle Zac said. "Wake up."

Will woke up, sitting in his driveway, in the driver seat of the Corvette, the car still running. "Don't Dream its Over" by Crowded House played softly out of the car's radio.

SIX

The annoyance of waking up before the best part of a dream vanished when the realization of where he was set in.

He began to shake, and his stomach fluttered. How had he gotten home? He was asleep at the wheel and dreaming. Perhaps if he were half-asleep, he could've explained it away. But that wasn't the case, and he knew it. He should be dead, with his precious new car wrapped around a tree, or a telephone pole, somewhere between here and Katie's house.

He sat for a moment, trying to rectify the situation in his head.

His uncle called him *Ace* in the dream, a nickname he had given Will way back when he beat his uncle at a game of cards with some aces. Somehow it stuck, but it was only something that Zac called him.

Will took a deep breath and let it out. He pressed the button on the garage door opener, and pulled the Corvette into the garage and stopped the engine.

The close call had shaken him to the core, and it bothered him that he couldn't explain his good fortune. Perhaps he wasn't driving faster than his angels could fly.

He closed the car door after he'd gotten out, and as he reached for the doorknob to enter the house, he got a crazy idea.

"Wait a minute," he said, turning back and approaching the car.

He gave the vehicle a suspicious look, opened the door, and sat back down in the driver's seat.

He put the key in the ignition and turned it, just enough for the electronics to turn on, but not enough to crank the engine. He looked down at the infotainment screen.

"Auto pilot," he said, loud and clear.

Text came across the screen, it read: *Engage autopilot?*

"No way!" He was in shock.

He thought for moment. "Auto pilot history, err … auto pilot recent history," he said.

Text began to run across the screen again. *Driver unresponsive, auto pilot engaged at 9:23 pm.*

He glanced at the time, that was about 10 minutes ago, about the time he would've dozed off behind the wheel.

That was incredible! And it explained a lot. Will knew his uncle was a software wiz, but he had no idea he was capable of something like this. He had turned an old car from the 1990s into one of the smartest of smart cars. But somehow that didn't shock him. This was Uncle Zac's dream car, it's what he wanted, and he made it his own dream of what it could be.

Will sat there, inside the car that had just saved his life

after he had fallen asleep on the way home from Katie's house.

There was just one thing that confounded him about the car's advanced technology; it didn't talk. The infotainment system was silent. He'd even tried out the GPS, and it displayed the map and driving directions, but it didn't vocalize the turns to make. He was sure Uncle Zac would've had the infotainment talk, but it didn't, or did it?

"Activate…" *Not audio…* Will thought, *hmmm.* "Activate infotainment voice?"

"*Car voice temporarily disabled,*" the text read across the infotainment screen.

"So, the car has a voice," he said, noticing it referred to it as 'car voice' as opposed to 'infotainment voice'. "I wonder why it's disabled."

He tried to navigate the menu on the touchscreen for a moment.

"Enable car voice," he said.

"*Car voice temporarily disabled,*" the text appeared again.

He's sighed. He was too tired to fight with it tonight. He took the key out of the ignition and got out of the car.

He reached out, and lightly pat the hood of the car as he walked to the garage door that led to the house. "Thanks for saving my life tonight, buddy."

He gave one last glance from the doorway into the house. He smiled as he turned out the garage light and went inside.

As he laid back in bed, Nala came bounding up the dog ramp at the end of the bed and cuddled up next to him.

"Hey girl," he said, as he gave her head a pet.

He looked up, and saw his mother standing in the doorway.

"I really like Katie," Beth said.

"Yeah," Will replied. "There's something special about her."

His mother smiled. "I remember back when I realized that there was something special about your father. We were in high school, and he asked me to go with him to a school dance." She ducked her head and smiled. "It was kind of a silly theme, the 'Out of This World' dance."

Will smiled. "Yeah, that's kind-a goofy."

"But the decorations were so great," Beth went on. "There were stars and the moon, and huge papier-mâché planets, back then we counted nine."

"Yeah," Will said. "Before Pluto-Gate."

"I remember your father and I were dancing next to Saturn, when he leaned in and kissed me. I knew then and there, in my heart, he and I really had something special that would stand the test of time. I knew he was the one for me."

Though he still missed his father very much, hearing old stories like that from his mother always warmed his heart. It helped him still believe that a fairytale true love could exist, in a very cruel, un-fairytalelike world.

"Well, I'll let you get some rest," Beth said, as she eased back from the door. "Love you."

"Love you too, mom," Will replied.

As he laid there, he heard his phone on the nightstand alert him of an incoming text message.

It was from his ex, Mandy.

Hey, it's been a while. I'd love to catch up sometime, she messaged him.

Will put his phone back down on the nightstand. *It'd been a while? The longer the better.* Will thought.

It was Thursday afternoon in the school parking lot. Kahlil threw his bookbag in his pickup truck, and was about to get in, when Will pulled up behind him.

"Hey Kahlil, wanna ride?"

Kahlil turned around and grinned when he saw Will in the Corvette. "Yeah, you know I want a ride."

Kahlil strolled over and did a quick walk around the car. He then opened the door and plopped down into the passenger seat. "This sits low."

"What do you think?" Will asked.

"It's nice, man," he replied. "If you had to get an old car, you made an excellent choice."

Will pulled out of the parking lot, and on to the road for a drive to show it off to him.

"These cars are wasted on old guys," Kahlil said with a laugh as Will pulled the car around a curve.

"I've never felt as connected to the road as I do when I drive this Corvette," Will replied.

"Well, we're almost sitting low enough to be connected to the road, so that makes sense. It doesn't seem like the door is going to fall off of this one, so that's another plus," Kahlil kidded. "Things are starting to look up for you, new car, new girl. How are things going with her anyway?"

"Incredible," Will replied. "We've been hanging out for

two weeks, but it almost feels like two years. She's just so easy to talk to. You ever meet someone, and it feels like you've known them forever?"

"Yeah, I think so," Kahlil said. "When Audre starts talking about clothes, it definitely feels like forever." He cut his eyes at Will and smiled.

"I feel like things are moving fast," Will continued. "But it feels right … you know, because it's her."

"Of course, it feels right, right now," Kahlil shook his head with a skeptic's judgmental look. "Just be careful."

"Why? Did you hear something?"

"No, I haven't," he replied. "Hey, I like the girl, from what I know about her." Kahlil thought for a moment. "Let me put this in a way you'll understand: relationships are like a car, if you're speeding too fast, there's a good chance you're going to lose control and end up in a nasty crash. Like I said, just be careful."

"That's pretty easy to understand, but I appreciate the car analogy." Will nodded. "She definitely has some curves I wouldn't mind driving."

"*And* … you just made the analogy weird."

Will chuckled. "Sorry."

"But I figured you'd appreciate the car angle." Kahlil said. "Just remember the last time …"

"We don't have to talk about her," Will interrupted.

"I just remember how tough that was for you." Kahlil reached over and patted Will on the shoulder. "I just care about you, man. I don't want to see you go through that again."

Will smiled. "Thanks."

Will's Friday was spent in a daydream bliss about his car and his 'girlfriend'. He couldn't wait for the evening, and when it finally arrived, it found him in the stands at his high school football field, with Katie by his side. She was looking as beautiful as ever in her short black skirt and t-shirt, but honestly, she looked amazing no matter what she wore.

They cheered on the school's team, the Westside Dragons, as they took on their arch rivals, the Thoroughbreds.

You could tell just by the name; the Thoroughbreds had a reputation of being elitist schmucks. A lot of them lived in really big houses; teenagers that drove Mercedes and BMWs given to them by their neglectful parents. They weren't all bad though. Will knew a couple, and they were nice enough. But they were all bad tonight, the night of the big game.

The game was reaching its final plays and tension was in the air, rising above the smell of fresh popped popcorn. The home team was ahead, but just by a small margin. The opposing team was on a final drive in the last seconds to try to score and wrestle a victory away from the Dragons.

The seconds had run down, giving only enough time for one more play. The Thoroughbreds were on the 20-yard line, and a field goal wasn't enough points; they were going to have to score a touchdown. But at 20 yards, that was a real possibility, especially with their strong offensive line.

"Come on, Dragons!" Katie yelled.

"Go Kahlil," Will called out to his friend in the defensive line on the field.

The Thoroughbreds snapped the ball to their quarterback, and the play was on. The seconds ran to zero, this was it. It was now or never.

A collective gasp washed across the home audience as the Thoroughbred quarterback was quick to throw the ball, and easily put it in the hands of one of their offensive men on the outside, who looked to have a clear path to the end zone.

The Thoroughbred player tucked the football, and began to run.

Will's heart sunk.

"Oh no!" he heard Katie callout next to him.

The visiting crowd began to go wild.

As the Thoroughbred offensive player closed in on the end zone, Kahlil launched himself into the air, seeming to come out of nowhere.

There was a glimmer of hope. The home crowd was on the edge of their seats as Kahlil made contact, wrapping his arms around the Thoroughbred player, and pummeling him to the ground, just feet from the end zone.

The game was over; Dragons win!

The home crowd began to lose their minds in the stands. The fears and tension of the close points made the celebration that much more intense.

Will wrapped his arm around Katie and yelled as he threw his fist into the air in victory. The whole school couldn't help but be proud of their Kahlil, the hero of the game.

As the crowd began to disperse, Will pushed through some people and caught up with Kahlil, to congratulate him on the win.

"That was amazing," Will said as he approached Kahlil and gave him a high five.

"Thanks," Kahlil replied. "I just hope the scouts that were supposed to be here, were watching."

Will smiled. "There's no way they could have missed that."

Kahlil glanced over to Katie who was standing next to Will with a grin on her face.

"I don't believe we've had a chance to meet officially," he said, reaching out his hand. "My name is Kahlil."

"Oh, sorry," Will said. "I should have introduced you. Kahlil, this is Katie; Katie, Kahlil."

"It's great to finally meet you." Katie reached out and shook his hand.

"Nice to meet you," Kahlil said warmly.

"You're probably sick of hearing this, but you were great out there tonight," Katie said.

Kahlil laughed. "I'll never get sick of hearing that."

Kahlil turned back to Will. "Me and some of the guys…" He glanced toward Katie. "And their girls." He looked back at Will as he continued, "Are going to the fair a little later after we clean up. You two are welcome to join."

Will turned to Katie. She shrugged and smiled, and gave him an excited nod *yes*.

"I think we're in," Will replied.

"Cool, cool," Kahlil said. "It'll probably be an hour or two, but we'll see you there."

The football hero turned and joined a couple of his team buddies as they headed to the locker rooms.

Katie locked her arm around Will's and leaned her head

against his shoulder. "The fair sounds fun. Are you going to win me something?"

Will chuckled. "I'll try, but don't get your hopes up."

Katie laughed as they turned and headed back toward the car.

SEVEN

There was an hour or two to burn before going to the fair, so, after Will and Katie got some coffees at a local coffeehouse, Will decided to show her another local point of interest in his continual tour of the town he was giving Katie. It was a place commonly called Lookout Point.

The stars dotted the night sky, pinholes to the heavens, and Will had taken the roof off the Corvette, so the view was on full of display above them.

Lookout Point was an area on the outskirts of town, on the side of the large hill that overlooked the town. For generations it was known by the youth as a date destination, the view was inspiring, especially at night, and it took little effort to make the night seem romantic.

On some nights, you may have two or three cars distanced from each other, enjoying the view. But tonight, with the fair in town, and the big football game, Will and Katie had the entire area to themselves.

It was a clearing surrounded by a dark, secluded wooded area, and on a night like this, it was the perfect place for some privacy. Will pulled up to a secluded vantage point to see the town's lights, and turned off the engine, but left the radio on.

"You didn't bring me out here to kill me, did you?" She kidded, as she took another sip of her frozen coffee.

"Of course not," he replied. "This is another stop on your local destination tour." Will held out his hands as if he were presenting something. "Lookout Point."

"Maybe Make-Out Point," she quipped.

Will smiled. "Sometimes people call it that too."

"Or maybe Murder Point." She smiled at him. "There are devious outcomes any way you want to spin it."

Will shrugged. "I'm just the tour guide."

"A tour of what, though?" She kidded.

With the roof off the Corvette, they could gaze at the myriad of stars across the clear sky. The town's lights below looked like stars as well, some stationary and some moving about. At this distance, it was as if the ground was a fun-mirror of the stars in the sky.

He reached out, and took her hand. She leaned over and they began to kiss. He ran his fingers through her long hair as their passionate kissing continued.

After a couple minutes of fervent making out, they eased back into their seats and smiled, they had to catch their breath for a moment.

"This is really beautiful." She looked out at the view. "A fine place to get murdered. So how many girls have you brought here?"

He laughed. "Just one, you, tonight."

"How did you know about this place, then?" She asked with playful suspicion. "And how did you know just where to park?"

"Me and some of the guys have driven up here to check it out, you know, people talk about it."

"So, it really is Make-Out Point," she kidded.

"Ha-ha," he gave her an exaggerated sarcastic laugh. "Did you want to get out and look?" He asked.

"Sure."

As they walked around to stand in front of the car, he put his arm around her shoulder as they gazed out over the infinite sea of stars and lights they beheld.

"This is really romantic, you're getting big points," she said.

"I didn't realize we were on a points system."

"Oh yeah; you've never heard of boyfriend points?" She went on as if it was common knowledge. "You want to be enrolled in the Boyfriend Points Program, right?"

"Of course," Will grinned. "By the way, are there any rewards involved for reaching certain scores?"

"Maybe." She looked into his eyes, leaned in and kissed him on the lips. Her lips were soft and sweet, and he could catch a hint of her cherry Chapstick. She kissed him like she meant it, like a girl who was giving him all of her heart.

It was in that moment that he realized, that he might be in love with this girl, or at least completely head over heels for her.

They eased away from the kiss, not breaking eye contact until she chuckled, and smiled at him to ease the seriousness of the moment. They turned back toward the lights of town.

She leaned forward as she scanned over the landscape. "Look, you can see the fair down there," she said, pointing her finger.

He looked down and could see the fair lit up, Ferris wheel spinning slowly into the air. He looked back at her. His eyes chased the soft lines of her face, and he traveled them up to her eyes.

Her eyes seemed as deep and rich as her soul, eyes and a soul he felt like he could get lost in forever.

"I can see the stars reflecting in your eyes," he said.

"I can see my heart reflecting in yours."

He gave her a curious look, as he tried to decipher what she had just said.

"You have my heart, you big goof," she clarified as she gave his arm a soft playful punch.

"Your Eyes" by Peter Gabriel began to play over the car stereo.

"All those electronic glitches make your car so much better," she said.

"I know, it has perfect timing."

He took her in his arms, and they began to sway to the music, slow dancing under the stars. They barely moved their feet; it was all in the sway.

After the song was over, they slid up, side-by-side onto the hood of the car, being careful not to scratch it, laid back against the window, and gazed up at the sky. The evening began to grow cooler at their high elevation, but they were comfortable, warmed by the still-toasty engine beneath the hood.

She cuddled up next to him and put her head on his chest. Her soft fingers always felt a perfect fit in his hand.

She looked up at him. "Thanks for the dance."

He smiled at her. "Anytime."

She grinned and turned back to the stars. "Good."

He glanced back up at the sky as well.

"I love looking at the stars with you," she said. "Let's never stop."

"This Year's Love" by David Gray began to play from the car's stereo. It was odd that it seemed unprompted by their conversation, but it was a perfect song for the moment.

There was no threat of rain, but Will put the top back on the Corvette after they arrived at the fair. He didn't want anybody messing with the car.

Kahlil and his group of football buddies had already been at the fair awhile when Will and Katie came walking into the festivities from the ticket line.

The night's football hero's face lit up when he saw them approaching.

"The Legend," Will greeted his friend as they approached, "The Thoroughbred slayer."

"We sent them to the glue factory," Kahlil replied, reaching out his hand to shake Will's, and as they shook hands, he pulled Will close for a hug.

"I thought you must have changed your mind," Kahlil said.

"Yeah, sorry, we got lost on the way," Will kidded.

Kahlil smiled. "I bet."

Will glanced around at the guys with Kahlil. "Hey, what's up, guys? Great game tonight."

The guys offered Will and Katie a warm welcome.

"We've just been riding rides, playing some games, and eating some delicious straight-up heart-attack food," Kahlil said.

"That sounds great," Will replied.

"Good to see you too, Katie," Kahlil said, then turned to the girl by his side. "This is my lady, Audre. You may recognize her, she's one of the cheerleaders."

"Good to meet you," Katie said.

"You too." Audre returned a genuine smile.

One of the guys in the group with Kahlil spoke up, "Hey, we're going to head to that weird mirror house, we'll catch back up with you guys in a bit."

"That's cool, go ahead," Kahlil replied.

The other couples left Kahlil, Audre, Katie, and Will there.

Audre turned to Kahlil. "I don't know how you're a big tough football player, and you're still scared to go on the tilt-a-whirl with me," she kidded him.

"You seriously want me to throw up on you?" Kahlil asked her.

"Come on, I don't want to go alone," Audre said.

"I'll go with you," Katie said.

Audre looked at her. "Really?"

"Yeah, it'll be fun," Katie replied.

"Great." Audre got on her tiptoes and kissed Kahlil on the cheek. "Looks like you're off the hook, baby."

Kahlil looked at Katie and mouthed the words *thank you.*

"Let's go." Audre nodded to Katie with the excitement of a girl freed, who'd been denied a tilt-a-whirl ride all night.

As the two girls left them there, the guys glanced around for something more their speed. They decided on a ball throwing game. Knock over enough small fuzzy figures, and they could win a small prize.

"Man, there's something different about you," Kahlil said in between a couple of his throws. "It's like you've got a glow about you."

"I think I'm in love," Will replied.

"Whoa, slow down man. It's like I came up with that car crash analogy the other day for nothing."

Will smiled, "Okay, okay."

"I get it. That's great, man, I'm happy for you." Kahlil put his arm on his shoulder. "Like I said yesterday, just be careful. It's easier to fall in love than fall out of it."

"I will."

"But yeah, she seems great," Kahlil said. "Who knows? She might be the one. I approve of this one so far."

"That's reassuring."

"And if it doesn't work out, know that Audre will fight her," he said in a kidding tone. "But seriously, she was so happy that you found someone, after your last one."

"Mandy was nothing compared to Katie," Will said. "Sure, she was a good kisser..."

"And a professional, with certain skills," Kahlil added. "Don't forget, people call her *Handy Mandy* for a reason."

"People call her that?" Will asked.

"You didn't know that?"

"No," Will replied. "But she didn't start doing all that stuff till after we broke up."

"Oh, really bro?" Kahlil said in disappointment. "I'm sorry."

Will rolled his eyes. "That's fine, I'd rather share that stuff with Katie anyway."

"You've got it bad," Kahlil said with a chuckle.

"Oh, and I asked her to the dance," Will said.

"And?"

"And she said yes, of course."

"That's great, man," Kahlil said.

"Also, my band got chosen to play a song at the dance," Will said.

"Nice, better not mess it up. Got to impress the new girl and all." Kahlil laughed, "But I'm sure it'll be good. I'll cheer extra loud."

Will and Kahlil got distracted by a scuffle behind them across the path. It was Doug and his cronies playfully pushing each other as they passed by the area.

"Great," Will said. "Those guys are here?"

"Them boys are gonna need to get dealt with at some point," Kahlil said.

"How do you even grow up to be such an idiot teenager? I mean, no matter how bad your home life is, how can you be devoid of any decency at all?"

Doug and his crew disappeared out of sight into the crowd. Will and Kahlil turned back to finish their carnival game.

When all was said and done at the booth, Kahlil had won a sizable teddy bear for Audre, and Will had the option of choosing a much smaller prize for his efforts. He picked a red and white polka-dot hair ribbon for Katie.

It wasn't long before the girls returned from the tilt-a-whirl, arm in arm, pal-ing around as if they were old friends.

"It looks like that went well," Will whispered to Kahlil.

"Good," he replied. "She can be her fair-ride-buddy."

"I won this for you, baby," Kahlil gave Audre the bear.

"He's great!" Audre grabbed the bear and squeezed it in a tight bear hug.

"And I won you this." Will held out the hair ribbon to Katie, a little embarrassed of the underwhelming prize.

"I love it!" Katie said, taking it from him and tying it into her hair.

The two couples hung out for a while longer, enjoying each other's company.

In time, Kahlil and Audre decided to leave; Will and Katie lingered a little longer at the fair.

"So how did you end up becoming such good friends with Kahlil?" Katie asked.

"Doug, actually," Will replied. "This was years ago … Doug was messing with me, and Kahlil noticed and stepped in."

"That's cool."

"Yeah, Kahlil is the kind of guy that won't stand by if he sees something that's wrong," Will said.

"He seems like a good guy."

"He is. After that," Will continued, "We started talking,

and really got along. We've been friends ever since. His girl, Audre is really nice too."

Brightly colored explosions began to fill the sky. Fireworks had begun to be shot, appearing high over the fair.

Will and Katie seized the opportunity for a spectacular view of the fireworks on the Ferris wheel, high above the fair, slowly going around, sharing a funnel cake.

"I don't think this night could get more perfect," Katie said as she cuddled up to him.

"Plenty of boyfriend points?" Will asked.

She smiled at him. "Plenty."

He put his arm around her as they watched more fireworks explode from the heights of the Ferris wheel.

When the ride was over, and they were walking away from the Ferris wheel, Will noticed a tall slender man, wearing a black hat beginning to approach them. There was an unsettling feeling that grew as the man approached. While hard to define, there was a darkness about him.

"William?" The man in the black hat said.

"Yes," Will replied, uneasy but curious. How did this creep know his name?

"I was looking for a proper moment to approach you. I represent an acquaintance of your late uncle," the man said. "First, he wishes to send his condolences on your loss."

"Thanks," Will replied, with a suspicion growing in his gut.

"My employer had taken an affinity for an automobile, one 1992 Corvette owned by your uncle," the man continued. "It is his understanding that you're now in possession of that car?"

"I am," Will replied, knowing where this was going before it went there. "But unfortunately, it's not for sale."

"My employer has prepared a very generous offer for you, that I think…"

"I'm sorry," Will interrupted him. "I have a sentimental attachment to the car. That same make and model, even color, are not that difficult to find, given a wide enough search on the internet."

"Like you, my employer is attached to that particular car," the man's voice grew sterner, and more menacing.

"I don't know what to tell you." Will's anxiety rose. "You'll have to excuse me; I need to get her home."

Will locked arms with Katie, turned, and quickly began to walk in the other direction.

"That man made my skin crawl," she whispered to him.

"Yeah, I know what you mean."

"Did you hear him? *I've been waiting for the right time to approach you*; hence he's been following us here at the fair."

"Yeah," Will agreed. "I don't know what's going on, but I'm not getting rid of that car."

"You shouldn't."

Will took a deep breath, and exhaled, "I just have a bad feeling that we haven't heard the last from that guy."

Katie locked on to Will's arm tighter as they walked.

EIGHT

Will and Katie continued together through the poorly-lit, gravel parking lot toward the car. "It's really dark out here," there was a note of apprehension in Katie's voice.

"And we had to park way out by the edge of the woods," Will replied. There were still plenty of cars parked all around, but all those people seemed to still be enjoying the fair. The parking lot was deserted, at least out where they had to park.

Katie gave a quick glance back over her shoulder. "You don't think that guy is still following us, do you?"

Will glanced behind them. "No, I don't think so, but I don't intend to stick around and find out."

"I think I was about done with the fair anyway."

Will looked around up ahead of them, trying to spot his car. "I think the car is right up here…somewhere." The gravel crunched beneath their feet as they walked a few more steps through the darkened lot.

"Hey!" Will heard Katie yell as she was pulled away, back behind him.

"Hey Puta!" Juan, Doug's cohort greeted him as he held her back by the arms. Just as Will turned around, he felt the heavy impact of Doug's fist to the side of his face. The punch knocked him off his feet and onto the ground.

Will shook his head, trying to get his bearings. As he looked up from where he sat on the ground, he saw Doug standing there, and Crazy Shane was nearby, behind him, holding his knife out in his hand as usual, caressing the side of the blade with his other hand like a real psychopath.

"Doug, what are you doing?" Will glanced over at Shane. "So what? Are you going to cut me now?"

"I don't know, maybe." Shane replied. "But right now, I'm just making sure you don't go anywhere, so Doug can finish the lesson he was going to teach you the other day."

"I can't believe you guys," Katie said, struggling to break free from Juan's grip.

"No, no, no," Juan said to Katie. "Puta deserves this, he has it coming."

"Let her go, man," Will said to Juan.

"I'm afraid not," Juan replied. "She needs to stay for the show."

Doug reached into his pocket and garnished a pair of brass knuckles.

"Oh great," Will said.

"Oh great is right," Doug said. "When I'm done with you, they're not going to be able to recognize your face." Doug took another step closer. "I told you it wasn't over between us."

Doug glanced over at Katie. "Maybe after she sees your makeover, she might take a liking to me instead," he said, blowing a kiss at her.

"Not in a million years," she replied.

"Maybe she won't have a choice." Doug shrugged his shoulders. "Or maybe she'll be next in line for a makeover."

At that, Will staggered to his feet. He knew that he couldn't win against this illiterate gang, but he knew he had to fight.

Doug looked over and chuckled. "That's it, at least you're going to take your punishment like a man, not a little boy."

Doug pulled his fist back, like a snake, ready to strike. "Here it comes."

There was the sound of a deep engine cranking up nearby, and tires spinning as they caught traction on the gravel.

All eyes turned as the pop-up headlights flipped 180 degrees up on the purple Corvette as it raced toward them.

"What?" Will said. "Who's driving my car?"

As the car accelerated, approaching the group, the front of the vehicle whipped around, and the back end of the car slid across the gravel sideways, hitting crazy Shane, sending him flying into a large bush.

In the confusion, Katie broke free of Juan's hold, spun around, and elbowed him in the chest, knocking the wind out of him. He stumbled back, wheezing, trying to catch his breath.

The spin of the car stopped with the tail-end facing Doug. The car began to accelerate, kicking the parking lot's loose gravel up from the back wheels, and launching them at Doug.

The wave of sharp small stones pelted Doug; he hid his face as he ran in the opposite direction.

The driver's side door of the Corvette flung open. "Will, get in!" A voice from inside the car said.

His stomach sank, he'd recognize that voice anywhere in an instant. It was his dead Uncle Zac's voice. But Will stood staring into an empty Corvette. "Get in the car, Ace!" the voice from the car insisted.

Will snapped out of it, and yelled to Katie, "Get in the car!" The passenger-side door flung open of its own volition, and she hopped in.

Through his baffled haze, Will found the wherewithal to jump into the car. The doors closed behind them, and the car took off, driving itself. In the rearview mirror, Will caught a glance of the three goons running for Doug's car.

Will's eyes were wide, as he was plastered to the back of his seat from the car's acceleration. His hands were in his lap, nowhere close to the steering wheel or stick shift. He watched the stick shift move on its own to the next gear.

He glanced over at Katie, who also looked to be in shock. "Are you okay?"

"Yeah," she said, looking as confused and afraid as he was. "There's nobody in here, you're not driving. How is this possible?"

"I don't know, I don't know," Will said, with a frantic tone in his voice. "The car is driving itself."

"I don't think cars from 1992 can drive themselves," Katie replied.

"Surprise?" His uncle's voice spoke through the speakers as the car flew out of the parking lot and onto the main road.

"So, I didn't dream the voice," Will said as he turned to Katie. "That's my Uncle Zac's voice. I can't believe it. My uncle must have programmed a self-driving artificial intelligence in this car…that uses his voice."

"What?" She asked, shaking her head.

"He was like this computer and software wiz," Will said. "He must have figured out artificial intelligence."

"Not artificial intelligence," the car interjected. "Intelligence, intelligence."

"What are you talking about?" Will asked.

"This isn't just a computer software program," the car explained. "It's me, Uncle Zac."

"You're kidding me," Will couldn't help but be skeptical. "That's not possible."

"Oh, it's possible," Zac's voice replied. "Way ahead of its time, like your uncle, but possible."

"Well, you sound as humble as my uncle," Will kidded.

"That's because I am him," the car went on. "I figured out how to transfer my consciousness to, for the lack of a better word, a server."

Will chuckled in disbelief. "You're telling me that you, this car, are actually my Uncle Zac?"

"Essentially, yes, Will," the car replied.

"This is heavy," Will said, shaking his head. "I'm supposed to believe that?"

"Look, I was waiting for the right time to ease you into the information, but you were in big trouble with those degenerates back there," Zac explained.

"Yeah, thanks for your help with that," he replied, still in disbelief that he was in a conversation with a car that claimed to be his uncle's consciousness. "How did you know what was going on? You weren't anywhere close to us."

"I've got sensors and cameras all over the inside and outside of this car, I'm constantly gathering and processing data from within and all around this car," Zac explained.

A look of horror came over Katie's face. "Make Out Point." She ducked her head in embarrassment.

Will cringed.

"Oh, don't be embarrassed," the car said. "I think you two are great together."

"Oh my gosh, please stop," Will interrupted.

"Okay, okay," the car said. "I can change the subject to those guys from the parking lot, chasing us in their Mustang."

Will looked behind them. "Those guys won't quit, seriously."

Doug drove a 2008 Ford Mustang. It was hard to miss, painted lime green, with some yellow stripes. It also had some modifications that let the muffler announce its presence from blocks away. There were also a few small menacing touches Doug had added to the car, like a red interior dome light, and an oversized spoiler. Perhaps the car itself wouldn't have been so bad if it didn't suffer from its association with Doug.

Doug always referred to his car as the *Mean Green Machine*, but other students commonly dubbed it the *Snot Rocket*.

"It's not always about the car, it's also about the driver," Zac said as the Corvette sped up, and drifted around a sharp corner. "That being said, this car is faster, and I can drive circles around those guys." The Corvette caught rubber as it increased speed.

"Did you know anything about this car talking or being able to do any of this?" Katie asked.

"No," Will replied. "I just thought there was a glitch with the radio."

"Oh, that was just me messing with you," Zac said. "Speaking of the radio…"

"Playing 'More Human than Human' by White Zombie" read across the infotainment screen; then the song began to play loudly.

"Music to drive to," Zac said.

The Corvette accelerated as it began to weave between the cars on the road. All Will and Katie could do was hold on for the ride. Katie put on her seatbelt; Will noticed and followed her example.

"Yeah, seatbelts are probably a good idea about now," the car said. "I meant to say that earlier."

"Sounds like something my uncle would play right now." Will commented as the music blared on. It looked as if they had gotten clear of the majority of the traffic, and they might be able to put some distance between them and Doug.

The Corvette screeched around another corner and sped back up. Katie looked nervous as the buildings and scenery on the sides of the road zoomed by in a blur.

"I don't want to die tonight," Katie said.

"I make no guarantees, but I'll do my best," Zac replied in his jovial jest.

Will reached over and grabbed Katie's hand. The tires on the Corvette began to squeal as Zac slammed on the brakes, the seatbelts held the two passengers tight.

Will and Katie screamed as their inertia came to an abrupt stop.

Will threw up his hands. "What was that for?"

A light brown dog trotted across the street in front of them. "Aw, how cute, a puppy," Katie said, short of breath.

As soon as the pup had made it to the other side of the road, safe, the Corvette floored it, and the tires squealed again.

The momentary stop gave Doug's Mustang the opportunity to close the gap between them. "They're coming up behind us," Will said.

"I can see that," the car replied. "Remember, sensors." The Corvette sped up.

"What are you planning on …" Will couldn't finish getting out his sentence, before the car threw itself into a drift in the middle of the road and spun itself 180 degrees to face the Mustang.

Doug and his goons looked at them in awe through their front window. Katie only offered a determined look, and one hand giving them the middle finger.

Smoke began pouring over the back tires of the Corvette as it accelerated in the opposite direction. It zoomed by the Mustang heading the other way.

Will looked in the rearview mirror to see Doug try to

do a 180-degree drift to follow them, but he spun out in the middle of the street, almost hitting a guardrail on the side of the road.

The Corvette zipped down the next side street and was soon out of sight of the Mustang in a few turns.

"That song is an oldie but a goodie," The car said as the song ended. Zac then turned the music down. "So, trust my driving now?"

"I mean, kind-of," Will replied.

"Not if I'm holding a cup of coffee," Katie kidded.

"Can we pull over somewhere so I can try to wrap my head around all this?" Will asked. "I need to get out and take a breath."

"Sure, but let's try not to take too much time," the car replied. "Your friends will be looking for us. I can outrun them all night, but do we really want to waste the gas?"

A couple blocks passed; the Corvette pulled into an empty parking deck. After rolling midway into the ground floor of the structure, the car stopped its engine and folded down its headlights.

"I'm sorry, Will," the car said. "I wanted to find a good way to tell you. I really did."

"But you died." Will shook his head in disbelief. "I went to your funeral. I feel like my head is going to explode. How am I supposed to process all this? How am I supposed to feel?"

"I don't know," Uncle Zac said. "Relieved? This is all unprecedented. This has never been done before, to my knowledge."

Will mulled it over in his mind.

"You can't tell your mother," Zac went on. "At least not yet. It'd be too much for her right now. And we have to see how this is all going to work. Maybe we can find a way to let her know, eventually."

Will let out a deep breath. "Okay."

"Actually, you can't tell anyone," the car said. "Both of you, this has to remain a secret." Will and Katie nodded that they agreed to keep quiet.

"Because that brings me to my next difficult topic," Zac said. "My death wasn't random. It was most certainly an orchestrated hit."

Will felt like he was going to be sick. Knowing his uncle was killed was bad enough, but knowing that it was premeditated murder somehow made it even worse.

"Just being in possession of this car puts you in more danger than I ever should have put you in," Zac explained.

"Why me?" Will asked.

"Are you kidding?" Zac said. "I love this car, and the only person I knew that loved it as much, and would take care of it as well as I did, was you. Am I wrong?"

"No," Will replied. "It's my dream car."

"I know," Zac said. "Mine too. That's *why you*. This car is even better than our dream car with all of the modifications I added."

"But it has a pesky uncle inside." Will chuckled. "We always saw this car as kind of a supercar. But now it's a supercar in a little different way."

"Exactly," Zac replied.

"You've done some amazing stuff to it," Will said.

"You deserved this car," his uncle said. "You just didn't

deserve the trouble that might come with it. Look, I have control of a lot of things in this car, but there's still things I can't do. Like fix everything in the engine, change the tires, the oil, you get the idea. And if it's something you can't fix, I've got a car guy named Tony."

"Yeah, okay," Will said, as he opened the door and got out.

The car's driver's side window rolled down. "Where are you going?" Zac asked.

"Nowhere, just stretching my legs and catching my breath." Will leaned against the car.

"Above anything else, we can't let the technology I built into this car get into the wrong hands," Zac warned. "The consequences could be disastrous."

"I understand," Will said.

"Do you?" The car asked.

"Yeah," Katie agreed. "Some creepy guy already tried to buy the car earlier tonight."

"What did he look like?" There was growing concern in Zac's tone.

Their conversation was interrupted by the sound of Doug's Mustang pulling into the parking garage.

The tires of Doug's car screeched to a halt about twenty feet in front of them.

"Get in," Uncle Zac said to Will. "I lost him before, and I can do it again. And I was barely trying last time."

Will stood by the side of the Corvette, hesitating to get back in.

Will noticed the red interior light of the Mustang, as Doug and his cronies got out of the vehicle.

They stood, side by side, facing Will and the Corvette; Shane had already brandished his knife.

"Dang, Butt-Face," Doug said. "I didn't know you could drive like that. Where's your other friend that sprayed me with rocks in the parking lot? Where'd you drop him off? I want to pay him a little visit too."

Will was silent.

"Well, I'll find that guy later," Doug continued. "It's mostly you that's going to get a beating tonight."

Doug hit a button on his keychain that popped the trunk of his car open.

Just as Doug had done that, a black Audi raced into the parking garage, and stopped to the side of them about half way between Doug and Will.

A man got out of the black car; it was the unsettling man with the black hat from the fair.

"That's the guy that wanted to buy the car," Katie whispered to Zac.

"Will, get in the car," Zac said in an urgent tone, in a low volume that only Will and Katie could hear.

Doug and his crew bowed up in front of the new arrival.

"Nice hat," Doug said, poking fun at the man from the Audi. "You look like the villain in a cartoon."

"Who are you, Puta?" Juan asked the new stranger in a threatening tone.

"I can't let anything happen to that Corvette," the man in the black hat said. "My employer won't allow it."

"Employer?" Doug scoffed. "Like, Will?"

"No," the man replied in a monotone voice. "Not…like, Will."

"So sorry, ese," Juan said as he walked back to the trunk of the Mustang and pulled out a crowbar. "Because first we're going to beat down Puta, and then we're going to smash his car. And there's nothing you can do about it."

No sooner had Juan said that; the man in the black hat raised his hand, brandishing a black, semi-automatic pistol with a silencer on it. Before another word could be said, or anyone could react, the man popped off a shot.

A slight mist of blood sprayed from Juan's hand, and the crowbar fell from his grip and clanked on the pavement below.

"You shot me!" Juan cried out, grabbing his hand with his other hand.

"Stop whining, I just grazed your hand, didn't even hit the bone, you baby," the man in the black hat said. He turned to Doug. "Have you ever thought about getting an ear pierced?"

"What?" Doug asked.

The man in the black hat raised his pistol and took another quick shot at Doug. The bullet grazed Doug's earlobe.

Doug grabbed his ear with one hand, then threw up his other hand. "Whoa, man!"

Shane threw up his hands in surrender, dropping his knife. The knife he was holding fell through the air, and by his own idiotic misfortune, landed, with the blade sticking into the top of his right shoe.

"Ouch!" Shane said through clenched teeth. But Shane remained frozen in place, in fear of the mysterious man that had them at gunpoint.

"Those shots could have just as easily been between your eyes. They probably should have, but I'm feeling extra charitable today. So, do I have your attention?" The man in the black hat asked.

Doug and his two goons nodded their heads in agreement.

"This is how it's going to be," the mysterious man continued. "If you come within 20 feet of that car, or Will, or orchestrate any harm toward either, I will come to each of your houses in the middle of the night, and not be so charitable next time. Don't bother him, don't even talk to him. You see him in the hall, pass on the other side. Do you all understand?"

The three thugs nodded their heads.

Will stood in terror of the man in the black hat, but if he was doling out protection, he thought perhaps he should press his luck a little.

"That goes for Katie too," Will said.

The man in the black hat glanced back at Will, rolled his eyes, and turned back to Doug and his boys. "That goes for Katie as well. Understand?"

"Yeah," Doug replied, blood running over his one hand holding his ear.

"Great," the man said, then motioned toward Doug's Mustang with his gun. "Now get out of here and I might let you live the rest of your miserable lives."

Doug, Juan, and Shane scrambled to get back into Doug's car, Doug holding his ear, Juan holding his hand, and Shane removing the knife from the top of his foot and limping as quickly as he could.

The Mustang cranked up, turned, and sped off to disappear the way that they came in.

Will stood in place, still frozen in the moment. Everything seemed surreal, and his gut felt hollowed out. He could hear Katie's breath trembling in the car next to him.

The man in the black hat put away his gun, and held out his hand toward the ground, as if to imply for Will to stay calm, despite the situation.

"Those guys needed a comeuppance," the man said. "I think anyone could agree with that."

Will stared at the man, a deer in headlights.

The man reached into his jacket pocket and pulled out an envelope and approached Will.

"Inside you will find details about the generous offer from my employer for the car," the man explained. "And a number where I can be reached."

Will took the envelope that the man handed to him.

The man looked down at his watch. "It's just turning midnight now. You have two days to accept the offer. So that means you must contact me by the end of Sunday."

"And if I don't?" Will asked.

"In that case, you will be offered a less attractive, but more persuasive, offer to part with the car," the man replied.

Will could tell that the alternative meant bodily harm to him, or the ones he loved.

The man spoke unaffected, as if it were all just business to him. "Take it home, look it over, and contact me," the man said. "And I hope you are wise enough to leave the authorities out of our matters. It's for the best, especially for you."

Will glanced down at the envelope. The man in the black hat glanced around and began to walk back to his Audi.

Will got back in the Corvette, and it started up. His face was glossed over, his mind unable to process everything that had just happened.

They followed the black Audi at a distance as it pulled through to the other side of the parking deck, then turned the opposite direction as they pulled out onto the street.

Will was quiet as the somber ride home began. His mind was too consumed by the traumatic experience to understand the night, or to contemplate what to do next.

NINE

They rode along, casually distancing themselves from the scene at the parking deck. "That … was terrifying," Katie said. "There goes my ability to sleep for the unforeseeable future."

"Me too," Will replied.

"That was the guy that killed me," the car said. "That's another reason I wanted you to get in the car."

"How do you know he was the one?" Will asked.

"What do you mean, *how do I know?* I saw him do it," Zac answered.

"That's something I don't understand," Katie chimed in. "You were killed unexpectedly, right?"

"That's correct," the car replied. "Though I'd been feeling an impending sense of danger, I guess it was still somewhat unexpected."

"Right," she continued. "How did you transfer your consciousness to the car at just the right moment? Or did you do it beforehand, and your body was walking around like a blank slate?"

"Ah, someone's paying attention," Zac replied. "I like her, Will."

"So do I," Will replied.

"Thanks." She ducked her head a little at the compliment. "I like you both too."

"Anyway," Uncle Zac continued. "The answer is *dual consciousness*."

"Dual consciousness?" she asked.

"Yeah," the car said. "If you think it's hard to wrap your head around it conceptually, try wrapping your head around it when you experience it. I was conscious in two places at one time."

"That sounds trippy," Will said. "But I don't understand how that would work."

"It was trippy," Zac continued. "But I don't know if *dual consciousness* is even the right word for it. It's more like one consciousness, split into two places. I was fully aware and processing stimuli from two places at once, but I was at one consciousness about it. It's like if one mind was experiencing things in bodies, in two different places at the same time."

"How were you…" Katie thought about how to phrase her question. "Of one mind in two different places? Some kind of telepathy?"

"A communications chip," the car explained. "While I was equally awake in both places, a small chip implanted in my head communicated with a chip in the car in real-time. That's how, even though my car wasn't anywhere near me when I died, I know who killed me."

"That's tech way passed anything I've ever imagined," Will said.

"That's what I was working on," Zack replied.

"Wait," Will said. "Wouldn't you be worried that they'd find the chip if they ever did an autopsy on you? I guess it's a good thing they accidentally cremated …" Will stopped mid-sentence. "Was it you?"

"Guilty," Uncle Zac said. "I don't know if they would have done one on me or not, the cause of death was pretty cut and dry, but I had to be safe."

"But how?" Will questioned.

"I have some wireless abilities built into the car," Zac explained. "I may have hacked into the funeral home schedule and bumped up the cremation."

"Incredible," Katie said.

"I was also still tied into some of the cameras in my house after I died," The car went on. "I saw some men break in, and comb through my house, leaving it looking undisturbed before the executor of the will could take stock of things. They were, no doubt, looking for records of the technology I was working on. Unfortunately, I was a little sloppy. While I didn't leave any notes about the consciousness tech, I did have some diagrams of the dashboard of a C4 Corvette, which they found. It's not a smoking gun …"

"Too soon," Katie said.

"Sorry," Zac replied. "It's not any kind of hard evidence of anything, but it may have aroused some interest in the car."

"Great," Will said with sarcasm.

"I had driven the car away from the house to hide it when I got shot," Zac said.

"Self-drove it?" Katie asked.

"Of course," Zac continued. "Anyway, so, they couldn't

get to it then, but I'm sure they've been on the lookout for it. I'm sure they realize that I have safety deposit boxes and other secret storage locations, but they're definitely after this Corvette as well."

"Obviously, I have no intention of entertaining the offer, but I wonder how much it is." Will held up the envelope the man with the black hat had given him. "Should I open it?"

"Yeah," the car said. "I'm curious as well."

Will opened the envelope and pulled out the piece of paper as his uncle drove along.

"Cop!" Katie pointed at an approaching officer's car.

Will dropped the letter in his lap, and put his hands on the wheel, to appear as if he were driving as the police passed by. As the officer faded in the darkness in the rear-view mirror, Will picked the letter back up off of his lap and read it.

"Thirty-thousand dollars," Will summarized. "And the hitman's name is Maxwell." Will folded the note up and put it back into the envelope. "Thirty-thousand dollars is not a bad offer. I might be able to get a ZR-1 version of this car in the same year…well, with some miles," he kidded.

"Playing 'Don't take the Money' by Bleachers" flashed across the infotainment screen, and the song played in the quiet background of their conversation.

"But he's not buying a C4 Corvette," the car replied. "He's buying a life, more specifically yours. That's the amount it's worth to Maxwell's employer not to be bothered with paying for the hit on you, and the suspicion it would bring to have someone close to me also get assassinated. And that monetary risk for the chance that there is some useful tech in this car … or there is a key or clue that would help them uncover my secret storage locations."

"I understand," Will replied. "That's a lot of money to be throwing around just at 'a chance' your tech is in there."

"Whoever it is has money to burn," Katie said.

"They really want the tech. The thing is," the car continued. "I really don't know who's behind it all. There're a couple people capable of it, but I don't know who for sure."

"You think it's someone you knew?" Will asked.

"It's possible, perhaps probable," Zac replied. "We have to be careful. If he can just throw money around like that, he has a lot of capital, and can have a lot of resources, and officials in his pocket."

"It's the kind of person who can pull some strings," Katie said.

"Exactly," Zac replied.

"You're not going to let them get away with it, are you?" Will asked. "There's got to be some way to figure out who did this, and expose them for it."

"Maybe," the car said. "Look, I didn't mean to get you involved in all of this. They're going to kill you if they don't get the car, but I would destroy myself before letting them get their hands on this technology."

"I'm not going to let you destroy yourself," Will said. "We don't even know who wants the tech."

"Whoever it is, sent a hitman to do his bidding," Katie said. "Spoiler alert, it's not going to be a humanitarian out to better the world."

"That's true," Zac agreed.

"What if we go to the police?" Will asked. "I know a cop named Joe. He sounds like he wants to get to the bottom of all this. He's got a vested interest."

"We can't go to the police, not with the caliber of people we're dealing with," Zac replied.

"What? Do you think Joe is dirty?" Will asked.

"No, I didn't say that." Zac replied.

"This cop's been on the force for a long time, he knows what he's doing," Will replied.

"You're going to get him killed," Zac replied. "I'm telling you no; that hitman is no joke. We, no, I, have to solve this puzzle, and I only have two days to do it."

Will felt Katie's hand grab his, he felt the concern in her tight grasp.

"One way or another, I refuse to let anything happen to you," Zac said.

"Do you think the hitman saw you drive yourself?" Will asked.

"I don't think so," the car replied. "He was way too nonchalant with offering you that deal, and two days. If he realized how far the technology had come, and that it was actually running in the car, he'd have probably shot you both, and tried to take the car tonight. My guess is that he saw us race out of the fairgrounds, being chased by Doug, and followed them, to make sure the car wasn't damaged. It's likely they think that my tech is simply hidden in the car, as opposed to operational in the car."

"Okay," Will said.

It wasn't long before they had reached Katie's house. Will had gotten out to walk her to her door.

"So … Tonight," he said, as they walked along. He was at a loss for what to say about the evening.

"Tonight, was both the most amazing and horrific night I've ever had," she replied.

"Me too."

"Like I said before, I don't know how I'm going to sleep a minute tonight," she said. "I'm so worried for you."

"Don't worry, Zac and I are going to figure something out. Remember we have two days." Will was putting on a brave face for her sake, hiding the inner freak-out he was experiencing.

She turned to him and grabbed his hands. "Call me tomorrow, I can come help you guys brainstorm."

"I will," he assured her, then gave her a light kiss on the lips.

She looked in his eyes, her own eyes a little glassy, and forced a smile through her worry. She then turned and finished the short walk to her door, offering one more wave before she went into her house.

Will returned to the Corvette, and they began their short drive home.

"What a night," Will said. "I don't even know what to think about first. Making out with Katie, you being alive, kind of, and in my car, you catching us making out, watching Doug and his pals get dealt with, or having to deal with the person who wants this car."

"Some good and some bad, it's a lot, I know," Zac said.

"At least this might solve your problems with those three psychos from your school."

Will nodded. "I hope so."

"Let's just get home, you try to get some sleep, and we'll figure it all out tomorrow morning."

"Yeah, wish me luck on the sleep."

That night, as expected, Will lay awake in bed, his mind racing through everything that had happened earlier that night. Though his heart and mind were overwhelmed, eventually the exhaustion won out, and he fell asleep despite Nala's light snoring by his side.

He opened his eyes in the morning, surprised that he'd been able to fall asleep. The events of the previous night seemed so unreal. Had he dreamed them all? They were all so far-fetched. Last night's happenings seemed ridiculous in the morning's rational light, but he knew it had all happened.

As he came down to the living room from upstairs, he noticed his mother sitting on the couch, eating some toast and watching the news. She glanced over, noticing him enter the doorway.

"Oh, hey, sweetheart. I didn't hear you come in last night," Beth said. "I saw that the Dragons won the football game last night."

"Yeah, it was great," Will replied. "Then Katie and I went to the fair with Kahlil and some of the guys on the team."

"That sounds fun."

That was all his mother needed to know.

As he entered the kitchen, Will considered making a quick sandwich. Somehow, despite the experiences of last night, he still had an appetite.

He picked up the loaf of bread. "Ah, mom bought wheat bread again." A disappointed sigh escaped his lips.

Will wasn't much familiar with Buddhism or the Four Noble Truths, that's probably why he always misinterpreted the quote: "life is suffering". Because whenever his mother had shopped for healthy food, to him, wheat bread was certainly life's Duḥkha.

Will grabbed a banana from the kitchen, and went out to the garage.

"Good morning, Will," Zac said. "Did you sleep at all?"

"Yes, I was surprised. I don't know how."

"That's good."

It occurred to Will that there was so much that he still didn't know about his uncle's situation. Was his computer always on? Or did he power down at night in some kind of sleep mode?

"Did you sleep?" Will asked.

"I no longer have my body, so I no longer require sleep."

"You're not going to run out your battery?"

"My consciousness components have an alternate power supply, it'd be a lot to explain at the moment, but let's just say it's not really a pressing problem, per se."

"If you don't need sleep, I guess you could get a lot of books read," Will kidded.

"I can process a digital book in less than a second,"

the car replied. "So yes, a lot of books, and a lot of other data."

"It takes me a lot longer to *process* a book. Just don't spoil any endings for me." Will chuckled. "You know you're starting to speak more and more like a computer."

"I'm sorry, inhabiting a digital server steers me more toward logical evaluation, but the heart is still in there, not a real heart, but you know what I mean."

"It's okay," Will said, patting the side of the car. "It's like I got you back from the dead, so I can't complain. So, did you figure out any ways to deal with our situation yet?"

"I'm still running through new possible scenarios," Zac replied. "The complexity lies in the fact that we are not only dealing with the lethal hitman, but also the man behind the curtain. If we dispatch of the hitman, then the one who hired him will remain undeterred, and hire someone else to come after us."

"That does make it tricky," Will agreed.

"Yes, and requires a greater deal of trickery on our part," Zac said. "I am especially seeking scenarios that put you in the least amount of danger possible."

"Thanks, but we're in this together," Will replied.

"I admire your loyalty, but this is a problem I created, and I myself should remedy. I would forever feel guilty should anything happen to you."

"You need me, and don't worry, you can count on me."

"Thank you, Will," Zac said. "I think we may need some supplies, get in and let's go." Zac started the engine of the car.

"Cool your engine for a minute," Will said. "I have to

go get my license and keys. I have to at least appear like I'm driving."

"Don't worry, I'll let you drive sometimes," Zac kidded.

After Will had grabbed his wallet and keys, and told his mom that he needed to go for a drive to clear his head, he returned to the garage, and they were off.

Will's mom wanted him home by lunch, Uncle Zac assured him that this errand wouldn't take long.

After grabbing some coffee at a drive through, Will soon found himself in the parking lot of a posh storage facility.

The car popped open the glove compartment.

"Look in the owner's manual on Page 44. Will found the manual and began to flip through it. On page 44, he found a key-card wedged in the book.

"I have a storage space here under a false name, so it wouldn't be traced back to me," the car explained. "The key card should open the main door of the facility and the door to my particular storage area, unit 412. I was careful to note that we were not followed here, but I need you to continue to keep a low profile."

"412, okay, got it," Will said as he started to open the door.

"Wait for a second, you don't even know what you're looking for," the car said.

"Oh ... yeah," Will replied.

"There's a lot of stuff in there. As you walk in, on the right, on the bottom shelf, there's a small black box with a label that has the letter 'C' on it. Bring that whole box back."

"Okay, sounds easy," Will replied.

"Do your best to go unnoticed," Zac reiterated.

"Did my mom ever tell you about the times I snuck out of the house as a kid?" Will asked.

"No."

"Exactly," Will replied. "She never caught me."

The car couldn't help but let out a chuckle. "Don't get cocky."

"That's the first time I've heard you laugh as a car," Will said as he got out. "It's weird."

"You're weird," Zac replied. "And you're still *a kid*."

Will closed the door and headed for the storage units.

The key-card worked on the entrance, and Will walked into the building.

This was nice, most of the exterior walls were glass windows. It was clean and climate controlled. He wondered what it cost to have a unit in this building, he imagined it was twice as much as any normal storage unit he'd ever been in.

As he proceeded down the hall, he gave a casual glance up and noticed the security camera. Well, he'd been seen, but hopefully not noticed. He found unit 412, and used the key-card to open the door.

The door slid up and open on its own. Will walked inside, and swiped the key-card again on an inside sensor, and the door closed behind him.

This place! Will thought.

There was so much stuff stored in this unit, it was bigger than it looked from the outside. There were plenty of storage containers and boxes, all meticulously organized on shelves that lined the walls.

There was a temptation to snoop through some of the other storage containers, but his uncle would know if he took too long.

Will knelt down, and found the box on the right labeled 'C', and picked it up. It wasn't too big or heavy. With some loose fingers he procured the key-card again to exit the unit, and closed the door behind him.

Trying to make his quick walk seem casual, Will began to feel at ease, as if he was going to make a clean getaway. But then a man rounded the corner.

The man took a second glance at Will, and recognized him. "Hey," he greeted.

Oh great, Will thought. "Hello," Will replied, with a nonchalance that implied that he didn't recognize the guy, when in truth, he did.

Was his name John? He knew he had met the man at his uncle's funeral. He had come up to his mother and him, and been super awkward and weird. *Are you kidding?* Will thought. Not only had he been seen, but he had been seen by someone who recognized him.

"Hey, aren't you Zac's nephew?" The man asked.

Will wanted to say no, but he could tell the man knew it was him, and denying it would seem that much more suspicious.

"Yeah," Will replied.

"I met you at the funeral for your uncle, my name is John," he said. "I was so sorry to hear about your uncle, what a guy, what a guy."

If this guy said *what a guy* to him again, he might start hitting his head against the wall. "Yes," Will said. "I miss him."

John glanced around at their surroundings. "I didn't realize you had a storage unit in this building. I like it here. Been here awhile?" His voice had an almost suspicious, inquisitive tone; or maybe Will was reading too much into the odd delivery the man had.

What kind of question was that? Will thought. "I don't have a unit here," Will replied.

"Oh?" The man raised an eyebrow.

"I was picking up something for my friend, from his storage unit."

"Oh, okay." The answer seemed to satisfy the man, at least from what Will could tell.

"Looks like you got your hands full, do you need any help?"

"No, thanks, I'll be fine," Will replied, almost a little too adamant.

"You know," the man continued. "I thought that was your uncle's car outside."

"Yes, he left it to me," Will replied.

John raised an eyebrow. "That was nice."

"It was nice running into you," Will gave a polite lie. "I need to get going."

"Alright," John said. "Take care, Will."

Will walked quickly out of the storage facility, and to the car. The guy had recognized him, and remembered his name, kind of creepy if you asked Will. What kind of psychopath remembers the name of a nephew of someone you met once at a funeral? And now he knew that he had his uncle's car. But then again, if he was the one behind all of this, he already knew that Will had the Corvette. Maybe Will was being paranoid, but they really couldn't trust anyone.

Glancing over, Will saw the BMW i8 that John drove. *Yep, that car is still out of your personality league,* Will thought.

The passenger side door of the Vette popped open when Will arrived with the storage container, and he placed the box on the passenger seat.

Will glanced back at the storage facility, just to notice the guy, John, standing there, looking at him out the wall of glass windows. Will closed the passenger-side door and got in on the driver side.

"There was a guy that entered the facility…" Zac said.

"John? Yeah, he saw me," Will interrupted the car. "He recognized me, and talked to me."

"What did he say?"

"Just idle chitchat," Will replied. "Asked me if I had a storage unit there, and I said I was getting something for friend from their storage."

"Not a lie."

"The weirdo is still looking at us through the window," Will said, as he glanced back again.

"That's John, alright," the car said. "A bit socially awkward at times. Can't say he's harmless, but at the same time I don't know if he has what it takes, the capital or the crazy to be behind the scenes of what's going on."

"Who is he?"

"And old colleague of mine from one of the tech companies I used to work for. I heard he's done really well for himself there since I left," Zac replied. "Weird guy, really smart though. He might be running that company by now. He might have the capital to be behind all this now. He was one of the ones that approached me about my tech before I got killed as well."

"Let's get out of here, he's burning a hole in my head with that creepy stare."

"So, what's in the storage containers?" Will asked as they rode along.

"Cameras," the car replied. "We're going to set up cameras all around your house that I can watch. I can sound my alarm if there's any unwelcome guests. That way at least you can be prepared."

"Sounds like a good first step in a plan," Will replied. "Like Kahlil would say, a good offence is a great defense."

"He's a defensive football player, right?" Zac asked.

"Yeah, how did you know?"

"Just sounds like something a defensive football player would say."

Will laughed.

TEN

As Will and Zac drove along, out of nowhere, a police car began tailgating them.

"Why is there a cop right on my bumper?" Zac asked. "I wasn't speeding, or committing any other traffic violation."

"Oh," Will said with a sigh. "It's probably Officer Cade. I imagine he saw that it was me behind the wheel."

"He just likes to mess with you for no reason?" Zac asked.

"Yeah." Will stared into the rearview mirror, it was indeed Officer Cade.

"Sheesh, you've got a lot of *friends* in this town, Will."

Though Will was by no means a troublemaker, Officer Cade had followed or pulled him over a number of times, it seemed for no more than the lawman's mood at the time. Will felt the only thing he had in common with Cade was a mutual distrust and distain for Doug Hanger. For Cade, this stemmed back to when someone stole the 'l' from the 'public safety' sign in front of the station, leaving the sign to read 'pubic safety'. Cade was sure that Doug had done it, but could never prove it.

Perhaps Cade associated Will with Doug, as a punk high schooler, not realizing that Will and Doug couldn't be more different.

"That's Cade alright," Will said. "His motto should be *to harass and serve…his own ego.* I know plenty of good cops, but Cade is not one of them. He liked to talk a lot of smack about my old Camaro when I had it running."

"Ridiculous," Zac replied. "Do you want me to smoke him out?"

"I don't think he wants to do drugs with a car," Will replied. "Besides I didn't know you were into that scene."

"I'm not talking about drugs, dufus, I built a defense mechanism into the car where I can pump a bunch of smoke out of the car's tailpipes," Zac explained.

"Oh, that's usually a bad sign of some engine trouble," Will said. "Or…is it like rolling coal?"

"I'm not really down with that scene," Zac said. "Besides, if I'm not mistaken, that's something you do with diesel engines. What I do is different."

"How is the smokey end result different?"

"I only do it as an emergency defense against someone pursuing me, or as a lesson to someone tailgating, not to bully low/no emissions cars…or destroy the environment in general. But the amount of smoke output is similar," Zac said.

"Uh huh," Will gave a skeptic reply.

"You can just tell Cade the car's been smoking lately," Zac continued. "He already knows you fix up cars that have problems."

"You do have problems, and that'd be funny," Will said. "But maybe if I don't antagonize him today, he'll leave me alone."

"Suit yourself," Zac replied. "I know it's not much of a *defense* mechanism. Honestly, it's more-so just doling out justice for someone tailgating too close."

"Oh, it'll come in handy sometime," Will said with a smirk. "But to be clearer, why don't we call it *smokescreen* instead of *smoking out*?"

"Yeah, I like that," Zac said. "It sounds more superhero-y."

"That too."

The blue lights began to flash.

"Great, I was hoping he wouldn't actually pull me over today," Will said, annoyed. "And he's the biggest moron."

"Really?"

"Yeah, you'll see," Will replied.

The Corvette pulled over and cut off the engine.

A few moments later, Officer Cade came strutting up to the driver's side window.

"If it isn't Young William," Officer Cade said.

"Hello, Officer Cade," Will replied. "I'm not sure why you pulled me over today, what can I do for you?"

"Well, when I see a suspicious car, I just like to know who's rolling through my town," Cade replied.

"This car is suspicious?" Will asked.

"Both you and this car, to be honest," Cade said. "You get rid of the Camaro?"

"Yeah, I sold it."

"I guess there's a sucker born every minute," the officer

replied. "I know what my father, A. R. Senior, would've call that Camaro…a hunk of junk."

"Come on."

A smile grew on the officer's face. "You traded one hunk of junk for another?"

"It's not cool to call someone's awesome car *junk*," Will replied. "This car has power and style."

"Style?" Cade said with a chuckle. "I've taken dumps with more style than this car. And I'll call it, and you, whatever I want, dirt-bag." He smirked. "Hunk-o-Junk and Dirt-Bag, the new villainous duo in town."

"Keeping it real classy as usual," Will said.

"Maybe you shouldn't be talking back to an officer of the law," Cade said. "Because maybe I saw you commit a traffic violation back there."

"Come on, you know that's crap," Will replied.

Cade shook his head. "No respect for authority. You've got a real bad attitude, kid," Cade said, trying to flex the lower range of his voice.

Will's eyes were drawn to the infotainment screen of the Corvette.

Text ran across the screen; it was a subtle message from Zac.

It read: *Look in the rearview.*

Will glanced in his rearview mirror, and noticed that Cade's patrol car had begun to roll backward. Cade must've left the engine on, and accidentally left it in neutral. How do you even do that? Perhaps he was too eager to dispense justice.

Will watched, waiting a few seconds for good measure,

making sure the patrol car had a good rolling head start before saying something. But at a point, Will could no longer keep his laughter contained, and he began to chuckle.

"What's so funny, you little punk," Cade said.

"Your patrol car is withdrawing itself from this traffic stop," Will said.

Cade glanced back to his car. "Not again!" he yelled.

"Again?" Will laughed.

"Get out of here, I'll deal with you next time," the officer said, shooing him away with his arm as he turned to run back toward his car.

The tires on the patrol car cut to the side, and the car rolled off the pavement and onto the shoulder of the road.

"No, no, no, no!" Cade yelled, running for the vehicle as fast as he could.

The patrol car's tires cut sharp once on the grass, and the back end rolled over the edge into a ditch. The rear bumper of the cruiser slammed to the bottom of the deep drainage ditch.

Will burst out laughing as he continued to watch in his rearview mirror. "I wish I had some popcorn."

"Thank you, universe," Zac kidded. "It's so seldom that the universe exacts the karma someone deserves in the moment."

Will turned the key and started the Corvette. "He's going to need a tow to get out of that ditch."

"Plenty of good cops out there, putting their lives on the line every day," Zac said. "And we've got this moron patrolling our streets."

"Doesn't seem fair," Will said.

As Zac and Will drove away from the scene, Will glanced in the rearview mirror one last time, only to see officer Cade standing in front of the car. The vehicle's hood pointed toward the sky. Cade was throwing up his hands in frustration.

"Jealousy" by the Gin Blossoms began to play over the radio as Will and Zac rounded another corner to put the entire scene behind them.

After they arrived home, Zac instructed Will where to place the cameras around the house. Some Will could do from the ground outside, and some he had to do going out on the roof of his house from his bedroom window.

As Will was coming downstairs after placing the last camera on the roof, he walked by the kitchen.

"Hey Will," his mom called out to him. "You want pizza for lunch?"

"That sounds great."

"Good," she said. "It's already on the way." She seemed hesitant to continue, but spoke again. "So, do you remember Dylan from the funeral?"

"Not really."

There was a hint of nervousness in her tone as she continued. "He was a guy that your uncle Zac and I grew up with, and I hadn't seen in forever," she explained.

"Okay." Will's suspicion grew as he listened.

"Well, he showed up to the funeral, and we spoke briefly then," she went on. "And we've kind-of reconnected after that. I wanted you to meet him under a better situation. I don't know if things between us will progress at all, but you know I always want to be honest with you, and I care about how you feel, and I want you to like him and approve. He's bringing the pizza, I thought we could all have a nice lunch together."

Will was caught off guard by her words. He didn't know why they upset him so much, but they did. "So, you were picking up guys at Uncle Zac's funeral?" He didn't bother to hide the agitation in his tone.

She seemed a little shocked by his harsh response. "You know it wasn't like that."

He knew his mother didn't deserve his anger, but he couldn't help it. It'd been over five years since his father had passed away, and his mother had not dated or even attempted to do so once. This is the first time he had to deal with the thought of her moving on from his father.

"I don't think I'm hungry right now, and it may be a while till I am," he said, seeing her eyes get glassy as he walked out of the room.

He walked into the garage, sat down in the Corvette and let out a sigh.

"Did you have any trouble with the cameras?" Zac asked.

"No," Will said, pouting there in the seat with his arms folded across his chest.

"Okay, I'll go ahead and connect to them."

Zac explained to Will how to connect the cameras with his phone so that he could view them as well.

As Zac was connecting to the cameras, he interrogated

Will further. "Is everything okay? I can sense your elevated heart rate."

"Really?"

"Yes, my sensors inside this car are pretty sensitive."

"I guess," Will said. "It turns out my mom might start going out with some guy that she reconnected with at your memorial service," Will explained, doing air-quotes around the word *reconnected*.

"Really?" The car asked.

"Yeah, can you believe that? We're all there mourning you, and my mom is picking up dudes," he complained. "It's some guy named Dylan that you two grew up with."

"Yeah, I hate how your mom is out on the town every weekend trying to get some strange," the car said in a kidding tone. "She's always tramping it up."

"What?" Will picked up on the sarcasm. "I'm not saying all that."

"I'm trying to remember how much she's dated since your father passed away," Zac continued.

"None that I know of," Will replied.

"Exactly," Zac said. "You don't really think your mom was out to pick up a guy there on purpose, do you?"

Will was silent for a moment.

"This isn't even really about Dylan, is it?" Zac asked. "Or my funeral service, for that matter. This is about your father."

"How can she just move on?" Will asked. "It doesn't feel right, abandoning my father's memory."

"I've known your mom, well, for as long as I've been alive," Zac said. "I can tell you she hasn't moved on, and she never will. She will always keep your father with her, forever."

"Then how can she …"

"How can she not want to be alone?" The car interrupted. "Not want to share new experiences with someone?"

"It just seems so soon," Will said.

"It's been five years, Ace," Zac said. "I know that doesn't seem like a lot of time. But coping with things is different for different people, and it takes different amounts of time. But I promise you, she's not abandoning the love she had for your father."

"I guess," he begrudgingly agreed.

"I haven't talk to Dylan in a long time," Zac continued, "But growing up, he was a really good guy. Do me a favor: maybe lighten up on your mother some. She's had it really rough since your dad passed. And maybe go easy on Dylan. You just might find that he's an alright guy."

"I don't know," Will replied, mulling it over, realizing that perhaps he was being a little harsh.

"It's not going to be an easy adjustment," the car went on. "But I believe your dad would've wanted your mom to be happy. If you don't take the high road here, you're going to break your mother's heart. Look, you're going to move out in a year or two. Do you really want her to be alone?"

Will glanced down. "I guess not," he replied with a little hesitation.

"It was my memorial, if anyone should be bothered, it's me. And I'm not."

"I get the point," Will said.

"Trust me, she's experiencing guilt, and she doesn't deserve to, and you're making it worse."

"I guess I am kind-of hungry," he said.

"What do you mean?"

"Dylan's on his way with pizza for us," Will explained.

"Go, have some pizza, and play nice," the car said. "Do it for me. Plus, if your mom is dating someone, it'll keep her distracted while we get our situation sorted out."

Will took a deep breath, and let it out. He then got up out of the car and went into the house.

As he entered the living room, Beth noticed him. It looked as if she had shed a few tears, and was trying to choke down her emotions and not to make a scene.

"Hey sweetie," she said with a cracking voice.

"I'm sorry mom," Will said. "Maybe I am a little hungry."

"Really?" his mother asked. A light illuminated in her eyes, one that dispelled the shadows of sadness and guilt and replaced them with a glimmer of hope.

"Yeah," he said. "If you waited this long to go on a date, maybe he's alright. But if there's pineapple on the pizza, that's definitely a red flag."

"I agree." She laughed as she stood up and gave him a hug. "Thank you, Will."

It wasn't long after when Dylan arrived with the pizza. And as hoped, there was no pineapple on it.

They made small talk, to Will's dismay, this included his schoolwork and new girlfriend. When his mother brought up the subject of him receiving the Corvette from his uncle, Will became a little more guarded with the information, but he didn't think that Dylan or his mother noticed.

Dylan looked to be in his mid-forties, about the same age as his mother, and by first impressions, he seemed like a nice enough guy. But Will knew that he and his uncle couldn't afford to trust anyone at this point.

Like so many people in town, Dylan said he worked for the nearby nuclear plant, he claimed to be an engineer there. Will knew some of the other students whose parents were engineers at the plant; they were pretty well-off. So perhaps Dylan wasn't faking it with his Mercedes-Benz AMG CLS coupe outside.

If things with Dylan and his mother progressed, there's no doubt he'd be able to take care of her. Will supposed that wasn't a bad detail about the guy.

When the topic of Will's father briefly arose in the conversation, Dylan had nothing but positive things to say about his dad. Will gave him another hesitant check on the list he was keeping in his mind.

As they were finishing up their lunch, Will got a text. It was from Katie, asking him how he was, and if she could see him today.

When it came to the threat of life or death, she could've run away, distanced herself, but she was drawing closer, sticking by his side. Will took notice of that. He thought it said something about her character, and about the feelings that she had for him.

It was a sunny day in a quaint middle-class neighborhood. By all outward appearances, things were peaceful, and if people had any troubles, they were minor, like a neighbor's dog doing its business on a freshly cut front yard; or a white picket fence, that might have needed a fresh coat of paint. But appearances could be deceiving. No one would suspect the hitman woes that Will and Uncle Zac were facing.

At the suggestion, and under the guidance of Uncle Zac, Will had just finished installing an added feature to the garage door opener. It would allow Will to open the door from an app on his cell phone, but it also gave uncle Zac the ability to open it.

Will sat in the Corvette in the garage, with the car's top off and windows down, looking out through the open garage door at the neighborhood, waiting for Katie. He began organizing a few things in the small center console, when he heard someone's footsteps walking up.

"Hey stranger," a girl's voice said.

Will looked up, it was Mandy. *What was she doing here? Especially when Katie was going to be here any minute!* He had to get rid of her.

"Mandy, what are you doing here?" Will got out of the car and closed the door behind him.

"New project car?" She asked, seeming in truth, uninterested.

"Yeah," Will replied.

"Like my new necklace?" She asked, motioning to a diamond necklace around her neck. "It's from a very expensive designer." She was perhaps less showing off her expensive new jewelry, and more-so trying to draw his eyes to her low-cut shirt-line. She knew how to garner a typical guy's attention.

"It's nice," Will replied, just trying to be polite.

"It's nice, but it's not a big deal," she played it off, without really playing it off.

Will remembered why he didn't miss conversations with Mandy. She was the kind of girl that would start talking louder, and laughing a little too much in the middle of a group of guys because she loved the attention. And the guys would gather, like moths to the flame. Whatever she was talking about, whatever she wanted, was what was going on in the world. One would swear a hashtag beat inside of her chest, in place of a heart. She fancied herself a budding social media influencer. The nomenclature *social media influencer* itself turned Will's stomach a little. She was a good impressionist painting: pretty from afar, but an absolute mess up close. He wondered how they ever got along in the first place. Oh, she was pretty, at least on the outside, and a really good kisser, perhaps that's how.

"I was just thinking about you," she said, immediately changing the subject as she began to approach him. "And I know we hadn't talked in a while."

Will took a step back, beginning to get nervous. She was always a bit aggressive.

"You didn't return my text I sent earlier this week." She gave him a pouty lip. She then snapped into a coy head tilt and raised her eyebrows. "I was worried you were mad at me." She was such a bad actress when she tried to be alluring.

"I wasn't mad," he replied. "I just didn't think we had anything else to say to each other."

"Well, that's silly." She kept easing forward toward him, as he kept stepping back.

"Is it?"

"You know, I never liked how it ended between us," she continued.

"What, when you went off to be alone with Kyle at that party we went to?" Will asked.

"Who knows why it ended between us." She ignored his previous sentence.

"It's a mystery, Handy-Mandy." A vague reference to Mandy's indiscretion that culminated in the end of their relationship, was all Will had the energy to give.

His back hit the wall; he had backed up as far as he could go into the garage corner.

Getting right up in his face, she stretched out her arm and leaned against the wall behind him as she spoke. "We were so good together," she continued. "Remember when you used to say that?"

"Look, I've got a new girlfriend now," Will replied. "And I can only disappoint one girl at a time."

"Yeah, I've seen her around." An unenthusiastic look crossed her face. "She's okay, I guess. If you're into that whole *girl next door* kind-of vibe."

"She's wonderful," Will said. "And I don't want to mess it up."

Mandy sighed. "Look, I've had a couple of boyfriends since we broke up, and they weren't like you."

"A couple?" Will's question dripped with sarcasm.

"No one has treated me half as good as you treated me," she continued. "You're like the bar that I measure every relationship by, and they can never seem to measure up."

"Mandy…," he tried to interrupt her to stop her. She really had to go before Katie arrived.

"I've been thinking," she interrupted him. "And I think we should get back together. I think the upcoming dance would be a great chance for us to hit the reset button on our relationship."

"No," he replied, shaking his head.

"I can be that girl you always wanted me to be, I promise."

"Eh-hem," a voice cleared their throat at the front of the garage.

Will looked over, it was Katie, with one eyebrow raised and her hands on her hips. *She's going to kill me!*

"He won't hit a girl, but I will," Katie said to Mandy.

Mandy rolled her eyes as she backed away from Will.

Will mouthed the words *thank you* to Katie.

As Mandy began to walk away, she glanced back at Will.

"Think about what I said … a reset," Mandy said.

Mandy walked by Katie, who was cutting her eyes at her until Mandy got into her car and drove away.

Katie turned back to Will. "Did I interrupt something?"

"No, trust me," He tried to hide the nervousness in his voice. "I was trying to get rid of her, she's so stubborn."

Katie paused for a moment, just to make him squirm,

then a big smile crossed her face. "I trust you, I can tell when a girl is no good."

Will let out a sigh of relief.

"And you looked really uncomfortable backed up in a corner," She walked up to Will and gave him a kiss on the cheek.

"You're pretty amazing," Will said, still in a little shock that he wasn't in trouble.

"I know," she chuckled.

ELEVEN

Will and Katie sat in the Corvette, parked in the garage. The bright day outside was a stark contrast to the deep dark trouble they were in. Though everything in high school seemed of life-or-death consequence, this actually was.

Will noticed the red and white polka-dot hair ribbon in Katie's hair.

She smiled as she noticed him noticing it. "I told you I loved it."

"I've been running through scenarios, and some may work," Uncle Zac said, "I do have a self-defense mechanism."

"That's great," Will said.

"But it's untested, and it may fry my computer," Zac added.

"What?" The disbelief washed over Will. "Fry your computer? Like kill you?"

"Um, yeah, essentially," Zac replied with a forced nonchalance.

"You can't fry yourself," Will said. "We can go on the run and disappear before that's an option."

"Going on the run is no kind of life, and eventually they'd come after your mother to get to us. Hopefully it won't come to that," Zac said. "I may be able to outsmart them, but we don't know how smart they are, and what precautions they'll take."

"Could we take all of your conscious components out of the Corvette and transfer it to another car?" Katie asked.

"I love this car, but that's not a bad idea," Zac replied. "But it's a difficult process, and we don't have the resources to get that done in the timeframe we have."

"My father owns a huge car repair and customs shop," Katie said.

"I meant more high-powered computer resources, and someone with a little more know-how than you two." Zac replied. "No offense, but someone has to already be on a certain level for me to even be able to guide them through what to do."

"Oh," Katie replied.

"But that's good to know though, about the shop," Zac said.

"Or what if we could find an identical car," Katie asked.

"Also, not a bad idea," Zac replied. "But it might be tricky to find something identical, plus depending on how resourceful they are, they might know the VIN and would notice if we hacked it off this one and put it on another car."

"You'd be surprised," Katie said.

Uncle Zac chuckled. "Is this place your father runs legal?"

"Totally." She smiled.

"It's another good idea, but obtaining an identical car and having the work done probably can't happen in our timeframe either," Zac said.

Katie shrugged. "Just trying to help with ideas."

"No," Zac said. "They're great ideas, thank you. At least someone's trying to help."

"Sorry," Will said. "I was still getting over the thought of you frying your brain."

"It's like those old commercials, 'this is your brain on drugs', and they put the egg in the frying pan," Zac said.

Will pondered his words. "What are you talking about?"

"Never mind," Zac said. "But I'll do everything in my power not to let it come to any brain frying."

Will nodded that he believed him. He wished that his father was still alive. He would know what to do. When he was a kid, his dad always seemed to know what to do. Now Will felt like it was up to him to figure it out.

"I still find it strange that Dylan became an engineer at a nuclear plant," the car went on a different tangent. "That really doesn't seem like him, or at least the Dylan I used to know."

"Do you think he's lying?" Will asked.

"I don't think so, I don't know why he would," Zac's voice sounded unsure. "It's just an odd fit. I guess people change as they grow up."

"I know a reason he could be lying," Will's tone rang of suspicion that Dylan could be after his uncle's technology. "Could you hack the nuclear plant personnel files to see if he actually works at the plant?"

"Maybe, the security is going to be pretty tight, but maybe not quite as tight on just the personnel information," the car said. "I have a few tricks up my sleeve."

"You have a few tricks under the hood," Will said. "You're a car now."

Katie smirked, rolling her eyes at Will's silly semantics.

"But the more I run through possible scenarios in my mind, the more sure I am that I have to do this by myself," Zac went on. "I can't endanger you two. If everything plays out just right, I should be able to come out on top."

"What are you going to do?" Will asked.

"Well, here's what you're going to do," the car explained. "You're going to sell me to Maxwell."

"No way!" Will said, the emotion in his voice beginning to rise. "If I sell you to Maxwell, I legally won't own this car anymore."

"It'll be okay, Will."

"I just don't…"

"You have to trust me," his uncle interrupted him. "Wherever I am, wherever you are, I'll find my way back to you. I promise."

Will sighed. He knew that there was no talking his uncle out of it.

"Besides, motor vehicle records are pretty easy to hack and fix some paperwork in the future if it comes to that," Zac said.

Will nodded. "Oh, okay."

"If this interested party isn't expecting any surprises, I may be able to surprise them," the car said.

"You can't do this yourself," Will said. "Not without them

finding out your technology. I have to be there to make the transaction. He'll be suspicious if the car is just sitting somewhere. Maxwell will know it's some kind of trap."

After a short moment of processing, the car replied, "As much as I hate to say it, you might be right. But after you make the deal, you need to distance yourself as quickly as possible."

Will shook his head with a little discouragement. "Fine."

"Besides, I need you to record and back up the car's video, in case something goes wrong. We need to know who this guy is that's after my technology."

"Goes wrong?" Will asked.

"Things seldom go as smooth as planned, but I think this is our best shot. It's your best shot to stay safe, and my best shot to stay intact," Zac said.

"So that's it?" Will asked. "You've made your decision?"

"Yes, Will," the car replied. "Go ahead and call Maxwell and set a time. Set it for after school on Monday. You should go to school and act like everything is normal. Go through the motions."

"I don't like this plan," Katie said.

After letting out a deep sigh, Will stood up and got out of the car. He had serious reservations about his uncle's plan, but he pulled out Maxwell's contact number and walked over to the corner of the garage for privacy as he dialed.

It was a short phone conversation. He was to meet Maxwell with the car by an old abandoned warehouse, by the river at 4 pm on Monday.

After hanging up the phone, Will put it back in his pocket as he walked back to Katie and the car.

"Of course, we're meeting him in an abandoned warehouse by the river in a deserted part of town," Will said.

"I expected something like that," Zac replied.

"Come alone, and don't contact the authorities if I expect to leave," Will paraphrased the conversation.

"You need to be careful." The nervousness on Katie's face was evident. "Both of you."

Will nodded, insinuating that he would.

"Maybe tonight we could go for a drive," Zac said.

"Yeah, sure," Will replied, wondering if it would be one of their final drives.

That evening, after Katie had left, Will found himself driving the Corvette, carving some curvy mountain roads in the evening darkness. Though Zac usually had control of the car, he was letting Will drive tonight unimpeded.

"I get to drive tonight?" Will whipped the car around another curve.

"I figure it's got to be pretty disappointing to get a cool car, then never get a chance to drive it," Zac replied.

"I thought it might be in case things go south on Monday," Will replied.

"Maybe that too," Zac replied. "If things go south, you should take that thirty-thousand band get the ZR-1 version of this car."

"Don't say that. Things are going to work out fine."

"We'll have to take a drive up to Beulah when we have

some time," Will said. "There are some great curvy roads up there."

"That'd be nice. We should time it to see the Independence Day fireworks they do over the lake up there."

They were all nice plans that they might or might not live to fulfill.

After they traveled around a couple more bends, the car spoke again. "You know, some of my favorite memories are working with you and your father on this car."

"Mine too," Will replied.

"I hate that I wasn't around more," Zac said. "I meant to say, I'm sorry I wasn't around more. Before, and especially after you lost your dad."

"You were busy," Will replied. "Don't worry about it, really."

"I could've made more time, at some point," the car said. "Sometimes I wonder if I wasted my life."

"Discovering the secret to immortality?" Will asked. "I don't think you wasted your life."

"Immortality at the cost of the people I care about the most?" Zac asked. "An uncle that just shows up to put you in the crosshairs of a hitman."

Will chuckled. "Nobody's perfect. And you're not absent…At least not anymore. Let's plan to keep it that way."

"Part of the reason I willed you the car was selfish," Zac said.

"How so?" Will asked.

"I wanted to make up for lost time with you."

"I don't think it's selfish if it's something we both want," Will replied.

"I'll do my best not to be absent anymore," Zac said.

Later that night, after an exhilarating drive through the mountains, Will and Zac were passing through town on their way home.

"I feel like I could keep this Corvette fixed up indefinitely," Will said. "The one thing that concerns me though, is what about when your computer system needs some tweaks in the future? I'm good with computers, but you're on a whole other level."

"Ah, Will, you worry too much."

Will took it as his uncle's not-so-clever way of avoiding his question. But hopefully it wouldn't be something they'd have to worry about for a long time…If ever.

"What time is it?" Will asked.

"It's 10:17, Will," Zac replied. "Thousands of functions, ahead of our time, and I'm reduced to being a talking clock."

"Having a talking clock with self-esteem issues is definitely ahead of its time," Will replied with a smirk.

"Touché," Zac said. "Speaking of the time, do you mind if we make a little detour on our way home?"

"It's getting late, but no, that's fine."

"Don't worry," Zac said. "It won't take long."

Zac took Will winding through the city roads for the next fifteen-minutes, to the other side of town.

"I thought you said *a little detour?*" There was a weariness growing in Will's voice.

"We're almost there," Zac replied. "I promise."

They rounded another corner into a nice subdivision of

condos. Zac pulled over to the side of the road, stopped the car, and flipped down the pop-up headlights.

"What are we doing here?" Will asked.

"Just checking on someone." Zac seemed intentionally cryptic.

Will glanced around, his eyes caught a familiar looking little red Porsche Boxster S in the driveway.

"Wait a minute." Will realized something. "It's that woman, isn't it?"

"The woman?"

"Yeah," Will continued. "The blonde woman that left flowers by the urn at your funeral. I saw her leaving the funeral in that Porsche Boxster."

"Her name is Samantha," Zac said. "She brought flowers to my funeral? That's nice."

"She seemed really upset," Will said. "Girlfriend?"

"Yeah," Zac said.

"She was really pretty, and looked a bit younger than you."

"She was."

"Man, it really is a shame that you died," Will kidded him.

"There's physical death, and there's *hearing an elevator version of a song you loved growing up being used to sell prescription drugs on TV* death … you know, death inside. Both are pretty bad." Zac kidded. "But seriously, Sam was great."

"Is she a model?"

"No, but could've been, for sure." Zac said. "She's employed at one of the technology companies I did some work for."

"Smart girls are the best," Will said.

"I agree," Zac replied. "And I feel like things were starting to get serious between us."

"I'm sorry."

"She could do it," Zac said.

"Do what?"

"Your question earlier," his uncle clarified. "She could make the digital tweaks if I needed them, I could walk her through it. She's knowledgeable enough."

"You still care for her a lot, don't you?" Will asked.

"Of course, I do, your feelings don't just disappear because you turn into a sweet 90's sports car."

"I guess not," Will replied with a chuckle. At least his uncle still had his humor about things. "So, are you ever going to try to contact her?"

"I don't know. My death has already caused her so much pain, and then to hit her with, I'm still alive, but a car," Zack said. "Anyway, how can I hold her again? My seatbelt? I can tighten the cinch, but it's not like that feels like a hug for me, or her. And I just don't know if it's selfish of me to put her through that roller coaster of emotions, because I can't part with her."

"I don't think it's selfish," Will said. "I know it was a little rough for me at first, but I'm so glad you're here. I'd much rather have the car version of you than no version at all."

"I don't know, maybe," Zac said. "It's complicated."

"I'm sure," Will replied, with a nod of his head. "But I would venture to believe that she'd still want you in her life if she had the choice."

"Perhaps," Zac replied. "You know, she's the only one that actually knows what I was working on, well, now with the exception of you and Katie."

"You told her?" Will asked.

"Pillow talk, what can I say? But I trusted her, and I still do."

"What did everyone think that you were working on?"

"A digital/neural transmitter," Zac said.

"What?"

"Imagine it," Zac said. "You'd be linked, you could close your eyes and access anything in a server with your mind. It would slash action and digital reaction time, be a new world for data access and digitally controlled devices."

"And gaming," Will said.

"Ah, typical teenager," Zac replied.

"What can I say?" Will shrugged. "That's mind blowing, is it possible?"

"Yes, duh, I used some of the concepts on my consciousness link to the car before I died," Zac explained. "But I was too busy working on this to work on that. I do have some preliminary stuff written up that would get someone smart enough headed in the right direction."

"Sounds like a technology someone would love to weaponize," Will said.

"There was a lot of interest in it, from a lot of sources," Zac said. "A little too much interest in the end. I was approached by a number of different people, and I turned them all down. Not only because I disagreed ethically with how some of the people were going to use the tech, but that's not what I was working on in the first place. I guess when someone found out I was 'done' with my project, and I turned them down, they figured they could just kill me, and steal the tech."

"It still makes me so mad that someone did that to you."

"We'll find out who they are, Will. Soon enough."

"Well, maybe Samantha already suspects that you're still around. I mean, if she knows that you were working on that project."

"No," Zac said with a chuckle. "She was supportive, but thought it was impossible, which she let me know in no uncertain terms."

"Oh."

"Man, I miss her," Zac said.

Another moment went by as they sat there in the dark.

"See that light on in her bedroom window on the second floor?" Zac asked Will.

"Yeah."

"She's reading before she goes to sleep," Zac said. "It's about to go out."

A short moment after Zac said that, the light went out.

"Like clockwork…still. Even on the weekend," Zac said. "She goes to bed at eleven."

"Does it help you to see that she's okay?"

"She's probably not okay right now," Zac said. "But it helps me to think that eventually she might be."

Zac started the engine and flipped up the pop-up headlights. They headed home for the night.

After their little detour, Will and Zac soon found

themselves driving through his subdivision, almost home. They turned the corner to the street that they lived on.

"Do you see what I see?" Zac asked Will, as they approached their house.

"Your night vision is better than mine. I don't notice anything," Will said.

"A couple houses ahead, parked on the other side of the road, it looks like a familiar Mercedes Benz," Zac said as they pulled into the driveway.

"Dylan?" Will said as he got out of the Corvette and began to walk toward the mysterious car.

"Will, wait," Zac said, but his plea fell on deaf ears.

Will walked down his driveway toward the street, intending to confront the mysterious car.

As Will approached the end of his driveway, the Mercedes's engine started, and the lights came on. It did a U-turn, and took off in the opposite direction. The car disappeared around the next corner.

After standing in the middle of the street for another moment, watching with his hands on his hips, Will started back to the Corvette.

"That really looked like Dylan's Mercedes," Will said. "I memorized the license plate, if you can look it up."

"Good thinking," Zac replied. "I can do that."

"I know you want to trust your old friend, and he seemed like a nice enough guy when we had lunch," Will said. "But there's something sketchy going on with that guy."

"I hate to say that you might be right," Zac replied.

"I don't know if I want that guy around my mom."

"It doesn't make sense, he used to be a stand-up guy," Zac said. "Not some crazy stalker."

"It's a shame," Will said. "I think my mom really likes him."

"Well, we don't know anything yet, let me check into him before you say anything to her."

"All right," Will said with a hint of skepticism in his tone.

"You should go in and get some rest, it's been a long day."

"Alright."

"I'll let you know if I dig up anything on Dylan, it shouldn't take me long."

"Sounds good," Will said.

Will pulled the Corvette the rest of the way into the garage, gave Zac the license plate number he'd memorized, then went inside to wind down for the night.

Will laid awake in his bed, mulling over the day, nervous about Monday. It might be the end of his uncle. It was a most dangerous situation and he just wished that he could do more to help. He tried to clear his head enough to fall asleep.

He pet his pup, Nala, on the head as she laid nearby. She must've heard Beth in the kitchen or something, because she got up, trotted down the dog ramp at the end of the bed, and went out of his bedroom door.

Will's phone began to vibrate, he had an incoming call. It was Uncle Zac.

"Hello?" Will said. "I was able to run the license plate, and it confirmed our suspicions, it was Dylan in that Mercedes."

"What a creeper," Will said. "I was also able to access the personnel files at the nuclear plant, and there's no record of Dylan there."

"So, he's lying to us," Will replied. "That's great, my mother is dating a con artist-stalker."

"It would appear so," Zac said. "It really confuses me, but it's true."

"Yeah, but it's like you said, we can't trust anyone."

"You're right," Zac replied. "Wait a second," Zac's tone turned more urgent.

"What is it?" Will became uneasy.

"Check your backyard cameras, it looks like someone is climbing over your back fence."

Will's pulse quickened; his stomach tightened up. He hopped out of bed.

Instead of checking the cameras on his phone, he scurried to his window, where he could peek out and view the situation in the backyard with his own eyes.

Will slowly eased up from beneath the window to look into the backyard. His high anxiety was soon laid to rest as he realized that it was his stupid ex, Mandy.

His feelings of fear and apprehension were replaced by ones of annoyance, and frustration.

"It's just my ex, Mandy," Will said with a sigh.

"That's good," Zac said.

"Well, it's not great," Will replied.

"It's better than the alternative," Zac said. "She's actually kind of cute."

"Until she opens her mouth and you realize she's a self-centered megalomaniac control freak."

"I was starting to get that impression this afternoon."

"She likes to pull every string in the marionette relationship."

"Yuck."

"Yeah, let me go," Will said. "I've got to get rid of her."

Mandy had stepped into the middle of the yard and was searching on the ground for a pebble to toss at Will's window to get his attention, when she glanced up and noticed him.

"Oh." She stood up and gave him a little wave.

Will opened his window, and called down to her in a hushed tone, "What are you doing here?"

She smiled and began to sway from side to side, starting in a seductive dance for him. "Why do you think I'm here? I'm here for you to ask me to the dance." She kicked off her shoes and socks to the side.

"You know there's no music playing, right?" Will said, watching her move back and forth. "And you know I can't do that."

She reached down to the sides of her shirt, and pulled them up slowly as she continued to move. "Sure, you can," she replied.

Pulling her shirt off over her head, she held it out, smiled at him, and dropped it onto the lawn.

"Come on, Mandy, I have a new girlfriend now," Will said.

She continued to dance in her bra, and eased her hands down to the button on her shorts.

"Mandy, no!" Will held out his finger, pointing at her to stop. "Don't do it."

With her best innocent flirtatious look on her face, she reached down slowly and unbuttoned her shorts. She worked them down her legs and to the ground as she continued her seduction.

She stepped out of her shorts and to the side of where they laid on the ground. "I'll stop when you agree to take me to the dance," she said.

"It's not going to happen," Will replied. "You're not getting cold yet?"

She smiled. "I'm getting the opposite."

Will rolled his eyes.

"Why can't you take me to the dance?" Mandy asked as she continued to sway in her underwear. "You can dump her," she said. "What have you two been going out for, a week?"

"Two weeks, thank you very much," Will corrected her with an air of being vindicated by that second week.

"Can't you see that I'm doing this for you?" She asked. "Remember back when we were going out, I was," she paused for the right words. "A little bit of a goody two-shoes?"

"You being a goody two-shoes was never the problem in our relationship." Will said. "And you weren't a goody two-shoes with Kyle at that party."

"Regardless," she went on with a slight roll of her eyes. "I wanted to show you that I was a little more relaxed these days, and open to things."

"I've heard," Will said.

She continued to dance. "We're going to get back together, Will, it's going to happen, you don't have to fight it." She slowly reached behind her back and loosened her bra latch.

She began to ease her bra down. "Whatever it takes."

Just then, a flurry of barks filled the air as Nala raced into the backyard.

Mandy was caught off guard, panicked, and started grabbing up her clothes off the ground.

As Nala reached Mandy, the fury in the small dog's barks increased. She grabbed Mandy's shirt in her teeth, and began to shake it wildly, as if she was trying to kill it.

Mandy grabbed the other side of the shirt, and attempted to wrestle it away from the furious little dog, while her other hand was trying to hold up her loosened bra over her chest.

Nala let go of the shirt, but then charged at Mandy, nipping at her feet and ankles.

"Call your stupid dog!" Mandy yelled at Will in frustration.

Will shrugged his shoulders. "She's a very stubborn little pup."

Mandy huffed in frustration as she grabbed up her clothes, and ran to the fence line.

Once there, Mandy scaled the fence in her underwear, with Nala nipping and barking at her the entire time.

After Mandy was over the fence, and had run off, Nala walked the back perimeter of the fence a couple times to make sure the coast was clear, and the intruder was indeed gone.

The little dachshund discovered one of Mandy's socks that was left behind in her escape. Nala grabbed the sock, and violently shook it in her teeth to teach it one last lesson. She would make an example of this sock, lest any other strange socks thought they would trespass in her yard.

Will covered his face, he couldn't help but chuckle to himself.

The small dog then used the bathroom, and trotted back to the house, seeming proud of herself and her guard-dog abilities.

Moments later, Nala came bounding into Will's room, up the ramp, and into bed with him.

Will glanced up to see his mother in the doorway of his room.

"Did you let Nala out?" He asked her.

"Oh, yeah, maybe." There was a smirk growing on Beth's face.

"Thanks." Will smiled back at her.

"Goodnight, sweetheart," she said to him, and then turned to walk down the hall to her room.

Will pet Nala on the head as she laid snuggled up to his side. "Good girl," he said.

Will's phone began to vibrate that he was getting another call. He picked the phone up from the nightstand, and saw that it was Uncle Zac.

"Yeah?"

"So, do you just have pretty girls throw themselves at you all the time?" Zac asked. "Because you're an okay looking dude, but it's starting to seem ridiculous."

Will laughed. "No, it's a new development. It's just

my girlfriend Katie, and my crazy ex-girlfriend, Mandy. I promise."

"Okay, I just didn't know if this was going to be a regular occurrence that I needed to brace myself for."

"No," Will replied. "I don't think I've ever been so wanted in my life."

Zac chuckled. "Goodnight, Ace."

"Goodnight Zac." Will hung up the phone and put it on his night table.

He then laid his heavy head down on his pillow.

TWELVE

The rest of the weekend passed all too quick, and Monday morning was upon Will before he knew it.

Will sat in the back of his first period biology class, unable to follow the teacher's lecture. His mind was churning with scenarios of how the afternoon would play out. Less on his mind was his own safety, he was worried about his uncle.

As the class bell rang, the students began to gather their things and file out of the room. Will was soon the last student left in the room. He took his books under his arm and approached the teacher's desk.

Mr. Denzie glanced up from some papers he was looking over. "Can I help you, Will?"

"Yeah," Will said. "What do you think constitutes a person ... you know, a life."

Mr. Denzie got a confused look on his face. "I'm not sure if I understand what you're getting at. You mean, biologically speaking?"

"I mean, I know we have our bodies and our minds, and who we are shaped by our experiences, and how we react to that external stimuli, and the fact that we are self-aware and have emotions and feelings."

"You're wondering if that constitutes a being?" Mr. Denzie asked.

"Say there's a computer program, and it exhibits evolution through external stimuli, it learns. It has emotions and is self-aware," Will said. "Would that constitute a life?"

Mr. Denzie rolled his eyes and let out a sigh. "You've been watching too many movies. Is this why you were completely zoning out during my lecture today?"

"Humor me, Mr. Denzie."

The teacher thought for a moment. "I don't know if your question is as much a biological question, as it is an existential one." The teacher went on. "I would say if it was truly self-aware, had emotions, and the ability to learn, it would be a life. Maybe one that we have trouble wrapping our minds around, but a life nonetheless."

"That's how I felt," Will said.

"Granted this would be almost impossible to test and know for sure," Denzie explained. "As computer programs can be written to outsmart tests. But if the elements were true and there was a definitive way to test it, I'd say yes. Does that help?"

"Yeah, thank you, Mr. Denzie," Will said as he walked toward the door.

"Next time ruin the computer science teacher's day with that kind of question," Denzie called out as Will closed the door behind himself.

Mr. Denzie had reaffirmed the weight of the situation at hand. His Uncle Zac's life was a life. Perhaps not one that he could fathom or understand, but a life worth the risk of trying to save.

Sometime, later in the day, Will was walking with Katie to one of her afternoon classes, when they happened across the school's memorial.

The memorial was essentially a large wooden trophy case, but with pictures, texts, and trinkets honoring lost students and faculty behind glass. Ones that had met their end while attending, working, or teaching at the school.

Katie's tilted head reflected her curiosity. "It's odd that the school has a long-term standing memorial section for students that have passed away."

"It's a nice thought," Will replied. "But depressing."

Katie pointed to a girl's picture in a slightly older section of the memorial. "Who's that girl?"

Will thought for a moment as he looked at the photograph. "That girl's name was Onyx. I think she died in a car accident."

"That's terrible."

"It happened years ago. I heard about it when I was a kid in elementary school. I was afraid of tractor trailer trucks for a while after that news story."

They stood in front of the memorial case for another moment.

Katie turned to Will with a concerned look in her eyes. "I just don't want to see you in this case."

He put his arm around her. "I'm going to do all in my power not to let that happen, I promise."

Katie wrapped her arms around Will and held him close.

Looking over Katie's shoulder, the corner of Will's eye caught someone walking by on the other side of the hall. It was Doug. His demeaner seemed subdued, and he had a bandage on the ear that had been shot.

As soon as Doug glanced up and noticed Will, he looked back down at the floor, and gave a wide berth, getting as close to the opposite wall as possible. The former bully passed in silence, not acknowledging Will's existence. Doug disappeared into a crowd of students down the hall.

"Katie," Will whispered. "Doug just walked by, without incident."

"Wow, that's great."

The fact that the bully was now impotent was a relief, but it only did so much to ease the tension of the day. Now if the hitman would just leave them alone as well.

After the final school bell rang later that day, Will gathered his things and walked out to his car.

As he crossed the parking lot and neared the Corvette, he saw Katie there, waiting for him.

Her face offered a concerned look, and she wrapped her arms around him as he arrived.

She held him close. "I'm so worried about you."

"I'll be okay," Will replied. "Wherever I am, wherever you are, I'll find my way back to you, I promise."

"You stole that line from the car," Katie said, a smile almost cresting across her face.

He looked into her eyes, "It doesn't make it any less true."

She smiled at him.

"Honestly, I'm more worried about Uncle Zac," Will said.

She reached over and gave a light pat to the side of the Corvette. "I'm worried for him too."

Will would have loved to have lingered there with her longer, but he knew that they needed to leave in order to get there in time for the deal. And he was ready for it to all be over with.

"We need to go," he said as he gave her a kiss, and pulled away from her embrace.

Will sat down in the car, and closed the door.

"So, you're using my lines to pick up girls now?" Zac asked.

"She's already done been picked up," Will replied. "I don't know, I couldn't think of something better to say in the moment, and that's what was on my heart. Besides, you heard her call me out."

"Yeah, I like her." Zac started the engine. "Are you ready for this?"

Will put on his sunglasses. "Yeah, let's go."

He watched Katie wave at them as they drove off.

"That girl is something special," Zac said. "Hold on to her."

"I'm going to try," Will replied.

After traveling a little more than 20 minutes through the winding city roads, Will and Zac had reached their destination: A desolate area of the city, and an abandoned warehouse by the river.

The walls of the building were constructed of sheet metal, attached to metal beams, not unlike the roof of the structure. Silver metal and rusted sections peaked through the outer white walls that were in desperate need of re-painting. The warehouse looked as if it would have provided the bare minimum of protection in the event of a storm.

Pulling around to the side of the building, they noticed the open back of the warehouse facing the river.

After passing a few large shipping containers that seemed to lay scattered at random near the building, they pulled into the open warehouse.

Zac stopped the car and turned off the engine. They sat there for a moment. They were a few minutes early. Maxwell hadn't arrived yet.

"Creepy abandoned warehouse aside, it's actually kind-of pretty down here by the river," Will said, trying to distract himself from his anxiety.

"Yeah," Zac agreed. "This area of town could use a revitalization."

"But if you revitalized this area, where would shady hit-men set up meetings?" Will kidded.

"Oh, sorry to be so insensitive," Zac replied.

Will gazed out across the water. "I wonder if he meets people down here so he can shoot them and toss their bodies into the river."

"Why would you say that right now?" Zac said, sounding disturbed by the comment.

"I don't know, just an observation," Will replied. "He could probably push a car into the river here too."

"Will, we should get out of here," Zac said, sounding as if he was just coming back to his senses. "I don't know what I was thinking, you shouldn't be here."

"This doesn't work without me," Will said. "Besides, it's too late to back out now." Will nodded toward the left of them, noticing that Maxwell's black Audi was pulling up.

Will got out of the car and eased the door closed behind him. He clutched the keys in his hand, hoping that Uncle Zac's plan would work.

The Audi's engine stopped, and the driver's side door opened. Maxwell gave a cautious but confident glance around as he stepped out of the car.

"I assume you were smart enough to come alone," Maxwell said.

"Just me and the car," Will replied.

"Good, it will be nice to take care of this without complications," the man in the black hat said.

"I have the title with me, but it's not in my name yet," Will said.

"That's not a problem, I can take care of that." Maxwell turned and retrieved a folder from his front passenger seat. "You can give me your signature on this bill of sale and the title."

"Okay." Will thought Zac might use the security defense feature he had told him about on Maxwell. But then

Maxwell would have to try to drive the Corvette for Zac to do it. Will tried to seem casual with his interest. "How are you going to take the car with you? You didn't bring an extra driver."

"As soon as we close the deal, I'll have a flatbed truck on the way," Maxwell said. "My employer doesn't want anyone else driving it."

"Ah, he's protective of the car," Will replied.

"I guess you could say that," Maxwell said, remaining vague. But Will knew it was due to his employer's interest in the potential of hidden technology as opposed to the car itself.

"Let me grab the title, it's in the glove box," Will said.

Maxwell nodded for him to proceed, but watched with a suspicious eye.

Will opened the passenger side door, and retrieved the title, keeping his hands in open view as he turned back around. He didn't want to get shot.

Will walked back, and approached Maxwell. The hair on his arms stood on edge as he got close enough to hand the paper to the hitman.

"Thirty-thousand is a very generous offer for your car," Maxwell said. "You were wise to accept."

"Yeah." Will tried to make a brave, but dark joke to ease the tension of the moment. "Maybe I could use it to hire you to finish off those guys from the parking deck."

Maxwell glanced at him and smirked. "I would almost do that for free," he replied.

Will's joke had paid off. The hitman seemed to become a little more at ease.

There was a noise that sounded like it came from behind one of the nearby shipping containers.

In the blink of an eye, the bill of sale had been dropped from Maxwell's hand, and replaced with a nine-millimeter pistol with silencer, that he procured from his jacket pocket.

"What have you done?" Maxwell cut his eyes as he raised the pistol to Will's head.

"Nothing, I promise," Will's voice shook as he spoke. "As far as I know it's just me and the car."

Staring down the barrel, this was the end, Will knew it. He thought of Katie, and how much he regretted not having the chance to grow old with her, and maybe have a family. He wished he had the chance to tell her that he loved her. A phrase that he felt inside, but had not worked up the courage to say to her. His mother crossed his mind, and how destroyed she would be when he was found. He thought about how strong she was, and how she had done the best she could since his father had passed. He wished he had the chance to tell her how much he appreciated her. This plan had taken a turn for the worst.

"I really thought you were smarter than this," Maxwell said as he glanced around, and then back at Will, his finger tightening on the trigger.

"Freeze!" A man yelled as he came from around the side of a shipping container. "Federal agent!"

The man stood, in one hand a revolver trained on Maxwell, and a badge in the other.

Will couldn't believe his eyes, it was Dylan, his mother's high school friend. In that instant, he didn't know what to think. Relief? Anger in the betrayal of his lies? Or fear that he would get blamed for notifying a federal agent? After Maxwell had killed Dylan, he would surely kill him. Will knew that there was no way Dylan was a match for Maxwell. Not after the precise gunplay that Will had witnessed in the parking deck the other night.

No sooner had Dylan told the hitman to freeze, did Maxwell swing his gun around to take a quick kill-shot at the federal agent.

It was instinct, a gut reaction, Will didn't have time to think. He lunged forward toward Maxwell, and shoved the hitman's arm, just as he took his shot.

Will's impact caused Maxwell's shot to miss Dylan, the bullet struck the wooden shipping container next to the agent's head, sending a mist of wood shards and dust into the air.

As Will was falling to the ground from his lunge, he heard another shot, but this one was from Dylan's gun.

The shot hit Maxwell square in the chest, and threw him back against his black Audi.

Maxwell's pistol made a clanking noise as it hit the concrete, after falling from his hand.

The hitman's body fell limp onto the ground next to his weapon. Upon impact with the ground, Maxwell's hat rolled away from his head on its brim, and came to rest near where Will lay on the ground.

Will laid there, shaking. It felt like he lacked the strength to get up. His nerves were shot.

Dylan put his badge away and lowered his gun as he made a brisk pace toward Will.

"It's okay, Will," Dylan said as he approached. "You're okay now."

No, he wasn't okay, Will thought. Not after almost getting executed, and what he just witnessed, and the fact that whoever Maxwell's employer was, would blame him for calling the feds. *And what?* Dylan was a federal agent?

The federal agent knelt down next to the hitman and took his pulse. Once he had determined that Maxwell was dead, he rose to his feet.

Dylan pulled out his cell phone and dialed a number. *"This is agent Jones; I need a discreet clean up and an extraction of a body. A one, Maxwell Romanoff, a.k.a. Black Hat Assassin. Single gunshot wound to the chest."* Dylan listened for a moment. *"Thank you I'll send you the location and I'll secure the scene until they get here."* Dylan hung up the phone, and returned it to his pocket.

"Hey Will," Dylan's tone turned softer, concerned for Will's emotional wellbeing as he turned back from his phone call. "Come with me."

Dylan offered his hand to help Will get back on his feet.

As soon as Will was standing again, Dylan led him away from Maxwell's body that lay lifeless on the concrete.

Their stroll took them near the edge of the river. Dylan continued glancing back every few seconds to keep an eye on the scene, making sure none of Maxwell's associates arrived, and no one stumbled upon the scene at random.

As they reached the water, Dylan motioned to a nearby spot. "Why don't you hang out here, and check out the river for a few minutes."

Will sat down at the edge of a small dock, facing the river's calming water that flowed by.

Dylan could see the trauma in Will's eyes, and he put his hand on Will's shoulder.

"Thank you for saving my life," Dylan said. "That was a brave thing that you did back there."

Will nodded, acknowledging his words.

Dylan had saved his life as well, but perhaps it wouldn't have been in eminent danger if Dylan hadn't made a noise behind the shipping container to begin with.

Will heard a vehicle pulling up behind them, and glanced back to see a black van pulling up to the scene with two men in it. Dylan seemed to recognize the occupants.

"Wait here while I go talk to these guys," Dylan said as he went over to the van.

What an incredible response time, Will thought.

Dylan spoke to the men for a few moments and then returned to where Will was.

"Do you think you're up to driving your Corvette?" Dylan asked.

Will nodded. "Yeah, I guess." It wouldn't be a problem, because Will knew he wouldn't actually have to drive.

"Why don't we go get some five-dollar coffee, and have a talk." Dylan gave a comforting smile. "I'm buying,"

Will took a deep breath, his soul still shaking from the ordeal. "Okay, but I want whipped cream on mine."

THIRTEEN

Will sat across from Dylan at a secluded outdoor table outside of a trendy coffee shop enjoying some coffee.

"So how are you holding up?" Dylan asked.

"I don't know," Will said with a sigh. "Disturbed." He was not only disturbed about the afternoon's events, but also the fact that Dylan had deceived him and his mother.

"That's understandable," Dylan said. "This whole thing's become a mess."

"Well, yeah."

"No, I mean we've been aware of someone in the shadows that is willing to stop at nothing to get his hands on some technology your uncle was developing," Dylan explained. "Maxwell, that guy that you were meeting, was a well-known hitman, and some of his hired muscle. We were trying to track him back to his employer, but now obviously that's not happening."

"Oh, I see," Will replied.

"I mean, the employer is crazy," Dylan went on. "He's

used these tactics before. He commonly uses extortion to get what he wants from people. Sometimes offering decent compensation, but with the threat of violence if the offer is turned down. We've been following Maxwell, and figured out this mystery man has been trying to track down your uncle's tech. I knew Zac, maybe not so much recently, but even back in the day, he was crazy smart. He's not going to hide his life's work in a 90s sports car that he gives to his nephew."

"Yeah, that would be crazy." Will cringed, hoping to bolster Dylan's misguided view on the matter.

"No, his files are in a safety deposit box, or storage somewhere, under a pseudonym to keep it safe," Dylan said.

"Huh." Will nodded, attempting to seem as clueless as possible.

"This guy doesn't even make offers sometimes … sometimes he'll just have Maxwell off them."

Will's eyes grew wider. "That's scary."

"Yeah," Dylan agreed. "You were in a lot of danger."

"How long have you been following me?" Will asked, a bit of nervousness beginning to nip at him.

"We've been tracking Maxwell." Dylan explained. "We followed Maxwell to the fair, and saw him approach you and your girlfriend. That's when we realized the imminent danger that you were in. At that point you really became a concern. I was already on the case, but I volunteered to take the lead and work extra to watch out for you and your mother, when we realized he was coming to squeeze you for the Corvette."

"Okay," Will said, somewhat relieved that they hadn't

been following them too long. It would have creeped him out if they were watching that make out session at Lookout Point.

"Then we caught him getting in his car and following the green mustang. We then followed him to the parking garage."

Will glanced down. "So, you saw that?"

"Yeah, that was a scary scene."

"You just let that happen?" A little agitation grew in Will's voice. "I don't like Doug and his thugs, but he could have killed those guys. That would have been okay?"

"You saw how quick all that happened."

"Yeah," Will conceded.

"We've been trying not to interfere, in the hopes that Maxwell would slip up and lead us back to his employer," Dylan explained. "But when he had his gun to your head, I couldn't let him do it. I got chewed out by my boss on the way over here for intervening, but I don't care. I just couldn't let him kill you."

"Your boss wanted you to let him kill me?"

"My orders were to not interfere, and follow Maxwell. Like I said, I couldn't just standby."

"So, was this all just a case?" Will asked.

"What do you mean?" Dylan seemed confused.

"With my mom? Was it just your job to get close to us so that you could try and catch this guy?"

"No, absolutely not," Dylan said. "Lying about my employment is part of the job, but I really do care about your mother, Beth."

"You'll have to excuse me if I have a hard time believing

anything you say," Will said. "You know my dad passed away five years ago, you're the first guy my mom has shown any interest in, and you're a complete fraud."

"Let me tell you a story," Dylan said. "Back in high school, I had the biggest crush on your mother. To me, she was the most beautiful girl at our school, and my knees got weak every time she talked to me. She's still gorgeous, by the way, maybe even more-so now. Anyway, I wasn't awkward or anything, I was cool, well, cool enough, but I didn't have a lot of confidence when it came to asking your mother out. She was different than the other girls."

Will took another sip of his coffee as he continued to listen to Dylan's story.

"When I finally worked up the courage to ask her out to the Out of This World Dance that year, she said that your dad, Steven, had already asked her the day before, and that she had accepted his invitation," Dylan went on. "I was crushed, broken to my soul. I didn't even end up going to the dance, I got one of my older friends to buy me some beer and I ended up getting trashed in my backyard, it was really depressing. That's another story though."

Will smirked. "That is sad."

"Yeah." Dylan cleared his throat and continued. "Anyway, it seemed like after that dance, she and your father were inseparable. I had lost my chance; I could see that they had fallen in love. What could I do? I wasn't a dirt bag; I wasn't going to try to win over a girl that was head over heels for another guy. It was obvious he loved her back too, he treated her like gold. It was little consolation, but at least he was treating her the way she deserved to be treated.

I may have lost my chance with Beth in high school, but I never ever lost my feelings for her."

"Are you serious?" Will asked, almost moved by his story, knowing his mother's story about that same dance. "So, what, if you started seeing my mother, would you just keep living a lie?" Will asked.

"I don't know, Will. I got into being a federal agent because I really didn't care about my life. Sure, I didn't want to get shot, but there's a certain amount of liberation when personal life doesn't matter. The work was exciting and distracting too. Not the paperwork part, but the *in the field* part," Dylan said. "But if I had a chance with your mother, I don't know if I would feel the same about putting my life on the line for this work. If things progressed, I think I would give this up."

"Or is that just something you'd say to get me to believe that you're not an agent anymore?"

Dylan chuckled. "No, it'd be the truth, I'm serious," Dylan said. "Sometimes it's not worth dying if there's a reason for living. I'm considering retiring after this case. Not retired, retired, but do something on the civilian side. But I can't even consider that, until this case is over and I'm sure that you and Beth are safe."

"I appreciate it." Will did appreciate it, and the conviction with which Dylan spoke, led Will to believe his words.

Perhaps he was wrong about Dylan, maybe just a little. Will knew that he still couldn't be trusted with any extra information, but perhaps he wasn't such a bad guy. For starters there wasn't pineapple on the pizza he brought the other day.

Dylan put down his coffee after taking another sip. "But here's where the situation gets a little sticky. With Maxwell out of the picture, our best link to this mystery person behind all of this is through you."

"Me?" Will asked.

"Yes," Dylan replied. "He still wants the car. Either he or an associate will be in contact with you soon, I can guarantee it."

"This is great." Will rolled his eyes.

Dylan took out his phone and typed a quick text message.

Will's phone received a text, he got it out and glanced at it.

"Oh, that's me," Dylan said.

"You have my number?" Will asked.

"I'm a federal agent, you should be surprised if I don't have it," Dylan replied with a chuckle. "This is my number, and I've also sent you another agent's contact."

Will opened the message and glanced at the other number.

"I was almost fired from the case when my boss found out about Maxwell," Dylan explained. "He said that I'm too close to the people involved, but somehow I talked him into leaving me on the case."

"That transpired quickly," Will said.

"Yeah, when I got chewed out on the car ride here," Dylan said. "It wasn't a pleasant conversation. But now an additional agent is going to be joining me. Agent Mitchell; Anne. I've known her for a long time, she's really good. She'll be working with us to try to catch this guy."

"Us?" Will asked

"Yes," Dylan said. "Depending on how you're contacted, we may or may not be able to intercept it, but however they choose to do it, you need to contact us immediately, so we can start forming a strategy. This individual is clever, that's why we haven't found them yet."

"I don't want to die," Will said in a moment of vulnerability. "Or have any of my family or friends get hurt…And I want to keep my car. And not be afraid anymore."

"We want all of those things as well," Dylan said. "That's why you need to work with us."

Will thought for a moment. "Alright," he replied.

Dylan looked over and nodded toward a woman sitting at a table near the door of the coffee shop. She picked up the iced coffee that she had been drinking, and approached their table.

As she arrived, Dylan motioned her to take a seat, then turned to Will. "Meet agent Mitchell, Will."

"It's nice to meet you," Will said.

"Likewise." She flashed him a professional smile. "I just want to tell you that we are going to do everything in our power to keep you and your family safe."

"Thank you," Will said.

"Think of us as your guardian angels," she said in a kind tone. "But you need to help us, by being upfront and honest about everything, so that we can do our job."

It was odd, she had a very nurturing aspect that, despite the emotional upheaval he was experiencing, eased his anxiety. He appreciated it, even if it was just momentarily eased.

She looked to be in her mid-30s, but seemed confident and emotionally put together well beyond her years. There was something about her that made it seem safe to confide in her. No doubt that came in useful in her line of work.

Will felt as if perhaps Dylan and Agent Mitchell could help get control of the situation and its madness, and maybe rein his life back in to normal.

"But this all must remain a secret, you can't tell your mother, or girlfriend, not even your imaginary friend," Dylan interjected with a smirk. "Confidentiality is the only way this works."

"I understand. And my imaginary friend has a big mouth," Will kidded.

"You see, that makes so much more sense to me," Zac said as they drove along, heading home. "Engineer, no, FBI agent, not my first guess, but believable for Dylan."

"They really sound like they are all about taking this guy that's after you down," Will said with a hint of optimism.

"Eh, yeah," Zac replied, something in his voice noting that he thought that there was more to it than that.

"How much do you think I should tell them? Obviously not about you," Will said. "But they sound like they want to help."

"Are you kidding? As little as possible," Zac replied.

"Really?"

"Yes," Zac said. "Why do you think they're after this guy, and don't say it's because they want to keep our family safe."

"I believe Dylan does, I mean, he especially cares about mom."

"Dylan doesn't call the shots, he's the one that wants you safe," Zac replied.

Uncle Zac began to play the Final Jeopardy music through the car speakers.

Will thought for another second. "This guy is hiring a hitman as muscle, maybe they see him as an underground crime lord?"

"Yeah, possibly," Zach replied with skepticism. "Or maybe they think if this guy is looking so hard for my technology, he might just find it, and perhaps they can follow him to it."

"So, you think they're after your tech too? Now you're starting to sound paranoid."

"Can I say yes without sounding full of myself?" Zac asked. "Yes. You've got to realize the weight and implications of what people thought I was working on."

"And in actuality it was something even bigger," Will replied. "I guess that makes sense."

"Of course, it makes sense," Zac continued. "And it adds a whole new level of complexity to things. While it's potentially nice to have some more muscle on our side, it's going to be hard to make a move undetected. We're going to have to play them like a hand of cards, Ace, and play them just right."

Text flashed across the Corvette's infotainment screen: "Playing 'Somebody's Watching Me' by Rockwell".

As Will and Zac rounded the corner home, they noticed Katie's Camaro in the driveway.

As they pulled into the driveway, she looked up from some homework she was working on in the driver seat while she waited.

The Corvette pulled around her and into the garage.

Will got out to meet Katie in the driveway.

She had already gotten out of her car, and rushed to him. She wrapped her arms around him, almost knocking him over.

"Stalk much?" Will kidded her.

"Shut up, you big goof," she said in her affectionate tone. "I'm just happy you're still alive."

Will almost couldn't believe that he was seeing her again, and holding her once more. He had gotten another chance, and wished he never had to let her go from his embrace again.

"What happened?" Katie asked. "How do you still have the Corvette?" She flashed a skeptical smile. "Did we win?"

Will sighed, still traumatized by the afternoon. "I don't really want to talk about it in depth."

She could tell he was stressed. "It's okay."

After holding her for another moment, Will spoke up. "Maxwell, the hitman, is dead."

"What?"

Will didn't know how much he should tell her. He wanted to tell her everything, of course, but emotionally he didn't feel like he had it in him to rehash all of the details. And he wasn't sure how much he should say about the agents' involvement.

"Evidently the authorities were tracking Maxwell, and they showed up at the deal. They shot him when he pulled a gun on me," Will summarized.

"He pulled a gun on you?" a wide-eyed Katie asked.

"Yeah," Will said, shaking his head as if he was trying to shake off the memory. "Maxwell is gone, but somewhere, someone still wants the car."

"You could've died today," Katie's voice sounded as if she was on the edge of tears. "I would've never forgiven myself if you'd died, and I had never told you …"

"Told me?" Will asked.

"I love you, Will," she said.

Will began to fall, as he so commonly did, floating through the universe contained within her eyes. "I love you too, Katie," he replied. He then kissed her softly on the lips.

"Hey, I could have died too," Zac's voice rang out from the garage.

Will and Katie turned toward him and chuckled.

"We love you too," Will kidded.

Katie lingered for just a little while longer, but had to leave. After all, it was a school night, and she had a lot of homework.

Will watched her back out of the driveway, and pull away.

"Saying the l-word already?" Zac asked. "Life sure moves fast in high school these days."

"You have no idea," Will replied under his breath.

FOURTEEN

Will had done his best to act as if everything was normal in front of his mother.

As Will shared dinner with his mother, he thought, *Acting normal never took so much energy.* But it worked, and she didn't seem to suspect anything amiss.

After dinner, Will sat at the kitchen table and did his best to concentrate, and get his head together enough to do some homework. But everything he read escaped him, replaced by flashbacks of his day, and of the last week. Those thoughts were followed by the anxiety of imagining the possible scenarios of what was to come. Glancing out a window to the backyard, he thought he saw a figure, or at least a shadow move, but there was no one there. But would there be one when he glanced again in a minute?

During the course of his attempts to study, his Uncle Zac notified him through the camera software, that agent Mitchell was checking out the perimeter of the house.

Having the agents watching them gave Will both comfort and stress. He felt safer, but more nervous that Uncle Zac would be discovered.

But should he really feel safer? Dylan's boss would have preferred Will be killed by Maxwell, rather than blow his cover. But he did feel safer with Dylan watching. He wasn't sure about all of his motives, but he trusted that deep down he was a decent person. Perhaps he was naïve, but in the short time he had spoken to agent Mitchell, he'd felt the same about her.

It was later in the evening, and Will lay in his bed. His faithful pup, Nala, was curled up by his side.

"Are you ready to attack Mandy if she comes back tonight?" He kidded Nala as he patted her on the head.

She let out a short, cute little growl, almost as if she knew what he had said.

Will's phone on the nightstand went off, and he reached over and looked at the number. He didn't recognize it, but thought that he should answer.

"Hello?" Will said.

"Hello, Will, this is agent Mitchell, we met at the coffee house earlier today."

"Of course."

"I was checking out the perimeter of your house a little earlier, and noticed what looked like functioning security cameras," she said.

"Oh."

"Yeah, I couldn't find them, or their network, and I was

wondering where they were, and if I could tie into them to keep a watch on the property easier."

Will's stomach twisted; he didn't know what to tell her. The cameras were also tied into the car's cameras. He certainly couldn't let her have access to those.

"Oh, those are dummy cameras." It was the first lie that came to Will's mind.

"Huh," she replied, sounding a little skeptical. "They're really convincing."

"Yeah," Will doubled down. "They're really nice, they look so real. My uncle gave them to us awhile back."

"Okay," she said, seeming to buy the lie, but Will wasn't sure. "That's a shame."

"Is Dylan there?" Will asked.

"No," Anne replied. "Do you need me to get in contact with him for you?"

"No, thanks," Will said. "Agent Mitchell, I was wondering if I could ask you something non-case related."

"Sure," she replied. "And you can call me Anne."

"You've known Dylan for a while, at least that's what he made it sound like."

"I have," she replied. "We go back a number of years. In fact, I've known him since I started at the bureau. He was already there."

"Be honest with me, in your personal opinion, do you think he's a sincere person?"

"Oh, absolutely," she replied without hesitation. "And I'm not just saying that. I've only known him to be a genuine and trustworthy individual. Maybe a little bit of a loose cannon in a raid, but that has seemed to somehow always worked out to be an asset in his favor. But I trust him completely."

"Thanks, Anne," Will replied. "That's good to hear."

"Does this have anything to do with your mother?" Agent Mitchell asked in a playful, suspicious tone.

"How did you know?"

Anne laughed. "I don't know if I should tell you this, but he's been talking about her long before this case."

"Really?"

"Yeah," she replied. "Your mother, Beth, was the one that got away, his long-lost love."

"He said that?"

"He has, in multiple ways over multiple years," she said. "If you're wondering if his feelings for her are sincere, I would say a thousand percent."

"That makes me feel better."

"It should," she said. "He's a really good guy. Is there anything else, Will?"

"No, that was it."

"Don't hesitate to call me if you hear or see anything, or if you're contacted by you-know-who."

"I thought that was the point?" Will asked. "We don't know who."

"Exactly," she said with a chuckle.

After Will hung up with Anne, he hopped out of bed, and went downstairs, followed by his four-legged shadow, Nala.

His mother was sipping a glass of wine on the couch in the living room when Will walked by.

"Are you okay, honey?" Beth asked as he passed.

"Yeah," he replied as he kept walking. "I just wanted to check something on the car."

"Alright."

Nala took a detour, and went to go sit with Will's mom on the couch.

Will entered the garage, walked to the Corvette, and sat down in the driver seat.

"I'm scared to call you on the phone," Will said. "They might have it tapped."

"That's probably a good idea, I can make it appear as if I'm calling from any random number, but they can still get to the conversation," Zac said. "And you know your phone is always listening anyway."

"I know," Will said. "It's usually in my pocket, but I left it upstairs for now."

"Good," Uncle Zac said. "I am going to start notifying you solely through the camera software if I see anything in my surveillance, instead of calling you."

"Sounds good." Will said.

"When Anne…"

"Anne?" Zac interrupted him.

"Agent Mitchell," Will clarified.

"What, are you two old buddies now?"

"No, she just said to call her Anne."

"Just don't let your guard down too much," Zac warned him. "These agents have to be slick for a living."

"Anyway, when she was checking the house earlier, she saw the cameras you had me put up."

"What did she say?"

"She wanted to link into them," Will said. "But I

told her they were dummy cameras, you know, to scare crooks."

"Perfect, that was probably the best thing you could've said. My car cameras are on there, I can separate them, but I'd rather not reveal the network that the house cameras are on."

"Yeah, that's why I think she bought the dummy camera excuse, she couldn't find them on any network in the area."

"I know." Zac sounded proud of himself. "I cloaked the network. The feds are good, but they're not that good."

Will chuckled. "You really are a computer nerd, aren't you?"

"At this point, a computer and a nerd," Zac replied. "And proud of it."

"As you should be," Will said as he got up out of the car. "I'm going to head inside, I just wanted to make sure I said the right thing about the cameras."

"That was perfect, Will, goodnight."

"Goodnight Uncle Zac." Will went back inside.

As Will entered the living room, he joined Beth and Nala on the couch.

"Hey," his mother said. "I thought you were going to bed, instead you're all over the place."

"Yeah, I'm going to bed in a minute. I just wanted to tell you…I know it's been hard since dad…" Will stopped.

"It has," she replied, sparing him the need to finish the sentence.

"I just wanted to tell you that I don't think anyone could've kept it all together better than you."

"I haven't always kept it together," she said with a chuckle. "A lot of nights were filled with crying after you went to bed."

"But you always took care of us," he said. "And I appreciate it."

"Oh, thank you sweetheart," she said as she leaned over and gave him a big hug. "You've always been my priority. And despite everything that was thrown at us, you turned out pretty good."

"That's debatable," he kidded as he leaned back on the couch after her embrace.

She reached over and grabbed her glass of wine, and took another sip.

"You know," Beth said. "It's so much harder losing a good man than losing a bad one. With a bad one, he breaks your heart, and you're crushed, but he was a jerk anyway. Losing a good man is like having your *happily ever after* get stolen away from you. And you can never really fill that void that was left. In time, you just learn to cope with it."

Will nodded in agreement. He knew that she thought his father was not just a good man, but the best. And his father always treated his mother like a queen.

"I don't know what brought all of this on," Beth said. "But I always love knowing how you feel and what you're thinking."

"I know mom," he gave a typical teenage dismissive reply.

"I shouldn't press my luck, right?" She asked with a smile.

"It's okay," Will said. "I love you."

"I know," his mom kidded. "See, two can play at the too cool game. Just kidding, I love you too…so much."

"And I guess it's alright if you want to go on a date with that Dylan guy, he seems alright."

Beth was a little surprised by Will's approval. "Thanks, sweetie," she replied. "That means a lot."

Will gave her a smile.

"Things with you and Katie going good?" She asked.

"Yeah, amazing. She's great."

"You know, maybe marrying your high school sweetheart runs in the family, who knows?" she kidded him.

He shrugged. "It wouldn't be a bad thing," Will said, with an embarrassed smile and a warm feeling inside.

"Whoever you end up with, I hope that you two are as happy as your father and I were," she said. "But I just hope that you get more time than we did."

"Me too."

"Well, you should probably get to bed, it's a school night."

"Sure," he said. "Goodnight."

"Goodnight, sweetie," she replied.

Will stood up and ascended the stairs, and was soon back in bed. Moments later, Nala came bounding up the dog ramp at the end of the bed, and snuggled up next to him.

After that traumatic Monday, the rest of the week seemed to pass without incident. It would've almost seemed like the world was returning to normal, except the occasional noticing of the agents' surveillance, and the looming feeling of impending danger.

Midway through the week, Will invited Katie to come out with him after school.

He wouldn't tell her where they were going, but it was finally revealed when Will pulled the Corvette into the parking lot of a greasy burger and fry joint.

"Another stop on your tour of places I should know about?" Katie asked.

"Kind-of," Will said. "I wanted to introduce you to some people. The food is good too, though."

A little bell on the door jingled as Will and Katie walked in the door. The place had an old diner feel to it, with a long bar, a row of tables in the center, and booths populating around the edges of the interior. Most important of all, it had that delicious greasy-food smell in the air.

"There they are," Pedro called out from a booth where he and Lucy were sitting.

Will walked Katie over to the edge of the booth to meet his friends. "Katie, this is Pedro and Lucy. These are the other peeps in the band I told you I was in."

"Nice to finally meet you," Pedro said. "I feel like he's been hiding you away."

Lucy smiled and waved. "Have a seat, you two. Oh

wait." She got up and slid into the same side of the booth as Pedro. "You guys can sit together."

"Thanks," Will said as he and Katie scooted into the other side of the booth. Will turned to Katie. "The milkshakes here are delicious."

"He's not kidding," Lucy said slamming her hand on the table as a playful punctuation to her sentence. "They're amazing."

Will and Katie ordered some milkshakes and some French fries to share as they hung out with Lucy and Pedro.

"So, Will has known Lucy ever since middle school or something," Pedro explained.

"Since the first day of middle school," Lucy corrected him. "When we bonded over making fun of our algebra teacher."

"Aw," Katie said. "That's sweet."

"To be fair, he deserved it," Will said. "He was terrible at explaining things, and when you'd ask a question, he'd treat you like you were an idiot."

"He absolutely did," Lucy agreed. "But we destroyed him in the notes we would pass back and forth. We burned him like my mom burns dinner."

Will glanced at Katie. "Her mom burns a lot of food."

"She blames it on the oven." Lucy rolled her eyes. "Will, remember that time you were over, and we had to rush to the fire alarm and try to fan away the smoke so it wouldn't go off, while my mom rushed our food out of the oven and to the backyard because it was smoking so bad?"

Will smiled, "How could I forget."

"Anyway," Pedro continued. "Then Will and I became friends last year. I've played drums since I was a kid and it took me, like, six months to find out that Will played guitar."

"What can I say? I'm a private person," Will said.

"I was like, let's start jammin', hombre," Pedro said.

"Then Lucy found out," Will explained. "And she said, *hey, you dorks are in a band? Count me in too.*"

"I took a crash course in bass," Lucy said. "Practicing all the time."

"She's really good now," Will said.

"That's awesome," Katie said. "I'd love to hear you guys play sometime. Do you have any gigs coming up?"

Lucy and Pedro looked at each other, then turned their gaze to Will.

"What?" Will asked.

"You didn't tell her?" Lucy asked Will.

"I've had a lot going on," Will said. "I guess it slipped my mind."

"Slipped your mind?" Pedro asked in awe.

"What slipped your mind?" Katie asked.

"We're actually performing a song at the dance," Will said.

Katie perked up with excitement, "That's great!"

"It's by far our biggest gig ever," Pedro said. "There'll actually be a decent amount of people at this one."

"Can you really call one song a gig?" Will asked, as if he were downplaying it.

"I can't believe you didn't tell her," Lucy said. "You wrote the song about her."

"What?" Katie exclaimed as she looked at Will with wide eyes and an excited smile.

"Thanks, Lucy," Will said with sarcasm.

Lucy shrugged. "Oh, was that a secret?"

Katie leaned up against Will and laid her head on his shoulder. "Now I really can't wait for the dance."

"Why don't you have some fries, Lucy?" Will said grabbing a big handful of fries and holding them toward Lucy's face to shut her up.

Lucy took the fries from Will's hand with her teeth, chewed and swallowed them.

"I'll take your fries, all the fries," Lucy kidded. "This guy." She pointed at Will with her thumb. "Don't let him undersell himself. He's a true performer."

Will dropped his head and sighed, he knew what story was coming.

"We were about to do a few songs at a talent show, and Will spilled a big drink all over his crotch right before we were supposed to go on stage," Lucy said with a chuckle. "It was hilarious, he was so upset."

"Oh, no." Katie glanced at Will and smiled.

"Will was paranoid that everyone would think he peed his pants." Lucy smiled wider as she continued. "So, he took a long sleeve shirt and tied it around his waist."

"I played it off as 1990s fashion influence," Will said. "And the shirt was flannel anyway, so that worked."

"Yeah, but I don't think they wore the bulk of the shirt in front in the 1990s, making it look like a flannel skirt," Lucy said. "Or as I prefer to think of it…a kilt."

"It wasn't ideal," Will replied. "But I don't think people

really gave it a second thought, except for Lucy, who likes to tell the story, and on occasion tries to speak in a Scottish accent and calls me her *Wee William*."

Katie laughed.

"Your Scottish accent is still terrible, by the way," Will said.

"I guess you're right," Lucy said. "Only a couple of girls happened to mention something about your shirt placement to me after that show."

"They did?" Will asked.

"Yeah, but don't worry, I didn't tell them about your wet crotch," Lucy said.

"Thanks," Will replied.

"No, I told them you 'got really excited' when you played a show." Lucy laughed. "And that you always got 'excited' when we performed live … it was kind-of your thing."

"Because he loves the music so much?" Katie kidded.

Will slumped his head down while Pedro and Lucy burst into laughter at her comment.

"Hey," Lucy said. "Then they asked when our next show was, so it was good marketing."

Pedro laughed. "I guess sex sells."

"Yeah," Lucy said. "But don't bring kids to the show."

Will didn't look up, exhausted by the direction the conversation had taken.

Katie laughed. "So, should I be worried?" It was obvious she was not worried, but playing along at Will's expense.

"Nah," Lucy said as she glanced at Will, seeming proud that she had sufficiently embarrassed him. "The girls were Skanksville."

After Will had dropped Katie off, he and Zac were making the short drive home, when, from out of nowhere, a car raced up behind the Corvette.

Will looked in the rearview mirror. "Where did that cop come from?"

"He was lurking in that last parking lot we just passed," Zac replied.

"Oh, I didn't see him," Will watched the patrol car tailgate them. "I wasn't speeding or anything."

"Zooming in on one of my rear cameras, it looks like your old buddy, Officer Cade," Zac said.

"Not today," Will said with a sigh. "I get so sick of him harassing me every chance he gets."

"Want me to smokescreen him this time?" Zac asked.

Will considered it for a moment. "Actually, I would love for you to smokescreen him."

"Great," Zac replied. "Because we're coming up on a perfect curve to do it."

Officer Cade had played this game with Will a number of times before, so he knew what to expect. Cade would tailgate for a minute or so to build up Will's anxiety, or perhaps the officer was just hoping that he'd make a run for it. Will never did, that would have just stirred up more trouble. After tailgating him for a while, Cade would pull him over and give him grief for no reason. Well, no reason except for not liking Will, or the cars he drove.

The key with the smokescreen would be the timing. Zac would need to deploy it before the blue lights went off, so as to better maintain their innocence. And they could feel fine about driving away, because they weren't in the process of being pulled over anyway.

They were approaching a sharp bend in the road. Will began glancing back and forth between the patrol car, and the upcoming curve. He could feel it, like another sense, it was almost time for the blue lights to start flashing.

"Come on, just wait a few more seconds," Will whispered under his breath.

Finally, when they had gotten close enough to the curve, Zac began to pour thick, dark smoke out of the tailpipes of the Corvette.

Will looked back at the huge cloud coming out of the back of the car. "Wow, that's a lot of smoke!" Will chuckled. "That's more than I was expecting."

"Yeah," Zac said. "Isn't it beautiful?"

The Corvette then sped up around the upcoming sharp curve.

There was the sound of squealing breaks, and an impact behind them. As they began to distance themselves, the smoke began to clear enough for them to see Officer Cade's patrol car, nose-first, down in the steep ditch at the side of the road.

"Officer Cade, ditched once again," Zac said.

Will laughed.

Watching in the rearview mirror as they continued to drive off, Will could see Cade getting out of his patrol car and throwing up his hands in anger.

Cade began to walk out of the ditch, but his foot slipped in the mud and he fell down, face first, and rolled backward into the muddy ditch.

"Deputy?" Zac asked. "More like Derp-uty."

"Oh, that pun was awful." Will cringed. "Even for you."

"You wished you thought of that pun, you don't have to pretend," Zac kidded. "Jealousy is an ugly thing."

Will and Zac rounded the next corner and left the scene behind.

FIFTEEN

Katie was looking forward to the dance on Saturday, and Will was too. But he couldn't relax, and his poor sleep was beginning to get the best of him. At least it was going to be a short school week. The students were getting Friday before the dance off.

On Thursday afternoon, since they were performing for the dance, Will, Pedro and Lucy were able to negotiate having a music practice during their corresponding free period. Not that they couldn't have found time on one of the evenings that week, but why not do it on school time? What better way to escape the school day doldrums? It helped to make the day go by.

Will had clung to the knowledge of this long upcoming weekend to help him get through the week, and his perseverance finally paid off when the end of school bell rang on Thursday.

As Will was crossing the parking lot, he noticed Katie standing by his car.

The sight of her always brought a smile to his face.

"Hey," he greeted her as he approached.

"Are you ready for the weekend?" She asked.

"Yeah, this three-day weekend couldn't have come at a better time," he said with an air of relief.

"So, what are you doing right now?"

"Um …" He thought for a moment. "I don't have any-thing pressing, except getting out of this place."

"I know what you mean," she replied. "I want to take you somewhere."

"So mysterious," he kidded her about the lack of infor-mation she was giving.

"It won't take long," she said, remaining cryptic. "I was thinking that you could drop off your car at home, and I could drive you this time."

Will's curiosity grew. "Sure, that's fine." He walked over to the driver's side door of the Corvette and opened it. "That sound good to you, Uncle Zac?" He asked the car.

"Any excuse to get my paint out of this sun sounds good to me," Zac replied.

"You're worried about your paint?" Will chuckled. "The more time passes, the more you sound at one with the car."

"I just figured I might as well get used to it," Zac said. "And just because I'm a car, doesn't mean I want to start looking like a slob."

"Valid point," Will said.

"And that means no trash on my floors too," Zac added.

"I got it." Will rolled his eyes.

Soon they arrived at Will's house, and with Zac parked

in the garage, Katie drove Will in her Camaro toward an unknown destination.

It wasn't too much longer before Katie was pulling into the parking lot of her father's automotive shop. She found a parking spot close to the entrance, and turned off the key.

Will was beginning to get nervous. "What are we doing here?" *She had brought him here to meet her father, hadn't she?* He had met Katie's mother, and she was delightful, but meeting a girlfriend's father is always a more daunting task.

"My father won't be around when you pick me up on Saturday for the dance, and he wanted to meet you," Katie said in a lighthearted tone, as if she didn't know the weight of what she was making Will do.

"You could've warned me, so I could've prepared my-self." Will glanced down at the clothes he was wearing. Not that he ever really looked slovenly, but now he was self-conscious about his attire.

"He's really nice, I think you guys would get along," she replied.

"But there's a different dynamic when you're dating someone's daughter."

"Maybe so," Katie said. "But you have nothing to worry about, he's really going to like you. But if you're not ready to meet him, you don't have to …I can tell him you were busy."

Will sighed. He was going to have to meet her father sooner or later, he might as well get it over with. "No, don't say that, I'll meet him now."

She grabbed his hand and smiled. "Thank you so much, Will. It'll mean a lot to him, and me."

Will offered a fake smile through his apprehension. He really would do almost anything for her.

As they got out of the car and began to make their way to the entrance, Will noticed a black C4 Corvette in the parking lot. It was a little older than his. He could tell by the side-gills as opposed to the side-scrape design, followed by other body, and light discrepancies. It was probably a late 1980s C4.

Katie noticed the Corvette and pointed it out. "The C4 is making a comeback…or maybe it never left."

"It's always had so much personality," Will replied with a smile. "Nice to see them still on the road breaking up the sea of modern car and crossover mediocrity."

"Yeah, and it's one of the older ones that have that cool retro digital dash."

"Have you been studying up?" Will asked.

She smiled at him. "I know things."

As they proceeded toward the front of the shop, Katie began to veer off away from the front doors.

"Hey Will, come over here for a second," Katie said.

She led him a few cars over, to the front of a shining black 1965 Ford Mustang that looked to be in mint condition.

"What do you think?" Katie asked.

Will began to circle the car, then looked inside one of the windows. The interior looked as immaculate as the outside did. The car had been kept up over the years, or painstakingly restored to show quality.

"This is really nice," Will said. "I knew a guy that had a '65 like this, but in nowhere near as good of shape."

"It's my dad's, he restored it," Katie said. "But don't worry, he doesn't peel-out into the crowd when he leaves car shows."

Will chuckled. "I don't think the stereotype carries over to the old Mustangs earlier than the Fox-Body style."

"I know, I'm just kidding."

Will took a couple steps back to look at the car as a whole. "Is it his daily driver?"

"Yeah."

"This thing could be in a showroom," Will said. "He did an amazing job on it."

"That's the perks of having an auto shop like this," Katie replied. "If it gets a ding, he can fix it."

"Nice perk."

"He could never have a car like this, and not drive it all the time." Katie smiled. "My dad says *if you're not enjoying life, what's the point?*"

"That's true," Will agreed. "I don't think I could have the Corvette and not drive it all the time. It'd be sad."

She put her hand on the edge of the Mustang's hood. "I was hoping you'd like it," Katie said. "I didn't know if you were a diehard Chevy, and hater to the rest."

"Oh, of course not," Will said. "I'm not a toxic car guy. I have my preferences, but so does everyone. I can still appreciate other cars, especially muscle, sports and performance cars. They have a lot of heart."

"That's how I feel too," Katie said.

They turned and walked to the front door of the shop.

Will's eyes grew wide as he entered the auto shop. There were so many supplies for all different types of cars. Beyond the fluids, wipers, and the standard fare of average auto parts stores, there was a great selection of OEM parts, and plenty of parts for modders.

She led him by the aisles and aisles of supplies, headed toward the front desk.

Will had some nervous butterflies in his stomach about meeting her father, but he tried to ignore the nerves.

There was a young man behind the counter that looked maybe nineteen or twenty years old. He was helping a customer that stood in front of him.

There was another man with his back to them, arranging some things on a shelf behind the counter.

As Will and Katie approach the front desk, the conversation between the customer and the young associate could be better heard.

"It dumped a pool of coolant all over the passenger floorboard of the car," the customer said.

The associate got a confused look on his face. "That sounds pretty bad." It was obvious that the store employee wasn't familiar with the problem the customer was having.

"Yeah, I'm really concerned about it," the customer said.

"I'm sorry," Will said, politely entering their conversation. "Is it that C4 Corvette outside?"

"Yeah," the customer said.

"Are the windows randomly fogging up as well, like after you turn the car off?" Will asked.

"Yeah, it was the strangest thing, it did fog up right after I stopped the car."

"Your heater core is shot," Will said.

"That sounds bad," the customer said.

"Yeah, kind-a," Will replied. "The replacement core isn't that expensive, the thing that kills you is the labor. There's a saying about that part. They say that the heater core came down the line first when they were building the car, and then they built the rest of the car around it."

"Yikes," the customer said, shaking his head.

"They actually have to get at it through the dashboard," Will explained. "You can bypass the core as a temporary fix, it's cheap and easy, but you won't have heat or defrost."

The customer nodded. "Okay."

"I'm sure they could help you with either option here if you didn't want to mess with it yourself," Will said.

"You don't work on cars, do you?" The customer asked.

Will smiled. "I barely have time to work on mine."

"Oh well," the customer replied. "Thanks for the advice."

"You're welcome," Will replied. "It's a great car; worth fixing. But I would avoid driving it until you get one of those options done, you don't want it to overheat."

The man nodded that he understood, and valued his advice.

The shop assistant also looked at Will with an appreciative look.

The man arranging things on the shelf behind the counter turned around. He looked to be a man in his mid to late 40s.

"Hi daddy," Katie said to the man.

"Hi sweetheart," he replied to her. He then turned to Will. "And you must be Will, I'm Mike, Katie's father."

"I'm Will, it's nice to meet you, sir."

"Katie says that you like to work on cars," Mike said. "It certainly sounds like you have a little experience."

"Oh, I'm sorry," Will apologized. "That was probably rude of me to butt into the conversation like that."

"No, not at all," Mike said. "I'm glad you did. If you hadn't, I would have. My guy didn't know what the customer was talking about, and the advice you gave him was perfect."

"Thanks, in general I'm better with cars that are older than me."

Mike chuckled. "Aren't we all?"

"This is a really nice shop you have here," Will said. "It's got a great selection."

"Thanks, we have a lot of stuff in the back too that you can request at the counter. Plus, the garage bays where we do all the work are in the back. Everything from maintenance and engine repairs, to modifications, and minor or major bodywork."

Will was more and more impressed with this place. "It's a big operation."

"Yeah, I like it," Mike said. "It's nice to be able to do something you love for a living. Well, most days I love it."

"I bet," Will agreed. "There's something about working on cars. They can be frustrating, but when you get them fixed, it's the most satisfying feeling."

"Provided you get them fixed," Mike kidded.

"I was brought up to believe that hard work builds

character. Maybe it's silly, but when I really make progress on a car, it makes me feel better about myself."

"Absolutely," Mike agreed. "That's not silly."

"And there's something about taking a really old car that's been forgotten and unloved for a while, and little by little, bringing it back to its former glory, or even better," Will continued. "When it's done, and you stand back and look at it, it's like you're standing on a mountaintop with your ratchet."

Mike smiled. It was obvious that it was an emotion that he sympathized with. "I think Katie might've been right about you," he said. "But it doesn't surprise me, she's a pretty good judge of character."

A smile grew wide across Katie's face. "Of course."

"Well, since time began," Mike went on. "Fathers have taken on the age-old tradition of intimidating their daughter's dates before a dance. And I was disappointed that I wasn't going to be around to do that on Saturday evening."

"Daddy." Katie put her hands on her hips, and gave him a look to rein her father in.

"I feel intimidated right now, if that helps," Will kidded.

"You don't have to be intimidated," Mike said with a smile. "I'm just messing with you. You seem like a good guy. Just be a gentleman, and treat my daughter nice. If she's happy, I'm happy…Within reason." He said, raising an eyebrow.

"Yes sir," Will replied, keeping a straight face. But all he could think about was that if Mike knew about Lookout Point, he might be a dead man.

"I won't hold you guys up any longer," Mike said. "I'm sure you're anxious to start your long weekend. I just wanted to get a chance to meet you, Will." He held his hand out to shake Will's.

Will gave him a good, firm, but not too firm, handshake.

"It was great to meet you, sir," Will said. "Oh, and thank you for fixing my moped the other week."

"It was my pleasure," Mike said, then turned to Katie. "I'll see you later tonight at dinner?"

"Yes," Katie replied with a smile. "Why wouldn't you?"

"You stay so busy, I never know these days," Mike replied.

Will and Katie turned, and began to walk away.

"I think that went well," Will whispered to Katie.

"Yeah," Katie said. "I know my dad, it really did."

"Hey Will," Mike called out from behind them.

Will stopped and turned back toward Katie's father.

"Do you by chance need a weekend job?" Mike asked. "That could evolve into a summer job, or more?"

"Yeah, that would be great," Will replied.

"Excellent," Mike said. "I know this weekend is busy, but we'll talk soon. I'll get your number from Katie."

"Thank you."

Katie linked her arm with Will's and pulled him away.

"I told you, you made a good impression on him," she said.

"I guess so," Will replied.

Soon Katie had brought Will back to his house, and they were standing in the driveway in each other's arms.

"Well, I better get going," Katie said. "My mom wants to make some alterations to my dress."

"That's nice of her."

"Yeah, we bought the dress, and I thought it was great as it was. But one of her hobbies has always been working with fabric, and it makes her really happy. She said she had some small alteration ideas, and I promised to hear her out."

"She probably wants to cover more skin." Will cracked a smile.

"Don't worry, I won't let her do that," Katie smiled back at Will. "Oh, that reminds me…" She got her phone out and texted Will an image.

Will procured his phone from his pocket and looked at what she had sent. The image was taken too close to make out what it was, the color was the only thing that could be ascertained from the picture.

"That's the color of my dress," Katie said. "In case you do the whole corsage thing." It was a not-so-subtle hint of something she was hoping for.

It didn't stress Will out; his mother had already volunteered to get the corsage for Will to give to her. He'd just forward the color picture to her.

"Okay, thanks," Will replied as he put his phone back in his pocket. "I'll look into it."

Will loved to see the way her face lit up when she talked about the upcoming dance. He could tell it meant a lot to her, and he would do all he could to make it the best night of her life.

She kissed him on the lips, then left his embrace. Giving him one more smile and wave as she backed out of his driveway, she drove off down the street.

Will was greeted by his four-legged family member, Nala, as he walked in the front door. He let her out into the backyard to run around and tend to her business. When she came back in, he fed her.

Will was excited by the prospect of working at Katie's father's shop. The aspect of working with her father was intimidating, but Mike seemed laid back, and somehow Will knew that it would work out just fine. The new job could potentially mean a discount on parts, and access to tools to do some larger automotive jobs.

Will thought that Uncle Zac might be excited to hear the news; he should go tell him about it.

Will opened the door and stepped into the garage.

"Hey Zac." As the words escaped his lips, he stopped in his tracks.

The garage was empty, the Corvette was gone.

SIXTEEN

Just as Will's stomach began to sink into a panic that the Corvette had been stolen, an alert went off on his phone.

It was Uncle Zac contacting him through the security camera network: *I'm parked a block over on the street behind your house. I can see the fed's surveillance vehicle from the house cameras. Sneak out the backyard, through the neighbor's driveway to meet me. Bring a flash drive.*

It was a relief to hear from Zac.

"There goes a peaceful evening," Will said as he hurried back into the house.

After grabbing a flash drive from his room, Will snuck out the back door, across the back yard, and to the fence.

As he scaled the fence, his mind flashed back to Mandy scaling the fence the other weekend. After having to jump the fence himself, he realized that Mandy was in better athletic shape than he gave her credit for. Then again, you can push yourself to do extraordinary things when being chased by a vicious attack dog coming at your shoes and ankles.

Will snuck down the neighbor's driveway undetected, and saw the Corvette in the road as he reached the street.

As he hopped in the car, Zac started the engine and pulled away.

"What are we doing?" Will asked.

"I wanted to run an errand without our babysitters," Zac replied. "Did you bring a flash drive?"

"Yeah, I've got it right here." Will dug the drive out of his pocket.

"Great, you can find a place to plug it in, in the glove compartment." Will leaned over and opened the glove box, found the USB plug, and inserted the flash drive.

"Got it on my first try," Will chuckled. "You know how it always takes a bunch of times to get a USB to go in."

"Yeah, sounds like you'll be going after my old job soon," Zac said with sarcasm.

"Shut up," Will smirked, picking up on his jab.

"So, how'd you sneak out past the surveillance team?" Will asked.

"Well, technically it's a team, but usually it's just one of them at a time. I watched on camera, and they followed you and Katie." Zac said. "When they probably should be watching me a little closer."

"Jealous?"

Zac chuckled, "No."

"When will this crazy surveillance end?" Will asked.

"Well, when they get their suspect, or my tech. Or both. So, I was thinking more about that project that everyone thought I was working on."

"The neural/digital connection connector thing?" Will asked.

"Yeah, you were listening," Zac replied. "Remember I said that I had some preliminary stuff written?"

"Yeah."

"Well, I've been doing a little more work on it, you know, in my spare time alone in the garage."

"Alone in the garage? Your tone sounds like you might need a hug."

"Ha!" Zac replied.

"Are you going to finish the project?" Will asked.

"Well, I can't, in my current state," Zac replied. "But I know who deserves to have this project. And I've given them more than enough of a head start with my extra work on the project."

"Samantha?"

"Yes," Zac said. "I just wanted to give her something, something meaningful. If she finished it, and I know she could, she would become a titan in our circles, and be set for life."

"You're not worried that she might meet the same end that you did?"

"She can do the research in secret, which is something she'll know to do," Zac said. "Especially after what happened to me. I was not secretive about the project on purpose, with the intent of using it as a red herring to lead people away from my actual project. She even warned me that what I was doing was dangerous, I should've taken her advice more seriously."

"Aren't you worried about someone weaponizing it?"

"If we don't figure it out first, someone else will, eventually," Zac explained. "We might not be able to keep it out of the wrong hands forever, but we can channel who gets it first. And Samantha and I were always of the same mindset when it came to technology and ethics."

"Couldn't we just give this flash drive to whoever has been trying to hunt down the research and solve our problems?" Will asked.

"No, they'd know this wasn't everything. They knew I was finished with my project. That's why they thought it was safe to off me. The stuff on the flash drive is far from complete. They'd just keep coming at us."

"So, you're going to reveal yourself to Samantha?" Will asked.

"When you say it like that, it sounds dirty," Zac replied. "No, I still don't know how I feel about that. I'm loading my research onto the flash drive, and you're going to deliver it to her."

"Oh, what do I..."

"I'll tell you what to say," Zac interrupted him.

It wasn't long before they had made the trip across town and had arrived at Samantha's condo. Zac pulled up into the driveway next to her little red Porsche Boxster. He had briefed Will on what to say during the trip over.

"You got this?" Zac asked.

"Yeah." Will got the flash drive out of the glove compartment and got out of the car.

Once he reached the door, he rang the doorbell. A moment or two passed, then Samantha opened the door.

"Hello?" She asked.

"Hey," Will said. "You don't know me, but I think you know my car," he said, motioning to the Corvette.

Her eyes opened wide. "You're Zac's nephew?" She asked.

"Yes, my name is Will."

"My name is Samantha," she replied.

"It's nice to meet you," Will said.

"Would you like to come inside?" Samantha asked.

"Sure," Will replied, then followed her inside.

Her condo was nice, immaculately clean. It echoed of someone that either worked too much, or relaxed too little, or both.

"Can I get you something to drink?" She asked.

"I can't get too trashed; I've got to drive."

"Yeah, you're his nephew, alright." Samantha cracked a smile. "You know what I mean."

Will smiled. "No thanks, I'm good."

He glanced around as he followed her to the living room. There were some framed pictures of his Uncle Zac, some of her with him, and one of them at the beach together.

"I'm not in the habit of just letting strangers in, but I recognized you from a picture Zachary showed me one time. He mentioned you on numerous occasions, and I saw you at the funeral as well."

"I saw you there too, leaving the flowers," Will said. "That was nice of you."

"That was a difficult day," she said with a sigh. "As has been every day since."

"Yeah."

She motioned to a couch in her living room. "Have a seat," she said as she sat across from him in a chair.

"How are you holding up?" She asked.

"I've been getting by."

"He told me that he was going to leave you that car," she said. "Of course, we thought that would be many years from now."

"I wish it was," Will said. "I love the car though. It's almost like having a part of him still with me," Will said, giving a deeper meaning than she realized.

She nodded. "So, what can I do for you?"

"I believe I have something of yours." Will pulled the flash drive from his pocket and held it out to her. "I found it in between the seats of the Corvette."

She took it from him with a curious look on her face. "Huh, I don't recognize it."

She leaned over and grabbed the laptop that was sitting on an end table, and opened it. She inserted the flash drive.

"Property of Samantha Stone," she read. "And then it has my address. The other files are password-protected."

She thought for a moment. "Let me try something."

She typed a password. "That was it."

"What?"

"The password was the anniversary of the day we started dating," she said. "Zachary talked a tough game, but was always a big softy at heart."

Will leaned forward on the couch, eager to see her reaction.

A look of astonishment washed over her face. "I had no idea he had gotten this far with the project."

"Is it something good?" Will played dumb.

"Yeah," she said, her eyes getting a little glassy. "Your uncle left me some important research," she said as she continued to scroll down. "So much of it."

"That's great, right?"

"Yeah." She had a confused expression on her face. "You said you found this in the Corvette?"

"Yes," Will said. "I was cleaning it out and I found it wedged in between the seats. I could only open the file that had your name and address."

It looked like she was thinking. About what, Will had no idea. "Interesting."

"Maybe he meant to give it to you a while back, and it fell out of his pocket or something."

"Maybe," she replied with what sounded like a hint of suspicion.

Will wanted to leave before she asked too many questions. "I should probably get going," Will said, rising to his feet. "I just wanted to drop off your flash drive."

"Thank you so much, Will," she said, looking up from the computer screen.

She laid the computer on a nearby end table and stood up to walk him out.

"You should know that your uncle thought the world of you," she told him as they walked to the front of the condo.

"Thank you, that's good to know."

"This world is so much worse without him," she continued. "I know he meant a lot to you too."

"He did."

"If it ever seems like it's all too much, and you need someone to talk to, you know where to find me," she said.

"Thank you, Samantha."

She stood in the doorway as he left. "That's a great car you have there, take care of it."

Will glanced back at her. "I will, I promise."

She smiled at him.

Will got into the Corvette, backed out of the driveway, and drove off.

"Seeing Sam was bittersweet," Zac said as they drove along. "She's so beautiful, being without her hurts so bad."

"She's an attractive lady," Will agreed.

"Easy there, killer."

"Don't worry about me," Will said with a chuckle. "No one on earth holds a candle to my Katie."

"I know, I was just messing with you," Zac said.

As they drove through the city streets on the way home, they passed a C8 Corvette travelling in the opposite direction.

"That's nice," Will said.

"Some people aren't big fans, but I like them," Zac replied. "You should try driving a mid-engine car sometime, it's different."

"You could have put your tech in that car," Will said.

"Yeah, but it wouldn't have been the same. That's not

the same car that made such an impact on me as a kid," Zac explained. "An old car is like a time machine. You can use it to travel to the past. It can take you back to a time in your mind when anything in the world was possible. And sometimes that's all the inspiration you need to make something happen now, in the current time."

"Huh." Will took in his uncle's middle-aged wisdom. "But why not the ZR-1 version of this car?"

There was a slight pause before Zac's response. "Well, that's a good question."

Will laughed.

"Still, I think I did just fine with this one."

"I agree," Will said.

"Well, ready to go back under surveillance?" Zac asked with a sarcastic enthusiasm.

"I can't wait until the stakeout sees us roll up out of nowhere," Will said.

"You can expect a phone call from them."

"That's annoying," Will replied.

"I don't make the rules, Ace."

"I just hope they don't follow us to the dance this weekend."

"So, you're going to wash me before the dance, right?" Zac asked.

"It just sounds dirty when you say it like that," Will kidded.

"Touché," Zac replied. "I guess getting a sponge bath from you sounds kind-a weird."

"Please stop." Will laughed. "But yes, I'll make sure you get a good wash by then."

"You know to never spray wash the engine of a C4, right?"

"Yes, yes, of course," Will replied, almost annoyed that his uncle felt like he had to ask him.

Soon they reached their neighborhood, rounded the corner and pulled into the garage.

Will went upstairs to his room, and he hadn't stepped two steps past the doorway, when his cell phone went off.

"Hey Will," Anne, the federal agent was on the other line. "Where did you go?"

"I just went out to see a friend," Will said.

"It was so weird," Anne said. "I didn't see you leave, and I've been watching you all this afternoon."

"Am I grounded? I don't know what to tell you," Will said. "Do you want me to check in and out with you whenever I go anywhere?"

"You know we're just trying to protect you," she replied. "We're trying to keep you alive."

"Yeah," Will said. "But at a certain point I still have to live my life, I'm a senior in high school."

"I'm not telling you not to live your life, by all means do."

"I'm sorry for being on edge," Will apologized. "All of this has just been stressful."

"It's okay. Don't worry, Will," Anne said. "This will all be over soon. This individual will come out of the shadows soon enough, and we'll be here waiting."

"Are you and Dylan going to chaperone the dance on Saturday?"

Anne laughed. "No, but I wish. Do you know how long it's been since I've gotten dressed up and gone to a dance?"

"A while I take it?"

"Yeah, that's an understatement. I know it's a stereotypical thing for an older person to say, but enjoy this time while you have it. Cause it's gone so quick and then you're an adult, and working all the time."

"Hopefully I'll be doing something I love for a living."

"Good luck with that," she replied. "Those jobs are few and far in between. But it's possible."

"I'll cross my fingers." Will said.

"Did you get her a corsage?" Anne asked.

"Yeah, she sent me the color of her dress. And I, well, my mom is getting one that matches."

"Aw, that's great," Anne replied with a longing nostalgia in her voice.

"I've seen you and Katie together," Anne went on. "I've seen the way she looks at you, and the way you look at her. You two have something special. I hope you guys have a wonderful time on Saturday. Once this stuff with your uncle's research clears up, you can get back to some kind of normal life."

"I'd like that." Will answered her with sincerity, but thought it a little odd that she phrased it *stuff with your uncle's research*, as opposed to *stuff with the mysterious individual*.

It wasn't too much later when Will descended the stairs and went to the kitchen. He opened the refrigerator, but nothing looked exciting.

Beth walked into the room.

"Hi mom, are you getting hungry yet?" Will asked.

"I was going to see if you could fend for yourself to-night," his mother replied. "Dylan wanted to take me out to dinner. I hope that's okay."

"Oh," Will said. He was slightly annoyed, but it wasn't a big deal. The new found knowledge that Dylan was lying to her about his profession gave him a strange feeling in his gut, but he knew he couldn't do anything about it for the time being. More of that *acting normal* that he was beginning to perfect.

Beth walked over to the counter and began digging in her purse. She retrieved some cash, walked over and held it out to him.

"Why don't you get some delivery," she said. "Something tasty, you deserve it. Celebrate the end of the school week."

"Thanks, it's been a long week," Will said as he took the cash from her.

The doorbell chimed. At the sound, Nala made sure that everyone in the house was alerted that there was someone at the door.

"It's probably Dylan," she said.

"I'll get it," Will said, walking out of the kitchen.

Will opened the door to find Dylan standing there with a bouquet of flowers.

"For me?" Will kidded. "You shouldn't have."

"How are you doing, Will?" Dylan was really good at his *acting normal*. Of course, he'd been perfecting it for years.

"I'm still alive," Will said. "So that's good."

"It is," Dylan said.

"Nice that you could find some time out of your busy schedule," Will went on.

"To be honest, you really have to find a work/life balance," Dylan said.

Will nodded. "To be honest, interesting," he said, repeating Dylan's words under his breath.

Beth walked up behind Will and got excited when she saw the flowers Dylan had brought.

He held them out to her. "For you," Dylan said, his face glowing.

"Thank you," Beth's tone was warm and happy.

Will sighed. He looked at the way that his mother's face lit up when she received the flowers from Dylan. He couldn't bring himself to ruin this for her.

"You weren't messing with Dylan, were you?" Beth asked Will.

"No, not at all," Dylan said.

"I was about to practice the age-old tradition of kids trying to intimidate the guys taking their mothers out," Will kidded, reformatting what Mike had said to him earlier. "But you got here too soon."

"Being protective isn't a bad thing these days," Dylan said.

"Well, you two have a good time, and be careful," Will said, then dismissing himself from their presence. "And don't stay out too late," he kidded, calling out from the other room.

Minutes later he watched out the window as Dylan and his mother pulled away in Dylan's Mercedes.

Will ended up ordering Mexican food for delivery. He had a crazy notion, and got out the old video projector that they never used, kept in a downstairs closet. He hooked it up, and set it on top of the Corvette. It was angled to project on the large back white-wall of the garage. Will started a movie so that he and Zac could watch it together.

Zac had chosen Terminator 2 for tonight's viewing. He also wouldn't let Will sit inside the car while he ate his messy Mexican food. So, Will reclined in a lawn chair by the side of the car, munching on his dinner.

"Never thought I'd be sitting around watching a movie with my car," Will said.

"Yeah, it's a ridiculous idea," Zac said. "But I still enjoy watching movies. I'm glad you thought of it."

Will smiled, feeling like they were starting to make up for some of that lost time, even if it was in their own, decidedly odd way.

"You know, Terminator 2 was the first R-rated movie that I saw in the theater," Zac said. "We were 16, but my friends and I said that we were 17, and the girl at the ticket booth really didn't care."

"It's a good first one to have seen in the theater," Will said.

"It really was."

"Seems like the kind of thing that would speak to you," Will went on. "Technology taking over humanity."

"Maybe so," Zac said with a laugh. "And as for the Terminator movies, for me they could've just stopped after they made the second one," Zac said.

"Yeah, maybe they could've sent a terminator back to stop the future installments from being made," Will kidded.

"I'd watch that one."

"But I think what you've done is even more unbelievable than this premise," Will said. "I still can't believe it's you in there."

"Believe it, Ace," Zac said. "But I don't think I'll be cracking the code on time travel anytime soon."

"Wouldn't that be nice," Will replied. He thought about what he would give to see his father one more time.

SEVENTEEN

It was a little after 10 AM on Friday when Will was sitting on the couch in his living room eating some cereal. Nala sat by his side, watching him like a predator, waiting to swoop in if he happened to drop any tasty morsels.

Will's phone alerted him to an incoming text. It was from Katie's phone.

Coffeeshop around 11:30 AM? The text read.

Sounds good, Will texted back. *See you there.*

His heart warmed as he looked forward to seeing her. Through all this turbulent chaos, she had been his rock, and he couldn't imagine what it would have been like if he had to go through all of this without her.

Will arrived at the coffee shop a few minutes before 11:30, and stood around waiting. It was around 11:45 when he got a text from Katie's phone. She told him that she was running late, and to go ahead and order himself a coffee and sit down outside.

Will felt like the text was a little strange, that and the fact that she was running late. Ever since he'd known her, she'd been a very punctual person. Perhaps she was held up by some preparation for the dance.

He tried not to overthink it, he always overthought things. He decided to just do what the text said to do, so he ordered a coffee, and sat down by himself at a table outside.

Will glanced around as he took another sip. Across the street, and a little-ways down, Will noticed Dylan's black Mercedes. It looked as if only Anne was in the car, having followed him to the coffee shop. He sighed; those agents were like his shadows. They watched him closer than Nala watched him in the kitchen.

Will couldn't wait for this all to be over. He thought it strange that it was only her sitting in the driver seat of Dylan's car. When it was just her, she was usually in a different car. When it was just Dylan, or when she was with Dylan, they were in his Mercedes.

He got a bad feeling in the pit of his stomach, and his suspicion began to rise. Will looked around from where he sat, trying to notice if he saw anything amiss.

He caught Dylan drinking a coffee, sitting with his back to him at the table right behind him.

Are you kidding? Will thought. The constant surveillance was beginning to weigh on him.

"So how was your date with my mom last night?" Will said, not facing Dylan, but speaking just loud enough for him to hear.

"It was very nice, thanks," Dylan replied, still facing

away from Will. "We had a wonderful dinner, followed by going to see a movie."

"What genre?"

"Drama," Dylan said with a little bit of a sigh. "Your mom chose."

Will chuckled. "Did she have a good time?"

"She had a great time," Dylan replied.

"Good."

"You know," Dylan said. "I know you don't believe me, but it means a lot to me to have your blessing."

"Always treat her like a queen," Will replied. "And we'll always be cool."

"That's one thing I can guarantee you. As long as I have the opportunity to, I will always put her wants, needs, and happiness before mine."

Will still had reservations about his mother dating again, but Dylan's words helped put him more at ease about the situation.

One of the coffee shop's baristas came walking out of the café holding a small box. He approached Will's table.

Will looked up at him.

"You're Will, right?" The barista asked. "Waiting for Katie?"

"Yeah," Will answered.

The barista put down the small box that he was carrying in front of Will. "This came for you."

"From who?" Will was bewildered.

"I don't know," the barista said with an air of dismissal, as if his current involvement with the situation was already well above his pay grade. "Some delivery guy dropped it off."

"Okay, thanks," Will said in a haze of confusion.

The barista was quick to leave him and go back inside.

"What is it?" Dylan asked.

"It's a little box, let me open it," Will replied.

"Careful," Dylan said.

"I've got it," Will replied, his slight agitation more spurn by his anxiety at the arrival of the mysterious box than Dylan's question.

"Wait," Dylan said. "It might be something dangerous. And maybe we could get some prints off the box."

Not heeding his warning, Will eased the lid up and off the small box.

It was as if his heart got ripped from his chest. Inside was a small hair ribbon. Red with white polka-dots. It was the hair ribbon that Will had given to Katie at the fair. He knew in that instant that someone had taken Katie.

"Someone has Katie," Will said.

"Are there any instructions?" Dylan asked, attempting to remain inconspicuous, facing away at the other table.

"No," Will said. "It's just her hair ribbon."

Will's phone notified him of an incoming text message. He rushed to get the phone out of his pocket.

The text was from an unknown number, it read: *she's safe, and will remain so as long as you are good at following directions.*

"Is that them?" Dylan asked.

"Yeah, they just confirmed what I thought, she's with them," Will said. "Sounds like they're going to send me instructions."

"Alright, Will, we're going to figure this out, and get

Katie back safe." Dylan said in a calming voice to try to ease Will's anxiety. But there was no easing it in the slightest.

Dylan got out his phone and dialed a number. "Anne," Dylan spoke on the phone. "Contact has been made. They have Katie, Will's girlfriend. We're awaiting further instructions. Stay on the line, and be prepared to move."

Will's hands were shaking a little when he texted a reply back to the message he had just received: *Tell me what to do.*

Another text came back from the number: *Call the number below and I will let you know what to do next.* Below the message was a phone number.

"He sent me a number to call for further instructions," Will told Dylan.

"Hold on for a second," Dylan said, then put his cell phone back to his ear. "Make sure we're recording Will's phone," Dylan instructed Anne over the phone.

After a moment, Dylan lowered his cellphone. "Go ahead, Will. Try to keep them on the line, be calm and cooperative."

"Yeah, I want my girlfriend back," Will replied.

Will took a deep breath, and looked at the phone number. His insides had the jitters. Was it just going to be another hired gun? Or was he about to talk to the man who was behind it all?

Will watched his index finger slowly move across his phone screen. Will pressed the number on the screen to call it.

An ear-piercing blast shook the ground as Dylan's Mercedes exploded into a fireball where it sat.

"Anne!" The visceral yell came from Dylan's lips as he jumped to his feet.

In all the shock and confusion, it took a moment for Will's brain to process what had happened. His ears rang, he stood up and gazed toward the burning remains of the car, wide-eyed, frozen in shock.

As the sound of the blast began to subside, it was replaced with the sounds of car alarms and people screaming as they fled the scene.

As the horror of what had just happened began to set in, Will began to shake.

"What just happened?" Will said, then again in increasing volume. "What just happened?"

Will's mind kept flashing back to seeing Anne sitting in the car just a moment ago. A car that was now reduced to a burning frame and rubble. Tears ran down his cheeks as he realized that his phone call had detonated the car bomb.

Dylan was already on his cell phone, calling in the explosion to the FBI. No doubt this would be a big mess to have to cover up, but that's what they were good at, covering their tracks.

Will felt his phone go off again. Another message from the mystery number arrived: *Now that we're alone, we can proceed.*

It was clear that the individual that had engineered the car bomb either thought that Will was being followed by only one agent that day, or that the bomb would get both agents.

The message went on: *Meet my associate at this address. You have 25 minutes to get there. Make sure you are alone, and not followed.* Below the message was an address that Will was not familiar with. Maybe it was out past the west edge of town, toward the mountains.

"I have to go to some address, alone," Will said through his emotional trauma, his voice shaking. "I only have 25 minutes to get there."

"Will, you can't go alone." Dylan said.

"I have to," Will said. "They have Katie."

"Not only can you not leave this scene, but Will ..."

"I have to go alone," Will interrupted him, his voice and emotions elevated.

"They could kill you," Dylan said. "I can't let you go."

"What if it was you, and it was my mother they had?"

Dylan was quiet, not able to return an argument.

"If something happens to me, take care of my mom," Will said.

"At least give me the address," Dylan said.

"I can't, you know that."

Will hurried away, down through the chaos of people leaving the scene, and made his way to the Corvette. He glanced back, and saw Dylan starting to walk in his direction, getting back on his cell phone.

Will and Zac drove off, headed for the mysterious address given to Will.

"My GPS says that we can make it there in 18 minutes," Zac said.

"He didn't give us much extra time, I hope there's no traffic," Will said.

"Yeah, no time to stop for gas," Zac said.

"Do we need some? Because the gauge looks fine."

"No, we're good," Zac said. "But I've been meaning to tell you. Do you know where it says *Premium Recommended* by the gas cap?"

"Yeah."

"I feel like it should say "Premium Required," Zac dropped a not-so-subtle hint about car care.

"That's what I always use," Will replied, his mind distracted by the larger things at hand. "Weird time to bring the subject up, though."

"Yeah, I feel like anytime could've been awkward," Zac replied.

Will rolled his eyes. "Certain times more awkward than others."

They passed the suburbs and the city limits on the west side and headed toward the mountains on the outskirts of town.

"If anything happens to Katie, I'll never forgive myself," Will said.

"This is all my fault," Zac said. "It's the truth. We both don't need to be riddled with guilt."

"I can't help it," Will replied. "I'm a guilty person. I mean, not that I did something, just that I always feel guilty."

"Yeah, I know what you mean. But you didn't do anything; I need your mind to be sharp right now, not cluttered."

"Oh, and I can't believe…I…Anne."

"I need you sharp, Will," Zac reiterated.

Will wiped away a tear that escaped his eye and nodded that he understood. "Okay."

They could see on the GPS that they were closing in on their destination. The houses became sparser, and the trees much more plentiful as they went along. Soon the forest was all around them on both sides of the road.

Nearing the base of the mountain, they rounded another corner, and an old abandoned gas station came into view, ahead on the left.

"I think that's it," Zac said.

"The gas station?" Will asked.

"Yeah. That's definitely it."

The car slowed down as they neared the entrance.

The gas station looked like a run-down slice of Americana straight out of the 1940s or 1950s. As the Corvette pulled into the abandoned gas station, they noticed a flatbed truck parked at the side of the building.

Zac stopped the car and Will got out.

"Be careful," Zac said.

The building was constructed of wood, some of the boards had parts broken, and some boards had a little rotting. There was a thick green moss that had taken hold to one corner of the structure. The area that once served as two gas pumps had been reclaimed by weeds and vines with only small glimpses of its petroleum vestiges peeking out between the greenery.

"Hello?" Will called out as he took a few hesitant steps toward the dilapidated structure.

A muscular bald man that looked to be in his mid-40s, walked out of the front doors of the gas station.

"Will?" The man asked, glancing around. "You came alone, right?"

"Yeah," Will replied. "I brought the car, now where is the girl?"

"Calm down kid," the man said. "She's not here, but she's fine. The boss likes red-heads anyway. Let me have your cellphone."

"My cellphone?"

"Yeah, we're going to leave it here, it can be tracked," The man explained. "Also, lift up your shirt."

Will was confused but did as the man said.

"That's fine, you don't have a wire," the man said.

Will lowered his shirt and handed the man his cell phone. The man disappeared with it back into the building.

After putting the phone somewhere inside the abandoned gas station, the man came back out, and started walking toward the flatbed truck.

"Take off the parking brake and put the car in neutral, would you?" the man asked, seeming bothered by his part of the job.

Will walked over, got into the Corvette and put it in neutral.

"Katie's not here, I don't know what's gonna happen now," Will whispered to Zac through his stress.

"It's all right." Zac tried to ease his anxiety. "It looks like

I'm going for a ride, and then we'll take it from there. Just keep your wits about you."

Will got back out of the car and stood by the driver's side door. The truck backed up to the Corvette and tilted down its flatbed so that the car could be pulled onto it.

The man got out of the truck, hooked the chain to the car, and pulled the Corvette onto the flatbed, and tilted it back up flat.

"My employer wants me to bring you with me," the man said. "He wants to talk to you personally. He's got the girl with him. You can ride in the cab of the truck with me."

"Okay." Will stood there, staring at the man.

Will tried to remain calm, though his mind was racing. *Why does his employer want to meet me face-to-face? It will make it that much worse if I can identify the individual. There's no way that this person can make what they have done any better by explaining it. Wait…Are they going to kill me? But I have to go, for Katie.*

"Well, come on," the man said, nodding impatiently toward the cab of the truck.

Will snapped out of the zone that he was in, and walked around to the passenger side of the truck and climbed in.

The man got in, started the truck, and took a left, away from town, onto the road. They began to ascend up the mountain road in the slow truck.

There was an awkward silence in the cab as they rode along. But what was Will supposed to say to the man? *How does it feel to take part in kidnapping and extortion? Is it fun? Can you spell extortion? No,* Will thought. He didn't have much to say for or to the man about his career or life choices. As far as Will was concerned, the man could insert his own shoe all the way up his own rear.

Will noticed the man would frequently glance in his rearview mirror to make sure that they weren't being followed. No, they weren't being followed. No one was coming to save them; he and his uncle were on their own.

They continued along the long and winding road up the side of the mountain toward the top. The journey was made even longer by the anemic struggle of the flatbed truck trying to fight its way uphill.

For portions of their trip, when Will looked out the window, he could see between the trees off the side of the mountain. There was no road shoulder. The view was amazing, but there was the danger of the close drop off if one strayed a few feet off the paved road. Intermittent lines of trees would return to impede the majestic view from time to time, but then the view would be back again.

They continued onward and upward. As they neared the top of the mountain, the truck began to slow down. Will noticed a small unpaved road off to the right side of the street. The driver turned onto the small road and continued over what became little more than a wide trail through a heavily wooded area.

Their way curved around and met up with a clearing. As the truck proceeded into the clearing, Will saw a couple of cars parked off to the side of the open area.

There was a Mercedes-Maybach sedan with a dark tint

on the windows, and the other car…was a red Ferrari Testarossa.

It's Alex! The man that Will had met at his uncle's funeral. Will was furious, but knew he had to keep his temper in check if he wanted to get Katie back safe.

EIGHTEEN

Will could see two men standing where the clearing met the sky, admiring the view from on high.

As they pulled closer, one man turned around. It looked as if he might be a bodyguard. He was muscular, had dark hair and a semi-automatic pistol at his side. The other man, still looking off into the distance, was Alex.

As the flatbed truck slowed to a stop, Will got out, and began a brisk walk toward the man looking off the mountain's edge.

"Alex," Will called out to him. "You're behind all of this?"

"Oh, hello Will," Alex said as he glanced back at Will approaching. "I'm afraid I'm guilty."

"I don't understand, but here's the car." Will motioned back toward the car, trying to keep his temper in check. "Where's Katie?"

Sensing Will's heightened emotions, the bodyguard

placed his hand on the pistol at his side, but Alex motioned to the man that it shouldn't be necessary.

"She's perfectly fine, Will," Alex replied in a calming voice.

"How do I know that?" Will asked.

Alex let out a sigh and turned toward the Maybach sedan. He nodded to the bodyguard at his side, and the man walked over to the sedan. When he reached the car, he opened the back door of the Maybach. The bodyguard grabbed Katie by the arm and pulled her out of the car.

"Will!" She called to him, looking rattled, but physically unharmed from what he could tell.

Alex gave the man another nod, and the bodyguard motioned for Katie to get back into the car.

She rolled her eyes and complied with the order.

The man closed the door behind her and then walked back over to Alex and Will.

"Hey, what's the deal?" Will asked, after Katie wasn't freed.

"I just want to talk to you for a little bit, so that you can understand some things."

"Fine," Will said with a little bit of a huff. "I just can't believe you did this. At the funeral you seemed like such a decent human being."

Alex looked out at the view, and took a deep breath. After he exhaled, he turned to Will. "Take a breath, Will."

Will tried to calm himself enough to take a deep breath.

"There you go," Alex said. "Isn't it beautiful up here?"

"Yeah," Will patronized him. Though it was indeed a breathtaking view.

"I actually own this land," Alex said. "I thought about putting a house here for when I need to get away, but I can't stray too far from work."

"It's nice," Will replied, emotionless about it.

After another moment of gazing off into the distance, Alex spoke again. "I'm a very reasonable man."

"Says the guy that kidnapped my girlfriend," Will replied.

"I had, and have, no intention of harming her, yet," Alex said. "I just needed you to understand the severity of you coming alone and following my instructions to the letter."

"You had to kill the FBI agent?" Will asked.

"Yes, they were relentless. You didn't get mad at them for monitoring your every move?"

"It was annoying, but no cause to kill them."

"What an invasion of privacy. Big brother has gotten out of control over the last couple of decades," Alex said.

"They were just trying to look after me, I guess."

Alex chuckled. "Will, you don't think that they actually cared about you? All they wanted to do was try to take something that wasn't theirs and give it to the government. And they were trying to use you to get it."

"What do you know about the death of my uncle?" Will asked.

Alex thought for a moment. "Your uncle was an unfortunate victim of being at the wrong place at the wrong time. He was killed by some street gang, or at least that's what I heard."

Alex wasn't a good liar, Will thought to himself.

"Maxwell worked for you, right?" Will asked.

Alex narrowed his eyes as if he suspected that Will knew something that there was no way of him knowing. Likely the fact that he had ordered Maxwell to kill his uncle.

"Maxwell scared off those three high schoolers in the parking deck that were chasing me," Will said.

"Oh," Alex snapped out of his suspicion when he realized Will wasn't talking about his uncle, and it was something to take credit for. "Well, yes, I employed Maxwell. Weren't those kids about to assault you and your girlfriend, and destroy the Corvette?"

Will nodded in agreement. "Yes."

"Sounds like Maxwell was looking out for you, and did you a favor," Alex said.

"He did," Will said. "I appreciated that. They stopped bothering me after that incident."

Will began to gain control of his emotions, and pretended to ease into a more positive outlook about the situation to gain Alex's trust.

"That's great," Alex said. "Now I'm going to be straight with you, Will."

That was doubtful, Will thought. "Okay," he replied.

"Your uncle was working on some new technology at our facility right before he was killed," Alex explained. "Your uncle wasn't a paranoid person, per se, but he knew that he was working on something groundbreaking, something that would change the future."

Will nodded as he followed Alex's story.

"One day he took me aside and said, look, if something happens to me before I'm done, you're the only person that can finish it." Alex said. "It was a nice ego boost that he thought so highly of me."

"I imagine so."

"Anyway," Alex continued. "He said, 'I'm hiding a copy of my work in a place only you and I could appreciate.'"

"He said all that?" Will asked, patronizing him, knowing that this was all a lie.

"Yes," Alex continued. "And I knew right away that he meant inside his car, perhaps within the dashboard where no one would look for it."

"Huh."

"I know that sounds like a funny place to put the future of technology, but maybe not to a car lover like your uncle." Alex cracked a smile. "Your uncle and I had always bonded over the love of our dream cars from childhood."

Alex wants me to believe that he was Zac's confidant? His lies sickened Will's stomach. But Will knew he had to play dumb and play along. "So, what was he working on?"

"It was a software that would change how people interact with their computers," Alex said, keeping it vague.

"How so?"

"It was a way that a brain could neural link with a computer, and control it, kind-of like Bluetooth."

"Sounds amazing," Will said.

"Yes, but it's not done, and your uncle would have wanted me to finish it," Alex said. "This will be big. I know you love the car, but you need to look at the bigger picture, we're talking a major step in the advancement of technology. This is going to change the world."

"Yeah," Will said, his voice lacking any enthusiasm at all.

"I meant all of those things I said at your uncle's funeral, when we were driving in my car." Alex said. "I think you're one of the promising youth, and I think you're a good kid in general. I could've had Maxwell kill you and just take your car, but I wanted to give you a more-than-fair offer, and give you a little boost in the right direction."

Will nodded that he understood. *Is this a sick narcissistic game?* Will questioned in his mind. *Is this how he sleeps at night? In a delusional world where he pulls the strings of everyone and everything around him, and he's the humanitarian?*

"This needs to happen, Will," Alex said. "You need to realize it's a small sacrifice for the greater good of our species' technological advancement."

Alex could sense Will's hesitance to fall in line with his ideology. "I have an idea that might satisfy us both. What if you let me have the Corvette, I'll give you the thirty-thousand dollars, I extract what I'm looking for, then return the car to you? We both get what we want. Surely you'd like that offer?"

Will couldn't deny, if his uncle's consciousness wasn't in the car, that would seem like a very generous offer.

"Do I have a choice?" Will asked.

"We always have choices," Alex said. "We just always have to live with the consequences of those decisions."

Will understood the subtle threat in his words. "What if I say no to your offer?"

Alex looked over to the Maybach sedan and gave his bodyguard a twitch of his head.

The bodyguard marched back over to the Maybach, taking his pistol in hand. He opened up the back door of the car and pulled Katie out. The man then held the pistol up next to her temple.

"No!" Katies eyes widened as she screamed.

"Whoa, whoa, wait!" Will said. "I was just asking."

Alex gave the bodyguard another look, and the man lowered his gun, and pushed Katie back into the back of the Maybach. He walked back to Alex and Will as if he were an emotionless machine.

What kind of weird nodding sign language did Alex have with this guy? Will wondered.

"I'm sorry," Alex said. "Desperate times require desperate measures, and this is bigger than you or me. I can be a very generous person, but it's also contingent on playing by my rules."

"Fine," Will said. "Take the car. Can I really have it back when you're done with it?"

Alex smiled. "Will, you have my word."

Will knew that Zac would be mad at him for not cooperating from the start. Zac had wanted Will to just sell the Corvette and get away as soon as possible, not to risk he and Katie's life trying to negotiate.

"Wait here," Alex said as he walked over to his Ferrari's passenger door.

Alex opened the door and grabbed a small duffel bag, and closed the door back.

Alex joined Will again and held out the bag to him. "Here you go, the thirty-thousand."

Will's jaw dropped as he took the bag from Alex. He

opened the zipper, just enough to see the banded cash inside. It was easily the most cash he'd ever seen in person in his life.

Will began to reach in his back pocket. The bodyguard raised his pistol.

"I have the title for the Corvette," Will explained.

Alex put his hand up. "Keep it, Will," Alex smiled. "Remember, you're getting the car back."

Will nodded.

"So, here's what's going to happen," Alex said. "You can ride in the back of the Maybach with Katie, he's about to leave. The driver will bring you by that abandoned gas station to get your phones, then return you to town. I have some business on the other side of the mountain. The flatbed truck with the car will then go back to one of my warehouses. Then we will be done here, and you can go back to your normal life. I can get in contact with you when we're done with the car."

Going back to a normal life? That's something Will thought might never be able to happen at this point. Something struck Will, *what's to keep Alex from having the bodyguard just take he and Katie somewhere to kill them? The man had just held a gun to Katie's head moments ago. Was the duffel bag of thirty-thousand just a game he was playing to get us to cooperate? Followed by two murders and two shallow graves?* What could he do, but take the word of someone whose lies he had already lost count of?

Something else then came to Will's mind…it was a plan.

"I don't think we need a ride," Will replied. "We can walk."

A confused look washed over Alex's face. "What are you talking about? That's a long walk to get anywhere. It would take you hours just to get back to the abandoned gas station to get your phones."

"With all due respect, my girl just had a gun to the side of her head. The sooner we're done with your associates, the better, and I don't mind a little walk," Will said.

"I guess I can understand that," Alex replied.

Will looked over at the Maybach. "She's free to go?"

"Alright," Alex said. "But confidentiality is another stipulation of our agreement. You cannot speak of this to anyone, or reveal my identification to the feds."

"What should I tell them?"

"Tell them you met with a flatbed driver at the abandoned gas station. He had the money and the girl with him, and he took your car. You never met anyone of consequence, and even your description of the flatbed driver is hazy."

"Okay." Will played along.

"I'm serious," Alex said. "Maxwell wasn't the only 'professional' I have on my payroll."

"I got it," Will said.

Will ran over to the side of the Maybach, and opened the back door to let Katie out. She almost jumped out of the car, and into his arms.

The driver of the flatbed truck got out, and walked over to talk to Alex and the bodyguard.

"I was so scared," Katie said, shaking. "I'm so glad you're here."

"It's so good to see you, Katie," Will replied.

"Is this almost over?"

"The transaction is over," Will said, holding up his duffle bag of cash. "They offered us a ride back to town, but I said we'd walk. I figured we could quit while we were still alive."

"I'm good with that," she said. "I don't want to go anywhere with that creep bodyguard."

Will glanced at the men talking. "I know Uncle Zac wanted us to distance ourselves as soon as the transaction was over with, but I think he needs our help."

"What?"

"You're not going to like the idea I just had," Will said.

As Will and Katie began to walk across the clearing, Will glanced back and gave Alex a casual wave, as if Will was leaving on amicable terms.

Alex smiled. "Don't spend it all in one place," he kidded.

Katie glanced back and also gave a casual wave, but her hand only held up one finger.

"Katie," Will said with a chuckle. "We're trying not to arouse suspicion."

"Sorry, it slipped," she replied.

Soon they reached the end of the clearing and continued onto the rough unpaved road that led out to the main mountain road.

They began to travel down the unpaved road, but as soon as they were out of the sight of Alex and his cohorts, they slipped off into the woods.

Will and Katie snuck through the woods, circling back

around to the far side of the clearing. They peaked out at the men from their well-hidden spot in some heavy brush.

It looked as if their short meeting was wrapping up, the men were beginning to disperse.

Alex walked to his Ferrari Testarossa, the bodyguard to the Maybach, and the truck driver began to walk to the flatbed truck.

"Are you sure about this, Will?" Katie asked.

"Nope," Will said as he handed Katie the duffel bag of cash. "Go ahead and start heading out toward the main road."

Will snuck away from her, and out of the brush.

The Ferrari and Maybach drove away, one after the other, leaving behind the truck driver, who had almost reached his flatbed truck.

Will crouched down and ran behind the truck. He was careful to keep the truck between him and the driver the entire time, as the man made his way around the front of the truck to the door.

As the truck driver got in, Will crawled up onto the flatbed.

"Hey Zac," Will whispered. "I figured you could use some help."

"What are you doing?" Zac asked at a low volume. "You need to get out of here."

Will crawled around the car and unhooked all of the restraints that held the car in place.

The flatbed truck started up, and began to drive across the bumpy clearing.

The truck continued onto the small unpaved road that

led out to the main road. Despite getting bounced around quite a bit, Will was able to hold onto the edges of the flatbed, and not fall off.

As the truck reached the main road, the driver turned left, to descend the mountain the way that they had come up.

As soon as the truck had pulled out onto the main road, Will crept over to the control levers for the flatbed, and began tilting the flatbed down. He was pleasantly surprised that it worked while the truck was moving.

The brakes began to screech, as the truck slowed to a stop when the driver noticed what was happening. But it was too late by the time the truck was stopped, the flatbed had been lowered enough for the Corvette to roll down off the truck.

The low car scraped a little as it slid down onto the street.

"Yikes, sorry Zac," Will whispered.

As Will heard the driver open the door and get out, he let go of the controls, and hopped off the opposite side of the truck so as to remain undetected.

"What?" The driver said when he saw what had happened. "This old truck has been nothing but trouble," the man mumbled.

The vehicle had rolled back a car-length or so off of the truck.

"I swear I had that car secured," the driver said to himself.

The car had been stationary for a few moments, but the wheels began to move ever so slightly. The incline of the mountain was starting to get to the car, or perhaps that's what Zac was making it seem like. The car gave a slight creak as it began to ease forward.

Then, the car noticeably began to move, rolling forward.

"No, no, no!" The driver yelled as the Corvette began to roll downhill.

Zac inconspicuously steered around the truck as the Corvette rolled forward.

The car gained speed as it passed by the driver and continued going downhill before the man could react.

The driver began to chase the car, without a good plan on how to stop it if he was actually able to catch up with it. He seemed increasingly frantic as the Corvette rolled toward a curve that would send it over the side of the mountain if it maintained its straight course.

Defying what seemed the laws of physics would dictate, the Corvette rounded the curve, and eased to a stop around a bend.

The truck driver slowed to a stop, winded by his short run. He was, perhaps, one of those all-weights and no-cardio guys at the gym.

He walked to the curve, and looked down the huge drop off at the edge of the cliff. He then looked over at the Corvette in relief. "How did that happen?" He looked confused by how the car had stayed on the road, but seemed infinitely grateful it did. Alex would have killed him if the car had gone off the cliff.

The truck driver looked at the car for a moment, and let out a deep breath as he took out his cell phone and dialed a number.

"Hey, I'm sorry to bother you, but I'm having a little trouble with the car," the truck driver said. "The truck bed seems to have malfunctioned and tilted back down while I was driving, and I know I secured the car, but it rolled off."

He listened for a moment. "No, the car is fine." There was another momentary pause. "No, I don't see those kids around anywhere. I just need to get the car back on the truck, which I can do, no problem. I just wanted to let you know what the delay was." He listened for another moment. "You two don't have to come back, I can handle…" the man stopped as he got interrupted on the other end of the phone call. "Okay," the driver said. "But I'll probably have the car loaded back up by the time you two get back, but if you want to be safe." The man listened for another moment. "Hello?" After getting hung up on, he put his cellphone back in his pocket and turned back to the car.

With all the distraction of the runaway car, and the following phone conversation, Will snuck into the flatbed truck, which still had its key in the ignition.

Will put the truck in neutral, and jumped out of it. It began to roll forward and increased its speed.

The man stretched out his arms, and took a big sigh of relief. The truck driver then turned around, just to see his flatbed truck barreling down the road in his direction, mere feet away.

The man jumped back to get out of the way, but tumbled over the edge of the cliff.

The flatbed truck sailed off the side of the mountain, and flew out through the air, and down. There was the sound of a crash on the ground at a far lower elevation.

Will's stomach sank. Will was merely trying to send the truck over the side of the mountain, not kill the driver. He tried to remind himself that the man did the bidding for Alex, who was truly evil.

"Will, I can't believe you took him out," Katie said, as she came out of hiding, with the duffle bag of money, from some nearby woods. She walked up by his side at the edge of the road.

"I didn't mean to," he replied.

As Will and Katie stood there in a bit of shock, Will walked over to the edge of the cliff beyond the curve, hesitant to look down the mountain where the man had fallen.

There was a surprise waiting when Will gazed over the edge of the cliff. The truck driver hadn't fallen to his death, but slid off the edge of the mountain, and fallen to a lower cliff. It was a small protrusion from the side of the mountain, and the man was stuck there, with no way to climb up.

"Katie, I didn't kill him," Will said. "He's hanging out on a cliff down here."

Katie walked over and peered off the edge. "That's a relief." Not that she was concerned much for the man, she just didn't want Will to have been responsible for his demise.

The truck driver looked up from where he was. "Hey, you kids!" He yelled. "You can't leave me stranded down here!"

Will and Katie turned around when they heard the sound of the Maybach racing around the curve, back to the scene.

The car's tires screeched to a stop as the bodyguard noticed the kids.

Will and Katie backed away from the edge where they were standing and closer to the inside of the street.

The bodyguard whipped out his pistol as he jumped out of the car and walked a few steps closer. He stopped and pointed the gun at Will and Katie.

Will stepped in front of Katie.

"Big mistake, kids," the bodyguard said.

Alex pulled up in the Ferrari Testarossa behind them, coming from the opposite direction.

"This just got worse," Will said.

Alex got out of the Ferrari and held up his own pistol at the couple.

"The car is around the corner," the bodyguard called to Alex. "Looks like it's fine."

Alex looked at the curve, and the crushed vegetation there, and was quick to jump to conclusions about the truck driver's fate.

"My flatbed truckdriver and truck are gone?" Alex asked. "Did you have anything to do with this, Will?" His tone denoted that he already knew that he did.

Will shrugged. "I don't know, maybe he was really bad at driving. But good news, truck driver is still here," Will replied. "He's stranded on a cliff, over the edge."

"Hey! Down here!" The truck driver yelled from his ledge on the side of the mountain.

"Hang on for a moment," Alex called out to the driver. "We have to settle something up here, real quick."

There was a silent moment as they stood in a strange

kind-of standoff. But there was nowhere for Will and Katie to go, the bodyguard was in one direction of the road, Alex in the other. To one side of the road there was a ditch, and a flat stone wall behind that. The other side of the road had a cliff with a far drop off just feet from the edge of the pavement.

"This could have been easy for you, Will," Alex said. "I'm afraid it can no longer be."

NINETEEN

"There's nowhere to go, Will," Alex said. "You're going to need to come with us until we can figure this out. Or you can join the flatbed truck."

A smart car whipped around the corner, and skid to a stop behind the Maybach. The driver's door swung open, and a man jumped out with a pistol in hand.

"Everybody freeze; federal agent!" Dylan yelled at the men.

"What are you driving?" Will asked.

Dylan cringed a little bit. "It's a Smart car. Look, I had to commandeer a car back at the coffeeshop, and somehow I ended up with that."

"I guess it's not a surprise someone gave it to you to use," Will said.

"Yeah, they didn't care what happened to it," Alex said.

"Look, I'm not happy about it either," Dylan said. "Alexander Lewis, fancy meeting you here." Anyone familiar with the individuals with money in town recognized Alex.

"I thought you were trustworthy, Will," Alex said. "But it's becoming more and more apparent that you aren't."

"Will didn't tell me," Dylan said. "I tracked his phone to the abandoned gas station, and when they weren't there, well, I kept driving up the road, and here I am."

"You guys are relentless," Alex said. "Didn't I say that before, Will?"

"You did," Will replied.

"It's a gift," Dylan said.

"Is it?" Alex asked, then swung his gun up from Will, to point at Dylan, and pulled the trigger.

As the crack of thunder was heard from Alex's pistol, Dylan was struck, and fell backward into the ditch at the side of the road.

"No!" Will yelled.

Alex trained the pistol sight back on Will.

The Corvette's engine cranked up. The tire screamed as smoke poured out from the sides of the wheel wells.

"What?" The bodyguard said in disbelief. "There's nobody in it!"

The Corvette began to dart across the pavement, whipping around Dylan's Smart car and the Maybach. The Corvette then turned sharply, and drifted the back end of the car almost completely around, across the road.

Before the bodyguard could react, the back quarter-panel of the car spun sideways along the pavement and slammed into him, throwing him across the road.

The bodyguard stumbled to the edge of the cliff, he tried

to get his footing, but slipped over the edge. His gun flew from his hand, and his fingertips tried to grab onto the edge of the mountain. He couldn't hold on, though, and dropped down the steep side of the mountain, making a hard landing on the ledge, stranded with the flatbed truck driver.

The car stopped with its brake lights facing Will, Katie, and Alex.

Both doors of the Corvette flew open.

Alex stood in awe of the self-driving car that had come to the rescue.

"Sorry," Will said. "The car has a mind of its own sometimes."

Will and Katie scrambled to get into the car. Katie threw the duffle bag of cash into the back section of the Corvette behind the seats. The doors closed behind them and the car peeled out.

Alex ran to his Ferrari, and cranked the engine. The Testarossa's tires chirped as it took off after them.

"Zac, call an ambulance for Dylan," Will said.

"I'm on it," Zac replied.

Katie clenched her teeth looking out the window, as the Corvette hung on around a tight curve with a cliff to the side. The car then pulled into a short straightaway.

The Ferrari rounded the corner behind them.

"Alex is behind us," Will said. "How does this car stack up against a Testarossa?"

"Well, like I've told you before," Zac said. "It's partly the car, and partly the driver."

"You're instilling a lot of confidence," Will's sarcasm was thick.

Text came across the infotainment screen: "Playing 'Dead Horse' by Guns and Roses". The song began to blare over the car's speakers.

Zac hit the brakes and turned sharp, swinging the back end of the car around 180 degrees.

"It's time to party like it's 1992," Zac said, as the Corvette took off in the opposite direction back uphill, passing the Ferrari.

Alex quickly spun the Ferrari around, and began closing the distance between them.

"You're going back up the mountain?" Will asked. "Are you sure that's a good idea? That's a Ferrari."

"Backseat driving is for cars with backseats," Zac replied as the Corvette accelerated, pushing Will and Katie back against their seats. "Time to pretend this is Pike's Peak."

The Ferrari started to inch closer and closer. The Corvette slid around another corner. All Will and Katie could do was to hold on.

The Testarossa began to ease up the back left side of the Corvette.

The jarring blare of an oncoming car's horn blasted, and the Ferrari whipped back into the lane behind the Corvette.

As they rounded the next bend, there was another straightaway before the next sharp curve.

The Corvette caught rubber in fourth gear.

"This ends today," Zac said.

"Whoa, Zac, we're not going to be able to make that curve ahead at this speed," Will said.

"Well, neither will he," Zac said.

"Is that the best option?" Katie asked. "I would like to make the curve."

"Yeah, I agree," Will said.

"Don't worry." Zac continued to accelerate.

"This isn't *Forza* on Xbox," The tension in Will's voice grew. "We could die if you don't make this."

"No kidding." Zac brushed his comment off.

Will tried to stomp down on the brake, but Zac wouldn't let it move.

"No, Will, I can do this." Zac said. "You've got to believe me. Katie, you too."

"I believe you can do it," Katie said.

Will glanced at her, surprised by her faith.

She looked at Will and shrugged her shoulders.

Will took a deep breath. "Yeah, I do too." Will wasn't sure if he actually believed what he said, but in this moment, he had to believe it.

"Are you going to smokescreen him?" Will asked.

"I won't have to," Zac replied.

The curve was fast approaching. Will could feel his pulse quicken, and his breaths shorten. He reached out and grabbed Katie's hand as the Corvette thundered forward toward the end of the straightaway.

The Ferrari was keeping pace right behind them. No doubt Alex felt whatever the Corvette could do, he could do better.

"Pride cometh before the fall," Zac said.

"I hope you're talking about Alex," Will said. "Cause you're kind of cocky sometimes."

As the curve was upon them, Zac braked, and turned

the Corvette hard, Will could feel the back tires wanting to slip out from beneath them, but they were holding. Will and Katie held on, as Zac began to accelerate out of the curve, just barely keeping the tires on the pavement.

Will heard the Ferrari tires screech behind them as Alex lost control in the curve, and slid off the road. The passenger side of the car made a loud impact into the tree line by the mountain side of the road.

The Corvette spun around 180 degrees, and stopped in the road, facing the crashed Testarossa.

"Told you we'd make it," Zac said.

"I had complete faith in you," Will kidded.

"So, you just accidentally stomped the brakes earlier?" Zac asked with sarcasm.

"I hate to see such a beautiful car crashed," Katie said, gazing at the expensive Italian wreckage.

"Yeah, me too," Will agreed.

"I would've made that turn if I was driving the Testarossa. Like I said, it's part the car, part the driver," Zac said. "And being the car helps me know how hard I can push it."

After a moment, Alex eased the door open, and staggered out of the crashed supercar, with his pistol in hand.

Will looked in disbelief. "That guy can still walk after that?"

"That's an amazing car you have there, Will," Alex said as he limped a couple more steps forward. "You know this isn't over, it will never be over, until I get that car."

"You two get out of the car," Zac said to Will and Katie. "And stand a safe distance away."

"What are you doing?" Will asked.

"I'm taking care of this, once and for all. Like I said, this ends today," Zac replied.

"Don't do anything stupid," Will said.

"I have to," Zac replied. "For you and Katie."

Will and Katie got out of the car with their hands up in the air.

"Don't shoot," Will said. "We're stepping away from the car."

"Really?" Alex was rightfully suspicious, raising the gun at Will. "Why the change of heart?"

"My car wants to talk to you, alone," Will said.

"Wants to talk to me?" Alex looked at the Corvette.

"Alex, it's me, Zac," Zac's voice beckoned from the car.

Alex got a dumbfounded look on his face as he walked closer. "Zac?"

"Yes," Zac replied. "It's me. I'm afraid I wasn't honest with you before."

Alex tilted his head, not sure what to make of what the car was saying.

"I was never working on the neural/digital transmitter at your facility. I was working on consciousness digital transfer."

Alex's eyes lit up. "Are…are you serious? This isn't just some kind of program mimicking you?"

"It's really me in here," Zac said. "That's why Will has been so protective. The neural/digital transmitter was just a red herring."

"Do you know what this means?" Alex said, his enthusiasm growing as his brain processed the possibilities. He continued a slow walk toward the car. "We could essentially live forever."

"Possibly," Zac answered. "Live, in a way."

"This is technology beyond what I imagined possible, the world will never be the same," Alex said, a smile growing on his face. "And you put it in your car?" He chuckled. "Ah, that's so you. You've always been a little ridiculous, but that's what I liked about you. It all makes sense now."

"So now you understand the trepidation I had with surrendering the car over to be thrashed and trashed by your *researchers*," Zac said. "It's me."

"I understand, now," Alex said. "This technology is far beyond most of my employees. They would be like cavemen beating on things with sticks."

"I couldn't have put it better myself," Zac said. "But I have a project I think we can collaborate on. But I want to work with you, directly."

"I understand," Alex replied as his slow walk eased to a stop at the side of the Corvette.

"I can show you things that will shock you," Zac said.

"I bet," Alex said with a chuckle. "I'm imagining the possibilities of all of this, and a collaboration with you."

"Get in and prepare to be enlightened," Zac said.

Alex put the pistol in his pocket, and reached out his hand to the Corvette's door latch.

As his hand made contact with the latch, Zac sent a violent electrical current through the car to the door handle.

Alex began to shake, unable to let go, convulsing from the electricity coursing through his body.

The electrical current increased, and began to arc out from the doorhandle like fingers through the air, with a blinding glow, digging back into Alex's forearm and torso.

Katie covered her mouth, and turned her face in horror at the sight. Will put his arms around her.

Alex's body shook for a few more moments, he was then thrown from the car to the side of the road. Smoke rose in the air from the area where his body had landed.

The Corvette's engine cut off, and every electrical component in the car shut down.

Will and Katie ran up to the car.

"Uncle Zac?" Will said, his heart racing as he began to panic. "Uncle Zac?"

Katie wrapped her arms around him, as he began to shake.

Tears began to roll down Will's cheeks. "Uncle Zac," he whispered.

Katie turned Will around, and held him in her arms as he began to cry.

A familiar echo from his life rang back to him: no matter how good it may be, every story had a sad ending.

Will and Katie heard a moaning from the side of the road. Will couldn't believe Alex was still alive. They walked over to the edge of the road to see the man.

Alex looked in rough shape, but still alive. He groaned in pain.

"Ew, smells like burnt hair," Katie said.

"Where am I? What's happened to me?" Alex had never sounded to Will like a feeble, confused old man before. It was clear the electrocution had done some neurological damage to Alex, perhaps memory loss, and perhaps worse.

"Stay there," Will said. "We'll send someone for you."

It wouldn't be difficult instructions to follow, it didn't look as if Alex could get up even if he tried.

Will and Katie turned back to the car. The light show was well over with. There wasn't an electrical or mechanical peep from the Corvette.

Will reached out with caution toward the Corvette's driver's side door handle.

"Be careful," Katie said.

"As careful as I can be." He tried not to let on how nervous he was about what he was doing.

He gave the driver's side door handle a few light quick taps, and after feeling no charge, he grabbed onto the handle and opened the door.

"We're good," he said to Katie.

The couple got into the Corvette.

"Do you think it's still got enough juice left to start?" Will asked.

Katie shrugged. "If it doesn't, maybe you could pop the clutch?"

Will turned the key and the car started up without hesitation. The car seemed to be running as normal, with the exception of the infotainment system. The screen was black, and had no power.

Will sat there for a moment as the car idled. Sitting behind the wheel, his mind was flooded with thoughts of his uncle, and he began to get overcome with emotion once again.

"Do you want me to drive?" Katie asked.

"Could you?" Will asked. Indeed, he had a lifetime's worth of trauma just in this week. But so had she.

"Okay," she replied.

They got out, and after changing seats, Katie put the Corvette in gear, and they set off.

Will was quiet as they rode along, lost in his thoughts.

"This car drives great," Katie said.

"It really does," Will agreed.

"The gear shifts have a real mechanical feel, compared to more modern cars," she said. "I really like it."

"Yeah, me too."

"That was brave, what your uncle did," she said. "Only a hero sacrifices himself for others like that."

Will was quiet, nodding his head in agreement.

"I just hope we're worth it," her voice cracked with emotion as she spoke.

"He would have said *yes*, without giving it a second thought," Will replied.

As they rounded the bend to come up on the scene where Dylan had been shot, one of the lanes of the road was blocked, and there was an official in the other lane directing traffic.

Will saw an ambulance, and a few other sharply dressed individuals that he only could assume were federal agents.

"I hope Dylan is okay," Will said. "See if you can pull off the road somewhere."

"You go ahead, Will. I'll figure it out."

Will opened his door, got out of the car, and rushed toward the scene.

"Whoa, wait a second there," a man guarding the perimeter of the scene said.

"Will!" Dylan called out.

The guard glanced back at Dylan.

"Let him through," Dylan said to the man securing the scene.

The man stepped out of the way, and motioned Will to pass without a word.

There Dylan sat, with a sling on his left arm, resting on the back bumper of the ambulance.

"Are you okay?" Will asked.

"Yeah," Dylan said. "Well, in a lot of pain, but I'll be alright. The bullet didn't hit anything valuable, it struck me right up here by the shoulder." Dylan motioned to the location of the wound with his head. "It's a good thing Alex is a bad shot."

"That's a relief," Will replied. "He's not the best driver either, evidentially."

"Oh. I hit my head when I fell back, and I was out for a minute," Dylan said.

"How are you and Katie? What happened?"

"We're okay."

"Thank goodness," Dylan said. "Where's Alex?"

"He's laying at the side of the road, across from his crashed Testarossa," Will said. "You need to send some guys up there a couple miles." Will motioned in the direction that they had come from. "He's in rough shape, and pretty confused."

Dylan flagged down one of the sharp dressed men walking around the scene, and alerted him to the other situation up the road. The man rushed off to attend to the matter.

"Wow, how did Alex crash his Testarossa?" Dylan asked.

Will smiled and his eyes got a little glassy when he thought about Zac. "I guess he got out-driven by a Corvette."

"You never cease to amaze me, Will. Oh, you and Katie's phones are in the Smart car, I brought them with me when I found them at the gas station." Dylan said. "I'll have someone get them for you." Dylan flagged down another individual to go get the phones for Will.

Will supposed that was the one nice thing about Dylan being injured, people were waiting on him hand and foot.

"Hey," Will continued on a sincere note. "Thanks for coming for Katie and me."

"Anytime," Dylan said. "And now that this case is wrapping up, I think it might be a good time to put in my resignation."

"Are you serious?"

"Yeah," Dylan said. "I figured it's time to give civilian life a go. Besides, your mom would get mad if she caught me doing this stuff, and I can't risk that."

Will smiled. "She'd be *so* mad."

"I'm supposed to have a date with your mom tomorrow night," Dylan said. "I don't know how I'm going to explain this." He motioned to his arm in the sling.

"Oh, I'm sure you'll think of something," Will replied. "You're the king of *acting normal.*"

Dylan smiled.

Someone working the scene handed Will his and Katie's phones.

"Thanks," Will said.

"I'm okay here, Will. You should get Katie home."

"That sounds good," Will said. "Glad you're okay."

"You too," Dylan said. "And I'm glad all of this is over."

As Will was beginning to walk away, he turned back to Dylan. "Oh, by the way," he said. "Two of Alex's henchmen went off the cliff over there." Will pointed to a spot at the edge of the road. "They're stranded, waiting to get arrested on a cliff below."

"I'll get someone on that," Dylan replied with a grin.

"And a flatbed truck is crashed at the bottom of the mountain in that direction too," Will added.

"Good grief, Will, you and that Corvette are like a one-man wrecking crew." Dylan smirked. "Have you ever thought about becoming a federal agent?"

Will laughed. "Nope."

Will turned and walked toward Katie in the Corvette. "More like a one woman, one man, and one car wrecking crew, if anything."

TWENTY

After passing by Dylan and the chaotic remnants of the scene, Katie continued to drive Will down the mountain road toward town.

"It's finally over," Will said with a sigh.

"Yeah," she replied.

Will was sad that he had lost his uncle, once again, but somehow inside, Will always felt that having him back from the dead, even in car form, was too good to be true. He never quite trusted that the situation would last. But Zac went out, saving Will and Katie, and his sacrifice would never be forgotten. It would live on, every day, in whatever became of Will and Katie's lives.

After shifting the car, Katie reached over and grabbed onto Will's hand.

A blip of light flashed across the infotainment screen, catching Will and Katie's attention.

Words appeared across the screen … *Rebooting.*

"What?" Will asked, as a glimmer of hope lit in his eyes.

The reboot text left the screen, shortly followed by another message: "Playing: 'Back in Black' by AC/DC".

The song began to sound through the speakers.

"Zac?" Will's eyes teared up as a grin grew across his face.

"The one and only," Zac replied.

"Yes!" Katie said with a big smile.

"Wow, what do you give a computer for a hangover?" Zac kidded. "I haven't partied that hard since college."

"We thought you were dead … again," Will said.

"I almost was," Zac said. "That little stunt just about fried me, and I'm not talking about the good *getting fried*. Speaking of, did Alex get fried?"

"Oh yeah," Will replied. "Extra crispy."

"It was actually pretty disturbing," Katie said. "But good job."

"He survived," Will said. "But I'm not sure if he remembers his name."

"I was imagining it was going to be like when they opened the ark in the movie *Raiders of the Lost Ark*," Zac said.

"What was that, *I can show you things that will shock you*, and *get in and prepare to be enlightened*, you said to Alex?" Will asked with a smirk.

"Did you like those lines?" Zac asked. "I was giving him a bit of foreshadowing; all the best stories do that."

Katie chuckled. "I don't know if they're quite that cheesy when they do it, though."

"Yeah, for someone who never had any kids," Will said. "You got dad jokes for miles."

Zac chuckled. "I guess so."

Perhaps it's true, that every story had a sad ending, but this story wasn't ending today, or anytime soon for that matter.

It wasn't long before Will was standing with Katie at the door to her house.

"It's been a day," Katie said with an exhausted smile.

"I'm so sorry for everything that you've had to go through," Will said. "But you've been nothing but amazing."

"People say that relationships are hard work, but wow," she kidded. "But you're worth it." She flashed him a sincere smile.

"Oh, I almost forgot," Will reached into his pocket and pulled out Katie's red and white polka-dot hair ribbon that he had given her, that he received in the box at the coffeeshop when she had been taken.

"There it is," she said with a smile, taking it back from him. She made quick work of tying it back into her hair. "Thank you, I was worried I wouldn't see it again."

"Like you couldn't live without it," Will replied.

"It's special," she said with sincerity.

It made Will feel good that such a little item he had given to her had meant so much. His ex, Mandy, would have thrown it in the trash long ago. It was one of the myriad of differences that set the girls light-years apart.

"Well, I probably better go," Katie said. "Before my mom starts to suspect my crazy double-life."

"Well, hopefully that's over now," Will replied.

"Except for the talking car, of course," she said.

"Of course," Will replied.

"I'll see you tomorrow night," Katie said. "You're picking me up at 6:30, right?"

"I'll be here with my chariot," Will replied, nodding toward the Corvette. "Are you sure you're okay not getting a limo?"

Katie laughed. "Of course! I'm not really a limo-girl. Anyway, a limo has nothing on your car."

Will wrapped his arms around her. "I wish I never had to let you go."

"Me too." She looked into his eyes.

They kissed for a moment, like two people that had just cheated death, cause indeed they had. After another moment, he let her go.

As she entered the door to her house, she glanced back and gave him one more smile with a gleam in her eyes. She then went inside and closed the door behind her.

Will got back into the Corvette and rode off with a sense of relief he hadn't felt in a while.

As they rode along, Will started to feel like things were finally going to get back to normal. Maybe they'd even start looking up.

"Besides Katie's hair ribbon, do you know what else you almost forgot today?" Zac asked.

"What's that?"

"The thirty-thousand dollars you got away with," Zac said.

Will's eyes got big as he whipped his head around to

notice the duffle bag of cash still sitting in the back of the Corvette, where Katie had thrown it earlier.

"Happy early-birthday?" Zac said.

Friday night found Will in the empty bleachers of the school's football field with his friend, Kahlil. There was no game that evening, but the bright lights were on, illuminating the area.

Kahlil took another sip from a bottle. It was one of a six pack of beer that his older brother had bought for him. It was the tail end of a guys' night at Kahlil's house watching a cheesy action movie. The sports field was actually quite peaceful, when it wasn't overfilled with rowdy, belligerent fans.

"Get you one of these," Kahlil said, motioning to the other five bottles of beer still in the pack.

"Nah, I'm good," Will said, taking another sip of his soda.

"Man, I brought us this whole six pack," Kahlil replied. "I can't drink it all. Just try one."

"Okay," Will said.

"Yeah, that's what I'm talking about." Kahlil held out the pack and let Will grab one. "Beers with bros."

Kahlil grabbed a bottle opener and popped the top for Will.

Will raised the beer slightly as if he was giving a silent toast and then took a swig. Will had to stop himself from gagging, it was horrible.

"What do you think?" Kahlil asked, trying not to laugh, already knowing the answer by Will's expression.

"It's good," Will said, trying to be polite.

Kahlil laughed. "Don't lie, Will, it's okay if you don't like it."

"But I'm going to drink it." Will cringed as he took another sip. "Beers with bros."

Kahlil seemed amused by Will's struggling through the beer, but appreciative of his dedication to 'beers with bros'. He turned his eyes to the football field.

"You know, I've been playing on this field for four years now." Kahlil took another sip of his beer. "I'm going to miss it next year."

"Yeah, but aren't you still planning on playing college ball?"

"That's the plan." Kahlil took a deep breath. "And coach says that recruiters have been showing up to some of our games."

"If they were at that last game, you should be set," Will said.

Kahlil chuckled. "Yeah, maybe."

"What's wrong?"

"I don't know if I'm ready for all of this," Kahlil said. "You know me…" He motioned to his stopwatch. "I like running plays I've already practiced a thousand times. I know who I am here, and I know I can dominate. Out there is just…"

"Uncertain?"

"Yeah," Kahlil replied. "And what about Audre? What if we get into different colleges? Everything is going to get disrupted and change."

"It is," Will agreed. "But I've known you for a while. You've got a big personality."

"Oh, thanks." Kahlil's sarcasm was evident.

"No, I meant that in a good way," Will said. "You're going to be you, no matter where you end up. And all the other details will work themselves out."

"I guess." Kahlil didn't sound convinced.

"I know," Will said. "The future is coming for us, whether we like it or not. And if there's anyone I know that's going to land on their feet, it's you."

"Thanks, man." Kahlil patted him on the shoulder, grateful for the encouragement.

"Look at who's talking about the future now," Kahlil said.

"What?"

"I don't know anyone who's into more old junk than you," Kahlil said with a smile. "Old cars, old movies, old music, and old video games…But I've been noticing a change lately."

"How so?"

"I mean, you still like old stuff, but you've been a lot more in the moment lately. Whereas you used to always talk about how great things used to be, you know, before your father…But it seems like you're starting to be in the here and now more than you ever were before."

"Yeah, I guess so," Will agreed.

"I think Katie has been good for you."

Will took another sip of his horrible beer and almost gagged. "I agree. I think she's shown me that there are things worth being in the present for. Things I don't want to miss out on here."

"That's a hundred-percent true," Kahlil said. "You can

love and miss the things and people, and they're always going to be with you, inside. But don't miss out on the new memories happening here and now."

"She helps me look forward to tomorrow too."

"Her and that nice car you just got."

"Yeah," Will said with a smile.

"I think you're right," Kahlil said. "I think I'm going to be okay next year. I'll miss this place, but college is going to be wild. It's going to be a party. It'll be a new play, but I'll own it." Kahlil reached up and took his stopwatch from around his neck. He laid it down on the bleachers beside him.

"Eh, you're finally done with the stopwatch?" Will asked.

"Maybe so." Kahlil smiled. "I guess there's no time like the future. And maybe I should live it instead of measuring it."

Will shrugged. "Sounds like progress."

"You know, Will, you're going to be okay too."

"Yeah, I think so," Will said.

"But the key is that you've got to realize that you're okay on your own terms, by yourself. Then you can be okay together with someone else. If that makes sense."

"It does," Will replied. "I think I'm finally starting to realize that."

After sleeping in on Saturday morning, and going to pick up his tuxedo rental, Will stayed true to his word and gave the Corvette a good wash. This made Zac very happy, because as he said before, just because he was a car, didn't mean he wanted to start looking like a slob.

It was almost time for him to leave, and Will finally came downstairs in his tux.

Beth seemed overcome with pride. "You look so handsome," she said as she walked up to him and adjusted his bowtie. "You picked out a great tux, she's going to love it."

"Thanks, mom," Will replied with that teenage superpower of being immune from a mother's compliments.

"So, are you staying in tonight?" Will already knew the answer, but he wanted to hear it from her.

"No, actually Dylan is taking me out on a date tonight," she replied.

"Is that so?" Will raised an eyebrow to mess with her.

"It sounds like he got hurt at work," Beth said. "He's okay, but his arm is in a sling, poor thing."

"I'm glad he's okay," Will played dumb.

"I'll have to get the full story from him tonight," she said.

Good luck with that, Will thought to himself.

Will had come to appreciate Dylan over the course of his ordeal. He felt that he was a sincere and genuine guy. And though he didn't hold a candle to his father, Will thought that Dylan could make his mother happy, and that he would treat her the way she deserved to be treated.

Will wondered what Dylan would do now that he was retiring from the bureau. He imagined the bureau would probably set Dylan up with some cushy desk job. Maybe even at the nuclear plant, so he wouldn't be lying to his mom about his job anymore. But he could always just tell his mom that he switched jobs. Will realized he was overthinking all of this, he had bigger things to tend to … the dance.

"What are you thinking about, sweetie?" His mom asked.

"Oh, nothing," Will replied, snapping out of his nomad thoughts. "I just wanted to tell you that I think Dylan is a decent guy," Will said. "You could do worse."

"Thanks, honey."

"That being said, you two still need to behave."

Beth laughed. "Listen, mister, so do you."

"I always behave," Will replied with a big cheesy smile.

"Yeah, sure you do." His mother wasn't convinced. Her face lit up as she thought of something.

"What?" Will asked.

"I have something for you," she said, picking up a gift from a nearby end table.

A glimmer of light reflected off the watch. The metal band was a shining silver, and its numberless face was black as night. There were just the hands, and the silver dot in the twelve's spot. Will instantly recognized it as his father's old Movado watch.

"That's dad's old watch." Will was confused. "You polished it up."

Beth smiled. "Yeah, well, it's your old watch now."

He took it from her hand and put it around his wrist. It was a perfect fit. He had always loved the timepiece, and something about having it now made him feel simultaneously closer to his father, and more of his own man.

His mother smiled at him. "Time marches on."

He glanced up at her. "Does it always have to?"

"I'm afraid so," she replied.

Will glanced down at the watch. "I guess it does."

"Oh, don't forget the corsage," Beth said, snapping Will out of his sentiments.

"Oh, yeah, I almost forgot." Will went to the refrigerator in the kitchen, where it was being kept fresh.

As Will walked back into the room, his mother had the camera on her phone ready.

"Come on, mom."

"Just a couple, Will. In front of the fireplace."

Will placed the corsage down on an end table, and went to go stand in front of the fireplace.

As Beth was snapping pictures, Nala walked over and sat on one of Will's shoes. Will bent down and picked her up.

"And a couple with Nala," Will said.

Will pet her on the head, and she stuck her tongue out. Beth snapped a few more pictures of him with the puppy.

"I wish I could see Katie's dress," Beth said. "Get me some pictures of you two together."

"Okay, okay, mom," Will said as he put Nala down and snatched up the corsage off the table. He started toward the garage. "I've got to get going, I have to stop by Pedro's on the way."

"Have a great time tonight, and be careful!" She said with a warmth in her eyes as she watched him walking out.

"I will, love you, mom."

"Ready for tonight?" Zac asked as Will entered the garage.

"I think so," Will said as he put Katie's corsage down on the front passenger seat.

He looked back at his music gear packed tight in the back of the Corvette behind the seats.

"My guitar and amp barely fit in here," Will said. "It's definitely not the car for hauling all your band gear around."

"I'm sorry, I wasn't thinking of all your band gear when I bought this car," Zac said in a snarky tone. "I'll try to do better next time."

"Yeah," Will kidded. "Why didn't you get a minivan or a station wagon?"

"I hate both of those options, but if it's for the band …" Zac eased in some sarcasm. "By the way, I noticed you're bringing my Les Paul guitar. Always a good choice."

"That's what I thought."

Will got in the car, and opened the garage door. He looked out at the road; he was ready for tonight.

"In the span of forever, there's only one tonight. Enjoy it," Zac said as he cranked up the Corvette's engine.

"I'll do my best," Will replied.

Pedro didn't have a date to the dance, but somehow it didn't really bother him. Or if it did, he didn't let it show. But him going stag to the dance worked in Will's favor. Pedro had agreed to bring his guitar and amplifier to the venue, so that Will didn't have to worry about lugging it around, and he could enjoy his night with Katie.

Pedro's home was halfway across town. As Will pulled

up to Pedro's house in the Corvette, he saw his friend loading up the last bit of his drum set in the back of his old Honda Element.

Will pulled into Pedro's driveway.

"There you are," Pedro said as Will got out of the car. "I was starting to get worried."

"Sorry," Will replied as he started to get his gear out of the back of the car.

"Guitarists have it so easy, I swear," Pedro said. "Hauling a drum set around everywhere takes a lot more work. Can't wait until our band is successful enough to have roadies."

"That'll be nice," Will said.

"And cute female fans." Pedro smiled.

"Are you sure you don't want help unloading everything at the venue?"

"No." Pedro began to play *Tetris* with Will's guitar and amp to fit it into his vehicle. "I want you to have a wonderful dinner with Katie. I'll take care of everything else. There's even a sound guy at the venue that can set your guitar and amp up and sound check it. You get the royal treatment tonight, I guess. Just don't let it go to your head."

"I won't."

"That's good, because I've watched a lot of band documentaries where the lead singer lets things go to their head, and it torpedoes the whole band."

"I'll keep that in mind." Will replied with a chuckle.

"It happens, like, almost every time."

"I really appreciate you bringing my gear, Pedro."

"It's cool," Pedro said. "Just make sure you're there, and you're ready to go at nine pm."

"Nine pm," Will repeated it to himself, so he'd be more likely to remember.

"Yeah, nine," Pedro reiterated. "That's when we go on. Actually, just come back stage, like, five or ten minutes before."

"Got it," Will replied. He then glanced back at the Corvette. "I need to get going."

"Yeah, yeah, go on." Pedro shooed him away. "I'll see you there."

Will rang the doorbell at Katie's house, and after a moment, Michelle answered the door. "Will, don't you look handsome?" she said. "Won't you come in?"

He followed her inside.

She then noticed the corsage in his hand. "That's beautiful," she said.

"Katie sent me the color of her dress so it would match."

"That should match perfectly."

Will followed her inside the lovely home, through the foyer and into the living room.

"She should almost be ready," Michelle said. "I'll let her know that you're here. You can have a seat on the couch in the living room if you'd like."

Her mother ascended the stairs to let Katie know that Will had arrived.

Will remained standing by the entrance of the living room, in view of the staircase. He glanced around. The house was very nice, it was also very tidy.

He noticed some pictures on the wall of Katie when

she was younger. There was a nice one of Katie and her parents at an amusement park when she was very young. She had a smile so big. There was another picture when she was slightly older and had big hair; she looked like she was acting in an elementary school play. Will relished the fact that she'd probably be embarrassed if she realized that he had seen some of these pictures.

Michelle descended the stairs. "She'll be right down."

"Thanks," he replied.

"Are you excited about the dance?" She asked.

"I am," Will replied.

"She is too," Michelle said. "Katie's father was really disappointed he couldn't be here tonight, he wanted me to take some pictures."

"My mom wants some of those too, if possible," Will said.

"Sure," she said. "I'll make sure Katie sends them to you."

"Thanks."

"You made a really good impression on Katie's father, but I knew you would. It might be weird to say, but you two seem alike in many ways."

"He's really nice," Will replied. "And I love his shop."

"He said you might come work there."

"Yeah, I'm supposed to talk to him about that soon."

"He really wanted to give you a hard time, you know, intimidate you for taking Katie out, for fun," Michelle explained. "But he couldn't bring himself to do it, because he liked you too much."

Her words help put Will at ease about impressing her father, perhaps Will could just be himself around him.

Then Katie caught his attention out of the corner of his eye as she descended the stairs.

Will turned to look, and when he saw her, it almost took his breath away. She was beautiful. Well, she was always beautiful, but tonight she looked incredible. The purple dress she had chosen accentuated her desirable form, and flowed around her as she walked.

Will didn't realize his mouth had opened as he gazed at her.

Katie smiled when she saw the expression on his face.

There was no hiding how taken he was by her. "Katie, you're ..." Will was at a loss for words. "Wow, you look great."

She smiled. "Thank you, Will. You look great too."

As she reached the bottom of the stairs, Will took her hands and looked at her. Her hair, her make up, that dress ... Will didn't know what he had done for the universe to think he deserved such a treasure. His starry-eyed gaze was interrupted by her mother's voice.

Hey you guys, can I get some pictures?" Michelle asked.

"Sure," Will replied. "Oh, I have your corsage."

Will opened up the clear box and removed the corsage and put it around Katie's wrist.

"It's perfect," Katie said. "I have your boutonniere too."

Katie stepped out of the room briefly, but then returned with the boutonniere, which she pinned to his tuxedo jacket. It also matched her dress.

"Thank you."

After Michelle had taken more than enough pictures,

Will and Katie walked out the door, and got into the Corvette to leave.

"Katie, you look stunning," Zac said as he as she was putting on her seatbelt.

"Awww, thanks," she replied, seeming almost embarrassed by the compliment. "It's still just me under all this fancy."

After enjoying a delicious hibachi dinner at a local Japanese steakhouse, the couple set off for the dance.

TWENTY-ONE

Soon they reached the venue for the dance, a local auditorium that often hosted concerts and other large functions.

Katie and Will held hands as they walked in through the front doors.

It was clear that the dance committee had gone all out. The dance's theme, 'A Night on the Thames', lent itself to a number of elaborate decorations. These decorations included the detailed sides of fake buildings, other attractions, and a boat. Structurally, all of these were made of cardboard, but were designed with an artful touch. They must have recruited the drama and art departments to help make some of these props.

There were also white Christmas style mini-lights accenting some of the structures, and suspended above the dance floor as stars. There were red, white, and blue balloons scattered around the room as well.

The decor invoked the magic that the evening could bring.

Katie squeezed Will's hand in excitement. "Isn't this great?"

"Yeah," Will agreed. It truly was.

The dance was already well in progress by the time Will and Katie had arrived. They meandered around the edge of the dance floor, watching everyone dance.

"Hey guys," a voice greeted them.

They turned to find Kahlil and Audre standing behind them. Audre was wearing a flattering strapless blue dress, and Kahlil had a nice tux on. Audre had her arm locked around Kahlil's.

"Hey, you two," Will replied.

Katie gave an excited wave.

"Man, they killed it with this theme," Kahlil said. "These decorations look awesome. I don't even know where the Thames river is; never heard of it. But it's probably somewhere in America, they've got red, white and blue balloons."

Will shrugged. "I think I've heard of the river, but I don't know where it is."

"Oh, the Thames is a river that flows through London, England. England's colors are red, white and blue as well." Katie pointed at some of the decorations. "See, that decoration over there is supposed to be the Palace of Westminster." She turned and motioned toward another decoration. "And over there, that's supposed to be the London Eye."

"That Ferris wheel looking thing?" Kahlil asked.

"Yeah," she said with a smile.

"All right, Miss Geography," Kahlil said with a smile. "School's out, but I guess I learned something tonight."

Katie got a little embarrassed. "Sorry," she said with a chuckle.

"Well, we're going to hit up the refreshments," Kahlil said. "I heard they have a pretty good spread over by the big cardboard boat."

"Nice," Will replied.

"We'll see you guys around," Kahlil said as they walked away.

The last song ended, and a new one began. It was a slow tempo song, so Will thought he could deal with it on the dance floor. And if he bit the bullet and danced now, he might be able to get out of dancing later when faster songs played.

Will glanced out at the dance floor, and back to Katie. "Would you care to dance?"

Her face began to glow. "I'd love to."

Will held Katie in his arms as they moved across the floor.

"I didn't know you could dance," Katie said. "You're pretty smooth." She gave a coy smile.

"I call my dance style, 'swaying with purpose'," Will kidded.

"Well, I like it," she replied.

Will gazed at her as he swayed with purpose. There's never been a star in the night sky that shone as bright as she did tonight in his arms.

"Do you like my earrings?" Katie asked about the diamond studs that graced her ears. "My mom gave them to me; they were from when she was my age."

"They're nice," Will replied.

They finished the dance and stayed on the dance floor for the next song. It was, to Will's luck, another slow song. After that one concluded, they left the dance floor, and went to stand near the decoration of The London Eye.

Katie remained there, taking in all of the decorations and watching the other students dance, while Will left to get them some refreshments by the boat decoration.

Kahlil was right, there was a great spread of snacks. But Will was still full from dinner, and had his sights set on the punch bowl near the end of the table. He and Katie were just thirsty.

As he was preparing two cups of punch, he didn't notice Mandy walking up next to him.

"Hey Will," Mandy said.

"Oh, hi Mandy." Will was still feeling a little awkward about the last time he had interacted with her, and Nala had attacked her ankles. He thought a sock she left behind was perhaps still in his backyard by the fence, probably almost chewed beyond recognition by now.

He tried to hurry with the punch, so he could avoid getting entangled in a conversation with her.

"You look so happy, Will." Her voice had an introspective tone, which was uncommon from Mandy. "Happier than you ever looked when you were with me."

He was done pouring the punch, but now felt obligated to reply.

"I see the way that you look at her," Mandy continued. "I don't think you ever looked at me like that. I think I'm starting to realize that we're not going to get back together again."

"No Mandy, we're not," Will said.

He felt a little sorry for her. She wasn't all bad, just mostly. And he was sure that it was embarrassing for her to put herself out there like she did the other night in his backyard. And he oddly felt a little bad about her sock. He knew that she cared for him in her own, warped way. The best he could do was to give her some closure.

"Mandy, I just want to let you know that I forgive you," Will said.

Mandy glanced down toward the floor. "You know, I pretend that I don't remember what I did, but I think about it a lot. I'm sorry that I hurt you."

"It's okay now, we've moved passed that."

"We have?" She asked.

"As friends," Will clarified. "We weren't meant to be together anyway; it wasn't in the stars."

"Sometimes I think that, maybe I'm not a very great person."

"It doesn't take much searching to see that none of us are great people," Will replied. "But it's never too late to be a better person than you were the day before."

A warm smile graced her face. "Optimism and ability to see the good in almost anyone is *so* you, I'm going to miss it."

"You look nice tonight, Mandy. I hope you have a good time." Will said.

"Thanks for …" Mandy searched for the words. "Thanks for being you. She's a lucky girl."

Will picked up the punch he had prepared for he and Katie. "I'll see you around, Mandy."

"Bye, Will," she said.

Will approached Katie holding two cups of punch.

"Thank you, sir," she said as she took one from him and had a sip.

"Oh, that wasn't for you," Will kidded.

She smiled and rolled her eyes at his joke.

They stood off to the side of the action and watched others dance as they enjoyed their punch.

As the song came to an end, Mr. Finner stepped out from behind the thick burgundy curtains that hid the stage, which up to this point, hadn't been utilized for the festivities.

The principal had a microphone in his hand. He tapped on it a couple of times, and the thump reverberated through the room. As if him being there wasn't buzzkill enough, he had to kill the mood over the speakers.

"Is this thing turned on?" Finner asked into the mic.

"I'm turned on," a male student's voice heckled from the crowd.

Mr. Finner pursed his lips in disapproval of the comment.

"Hey everybody, I hope you're having a good evening and enjoying yourselves tonight," Finner said.

"We were," the heckler struck again.

"Anyway, we have a little treat for you guys," the principal continued. "A band made up of some students from our own school is going to perform one song for you tonight."

"Oh, crap," Will said, realizing that he had lost track of time.

Will tossed his cup, with a slight remainder of punch left in it, into a nearby trashcan and began to run toward the side doors of the stage.

"Without further introduction," Finner went on, "Here they are." It seemed he couldn't be bothered with remembering the band's name to introduce it.

The curtain was pulled open.

Pedro sat behind his drum set, and Lucy stood there with her bass. Both looked like deer in the headlights, bewildered, and not ready to begin without their other band member.

The stage was decorated nicely, with balloons and streamers of the same dance color theme. The stage was also adorned with the same white mini-lights that were strewn about other places in the room.

Will ran onto the stage, from left side-stage, and abruptly stopped himself in the middle of the scene at the microphone stand.

A few students in the crowd chuckled at his hurried arrival.

Will glanced backstage right on the other side, and saw Mr. Finner giving him one of his trademarked looks of disapproval.

Principal Finner was not a grinner, Will chuckled to himself.

"Hey," Will smiled and gave a slight wave to the crowd. He turned around and grabbed his uncle's white Les Paul off of a nearby guitar stand.

"Nice of you to be able to fit us into your busy schedule," Lucy whispered, as he walked by, back up to the mic.

Will glanced over at Lucy and gave her a wink. She smiled and rolled her eyes at him.

Will stood centerstage, in front of the microphone.

"All right, we're Oblivion Cubed," he said to the audience. He then began to play his guitar and sing.

Pedro and Lucy joined in. It was a slow tempo song, well suited for dancing, and the students on the dance floor seemed to find the rhythm quickly and began to dance.

Will's lyrics were sweet, the song about longing to hold the new girl who smiled like the sun, but didn't know his name.

He glanced down at Katie as he sang. She held her punch as she swayed back-and-forth to the song, with the biggest smile on her face. He couldn't help but smile to see her enjoying the song he had written for her.

Will glanced back at Lucy and Pedro during the musical break in the middle of the song. They both had grins on their faces, looking as if they were having the time of their life. It crossed Will's mind how lucky he was to have such great bandmates, and maybe if he started taking the band as seriously as they did, it could go somewhere, besides Pedro's garage where they practiced.

Will repeated the song's chorus onc last time:

"She smiles like the sun,
and I'll never be the same,
I just want to hold her,
but she doesn't know my name."

Will strummed the last chord of the song, and let it reverberate through the auditorium.

The crowd of students erupted into applause.

Will glanced at the other band members; they had accomplished looks on their faces. They had done it. It was easily their biggest gig, even though it was just one song. They finally had a good-sized crowd to perform for, and the audience loved them.

"Thanks," Will said to the students.

Will glanced down at Katie. She had put down her punch and was clapping enthusiastically, rocking up on the tips of her toes. It was safe to assume that she loved the song. And that's what mattered the most to Will.

Will caught sight of his friend, Kahlil, in the crowd. He and Audre were cheering, also impressed by the band's performance.

Kahlil gave Will a thumbs-up.

"Thanks," Will mouthed the word to his friend.

Kahlil glanced around at the crowd, and then yelled out, "One more song!"

The chant began to echo through the crowd, "One more song; one more song!"

It started with just a few voices, but then grew to an overwhelming majority of the audience.

Kahlil shrugged and smiled at Will; he had incited a riot of students calling for more.

Will glanced over to the side-stage were Finner stood. The principal rolled his eyes and gave in. He held up an index finger.

"Just one more song," Finner mouthed the words.

Will nodded that he understood, then stepped back to the mic. "Do you want one more?" He asked, egging the audience on.

The students began to cheer and applaud.

Will walked over to his amplifier and pulled the distortion pedal out from the back, and put it on the floor. He then went to his guitar case at the side of the stage and opened it. He retrieved some Kurt Cobain white oval style sunglasses and put them on as he walked back up to the mic, center stage.

"I always have these in my guitar case, just in case I need them," Will said to the crowd.

Will turned and glanced back at the band and smiled. He turned back to the mic and launched into a cover of "Lithium" by Nirvana.

The students were fixated on Will and the band, then when Will stomped the distortion pedal for the chorus section, the crowd began to move to the rhythm.

Will saw Katie in the crowd, dancing in place to the music, having a great time. He looked over to Kahlil, who pumped his fist in the air giving Will more encouragement to let loose.

The grunge sound washed over the crowd, and with the exception of a few people in the periphery of the auditorium, by the second chorus, the students were wholeheartedly into it.

Will yelled and rocked out on the Les Paul. He gave it his all, and the performance showed it. As the crunch began to subside from his last guitar cord, the audience began to applaud again.

Will saw Finner standing side-stage with his arms folded, looking annoyed. He didn't seem to be a fan of the song choice. Will gave him a smile that seemed to bounce off his grumpy force-field.

Will saw Katie clapping and jumping in place. Kahlil was cheering too.

Will turned back to the band.

"That was great," Will said.

"Our biggest gig was a success." Pedro was elated.

"I'll admit it, we were pretty awesome," Lucy said. "But we probably would have been better if Will was wearing that flannel shirt tied backward around his waist."

Will rolled his eyes and smiled. He then glanced back at Katie, who smiled at him, gleaming with pride.

"Go ahead, Will," Pedro said. "I'll get your guitar and amp. You can pick it up from my house tomorrow."

"Thanks," Will said as he put his guitar back on the stand.

"And if it doesn't work out between you two, give her my number," Lucy said.

An amused Will shook his head at her comment.

"What? She's hot," Lucy said with a mischievous smile.

"Are we allowed to tell you she's hot?" Pedro asked. "Asking for a friend."

"It'll work out," Will said to Lucy.

"How do you know?" Lucy asked.

"Fairytales always end with 'happily ever after'," Will said.

"Have you ever read actual fairytales?" Lucy asked. "They're pretty messed up, dude." She smiled at Will. "Run to her, Wee William."

Will cringed at Lucy's terrible Scottish accent, then headed to the side-stage exit, opposite Finner.

As Will descended the small set of stairs at the side of the stage, Mr. Denzie was standing at the bottom, waiting for him.

"Hey, Mr. Denzie," Will said.

"Nice job, Will, you did Kurt justice," Mr. Denzie said.

"Thanks."

"I know that you think that I'm tough on you," Mr. Denzie continued. "Maybe tougher than I am on some of the other students."

"Yeah, sometimes."

"It's just because I see this potential in you, that I haven't seen in many students over the years that I've taught here. If you really put your heart into something, I believe that anything you touch will turn to gold. I truly believe that, Will."

"Wow." Will didn't know what to say. He always thought that Mr. Denzie was just tough because he liked to be.

"You know where to find me if you ever need to be reminded of that," Mr. Denzie said.

"Thanks."

"Oh, and work a little harder in bio," Denzie added. "Now get out of here and go have a good time. I'm starting to make myself sick with all of this heart to heart."

Will chuckled. "I'll see you in class, Mr. Denzie,"

"See you there, buddy," Mr. Denzie replied.

As Will began to wade through the crowd of students across the floor, he found Arthur standing in his path.

"I know you never had the guts to race me with your

moped, but much respect for what you just did on stage," Arthur said.

"Thanks, Arthur."

"Well, it's back to the ladies," Arthur said as he strutted away.

An amused smile grew on Will's face with the morbid curiosity of what lady would have accompanied Arthur to a dance.

Will watched Arthur exit the dance floor and sit down at a table, only to pull out his phone.

"Ah, the internet ladies, if indeed they were ladies, and not catfishing middle-aged dudes," Will said to himself. Maybe love was in the air for everyone.

His eyes found Katie off to the side of the dance floor, staring at him with a grin across her face.

As he neared her, she wrapped her arms around him. "I have a new rock star crush."

"Who's that?" Will asked.

"You goof," she replied. "You all were so good up there. I can't wait to come hear you play a full set somewhere."

"I'll let you know where and when."

"I'll be there," Katie replied. "And let me know where I can buy a t-shirt."

Will received sporadic compliments from other students as the night went on. The positive attention was nice, but Will's favorite part of the night was dancing with Katie, his arms around her as they both swayed with purpose.

As they danced near the Palace of Westminster decoration, Will looked up at the clock tower part of the prop. He then looked up at the mini-light stars above them. He then looked back down at Katie. In that moment he knew that he cared for her more than he could've ever imagined caring for someone. They had something special together, a bond. He could feel it. And looking in her eyes, he could tell that she felt it as well. In that moment he knew that he would always love her, and he'd never be complete without her. He leaned in and gave her a kiss on the lips.

As they drove away from the dance, Will looked up at the starry night sky through the open roof of his car. And through the open roof a Corvette, came the realization that sometimes dreams still come true. "Playing 'Calling You' by Blue October" read across the infotainment screen.

Later in the evening, after the dance, Will and Katie found themselves outside of Will's bedroom window, on a blanket on the roof, underneath the stars.

"It's really nice up here," Katie said. "This is where we had our first date."

"Yeah, I guess." Will chuckled. "If you could call it that."

"So much has happened in the short time since then," she said. "It seems like it was a world away when were weren't together. I'm so much happier now."

Will looked at her and smiled.

"What are you thinking about?" she asked.

"I was thinking about how I'd do it all over again. I'd go through all that mess just to be with you."

She leaned over and began kissing him.

Katie laid back on the blanket on the roof as they continued to make out. He leaned over her as they kissed.

"You and the stars," she said, looking up at him with the night sky as his background. "Two things I could never get tired of seeing."

And if they were wishing on a star, the only wish to be made at the moment was for each other.

TWENTY-TWO

Sunday afternoon found Will beneath the Corvette. The garage door was open, letting the cool fall breeze blow in. Will tightened the oil drain plug beneath the car, and filled the car with new oil. When he was done, Will backed it down the ramps.

The song "Changes" by David Bowie, began to play from the stereo in the car.

"I like this song." Will chuckled as he carried the car ramps back to the wall of the garage where he stored them. "Appropriate for an oil change."

"Give me some credit, I like to think it's a little more cerebral than that. Bigger things are changing than the oil," Zac said. "It's just a great song too."

"Yeah, it is." Will returned the wrench he was using for the oil change to his workbench. "I wish working on everything in this car was as easy as changing the oil in it."

"It would take the challenge out of things," Zac kidded.

"Don't you like a good challenge? Like 'the minus world' in *Super Mario Bros.* on the NES?"

Will laughed. "When was the last time you played video games?"

"It's been a while," Zac replied. "As a kid I used to play that level for hours, trying to figure out how to get out of it. Only to learn when I was older that it was a glitch in the game, and once you were in, there was no way out until you ran out of lives. I was just futilely searching for some pattern or deeper meaning that wasn't there."

"Sounds like time well spent," Will said.

"Yeah, it was like a sad metaphor for life," Zac said.

"Isn't that, like, nihilism or something?" Will laughed. "You're so melodramatic, even for a 90s sportscar."

"So, it seems like you and Katie had a good time last night," Zac said.

"Last night was amazing, I'll never forget it for the rest of my life."

"Great," Zac replied. "On a side note, you know there are still cameras on the roof of the house."

It took Will a second, but then he realized that the cameras surely caught he and Katie's make-out session on the roof last night. He rolled his head back and sighed.

"Just thought I'd throw that bit of information out there," Zac said. "You know, for future reference."

A little red Porsche Boxster pulled up in the driveway, it was Samantha.

"Uh-oh," Will whispered to Zac. "This looks like trouble."

Samantha got out and walked toward Will in the garage.

As she approached, Will could see she had tears in her eyes.

"Hey, Samantha," Will greeted her as she reached the edge of the garage. "Are you okay?"

"He did it, didn't he?" Samantha asked.

Will knew she was talking about Zac transferring his consciousness to the car, but played dumb. "Who did what?"

"You know what I'm talking about," She replied, seeing through his ruse. She looked down at the car. "He's in the car, isn't he?"

Will didn't feel like it was his place to reveal his uncle Zac's living situation, if Zac wanted to make himself known, he would have to do it on his own.

"You don't have a good poker face," she said to Will.

"Surprise?" Zac said to her through the car speakers.

Samantha breathed out, as if she had been holding her breath for days.

"Zachary, I can't believe it," she said with an astonished look on her face as she approached the car. "Is it really you?"

"As much me as can be in a computer in the dash of a 1992 Corvette," he said.

She put her hand on the hood of the car as a tear rolled down her face. "I've missed you so much."

"I've missed you too," Zac said. "How did you figure it out?"

"Some of the timecodes on the files Will gave me on that flash drive were from after your death," Samantha explained. "It looked like you tried to cover it up on the surface, but when I dug a little deeper, I found your rookie mistake." She smiled. "You're so sloppy sometimes."

"I'm not a slob." Zac replied. "Maybe I wanted you to find it."

She smirked. "Yeah, nice save."

"How did you find us?" Will asked.

"How did I find you? Please…" Her tone was nonchalant. "A monkey with a computer could find you if they wanted to."

Will shrugged. "Good to know."

She turned back to the car. "I have so many questions, and things I wanted to tell you about, Zachary."

"People always used to think you were the quiet type," Zac replied. "Then I would say, 'Well, you haven't dated her'."

"Zachary, you've changed, but you haven't really changed," she said, smiling.

"You know, I could give you two some time to catch up if you want," Will said. "I'm done with the oil change."

"That would be great, Ace," Zac replied.

"Want to go for a drive?" Zac asked Samantha.

"Sure," she replied.

She looked surprised when the engine of the Corvette cranked up on its own.

"Oh, Zac likes to drive. It's kind of disappointing to get willed a cool sports car that barely lets you drive, but I've come to grips with it," Will said.

Will could see the fascination in her eyes, as if she was witnessing the stuff of imagination.

The driver's side door opened on its own. She got in the car and the door closed behind her.

"We'll be back…eventually," Zac said to Will. "Don't wait up."

The Corvette then pulled around Samantha's Porsche in the driveway and on to the road. The tires caught a little rubber as it sped away. They would spend the next few hours getting reacquainted.

Will didn't realize it at the time, but the events of the day would lead to a growing friendship with Samantha, as he would periodically see her when she and Zac would collaborate on technological theories and research. She would become the channel through which Zac's work could live on. His work, of course, combined with hers. They would both greatly benefit from Zac's advanced understanding, gained by being a computer.

Later in the afternoon found Will and Katie in the backyard of his home. They stood by an old oak tree that stood tall near the back fence. Will took out the old pocket knife that had been handed down to him through generations, and carved his and Katie's initials on the tree. He folded the knife and returned it to his pocket. Reaching out, she took his hand, leaned in and kissed him on the lips.

If life was a car, and the choices we made were the roads that we took, Will hoped Katie would be in his passenger seat for the rest of his journey. As indeed he hoped that he would also be in her passenger seat, from her perspective.

As he drove the Corvette, he glanced over at Katie's face, warmly lit by the setting sun. Her soft red lips smiled at him, and after shifting into the next gear, he reached over and took her hand in his.

Looking toward the future, no one can really predict what our lives will be. But in the end, what really matters, is how you got from point a to point b.

ACKNOWLEDGEMENTS

I'd like to thank Bob, Jan, Mark, Matt and Ashley at Deeds Publishing for their hard work to make this book a reality. Thanks to Rachel as well. And as always, thanks to Amanda Kate for her support and patience with my creative endeavors.

ABOUT THE AUTHOR

William j Barry was born in Newton, New Jersey, but moved to Florida, and then to Georgia at a young age. He went on to obtain a Bachelor's Degree in Psychology from the University of Georgia. William has enjoyed penning stories since grade school. They were a good outlet for his overactive imagination.

After college, William returned his focus to writing. He wrote a trilogy of young adult dark-fantasy novels: Sebastian and the Afterlife (2011), Agents of the Reaper (2012), and Forever Awakening (2014).

Besides writing novels, William also enjoys writing/recording music. He currently lives in Bogart, GA with his wife and two Dachshunds.